DAY OF THE ANTS

Robert D. Barclay

Copyright © 2022 Daniel Amson

All rights reserved

The characters and events portrayed in this book are fictitious. Any similarity to real persons, living or dead, is coincidental and not intended by the author.

No part of this book may be reproduced, or stored in a retrieval system, or transmitted in any form or by any means, electronic, mechanical, photocopying, recording, or otherwise, without express written permission of the publisher.

ISBN-13: 9781234567890
ISBN-10: 1477123456
KDP ISBN: 9798363628146

DAY OF THE ANTS

Robert D. Barclay

To everyone who keeps the creature features alive!

CHAPTER 1

The ant made its way up the sun-dried stick, sensing the change which had occurred in its environment. Twin antennae waved in the air, trying to make sense of what had happened. Warm, moist air passed over its sense organs, unmistakably the exhalation of a potential threat.

"Yep, that's an ant alright. Now please get it the fuck out of my face," Frankin grimaced, eyeballing the tiny insect as it explored the stick, searching for a path to escape.

Simon, who had been holding the stick up for Franklin's observation nodded before dropping the stick to the scorched desert ground, the insect instantly dismissed as it disappeared amongst the sparse yellow grass. "Well done, old man. But do ya know what type of ant?"

The older man pulled a rag from his back jean pocket and wiped the sweat from his brow. His eyes were constantly squinting against the harsh sunlight. The sun had begun to set and its low angle in the sun was almost blinding. "What difference does it make. An ant's an ant."

Simon laughed and kicked dust up from the ground as he surveyed the huge anthills they had found. "When you find a nest this big, it could make a big difference."

Putting his rag back in his back-pocket, the older man was inclined to agree as he looked over at the ant hills in the earth. Franklin had to admit that although he acted as if he'd seen it all before, he had never seen the likes of this.

There were three large ant hills, each one about five foot in height and about seven feet across at the base. Their surfaces were swarming with the insects, there had to be millions of them. They marched in numerous paths across the dried ground, traveling to and from the hills with seemingly military precision, forever busy.

"You reckon? An ant's a fuckin' ant, you young boys take everything too seriously."

Simon wasn't put off sharing his knowledge as he took a step towards the closest hill and crouched beside an endless column of the marching ants. "These, my senile amigo, are fire ants."

Franklin studied the moving column with a hesitant interest. "What, they breath fire or something?"

Simon laughed as he stood up straight. "Man, you must be the stupidest mother who ever lived."

"Smart enough to be your supervisor," Franklin shot back.

"Taken," Simon conceded. "They're Argentine Fire Ants."

Franklin shrugged blankly.

"From Argentina?" he said as a question, looking for any recognition in Franklin's face regarding what he thought was common information.

"Argentina? Fucking foreign bugs? Goddamn Mexican immigrants, always fucking things up," Franklin spat with distaste.

Simon winced but chose not to comment on the older man's racism. "They are nasty fuckers. Spread like wildfire. Nothing here eats 'em."

"That's why they call 'em fire ants? 'Cause they spread like wildfire?"

"No, that ain't why."

"Then why?"

"It's the sting. Hurts like a son of a bitch. Get enough of them, they can even kill a child. These bastards, they're big, too. Some of 'em look to be an inch long."

"That's bigger than normal?"

"I don't know…"

The look on Franklin's face showed that his distaste for the insects was growing by the second. "Could these be what's been attacking the boss-man's cattle?"

Simon regarded the ants thoughtfully. "Could be. I thought it would have more likely been Killer Bees to be honest. But it could well be."

"Killer Bees?"

"Yeah, you know, Africanised Honeybees."

Franklin shook his head. "More fucking foreign bugs."

Simon scratched the back of his neck, it felt hot from the sun. He stood back to full height and took a few steps back from the hills, wary not to put his foot in any of the columns. "Well, judging from the size of these hills, I'd say we have found our culprits."

Franklin nodded. A number of the ranch's cattle, a herd of four hundred head of longhorn, had been attacked by what appeared to be insect stings lately and as head wrangler and labourer, it had been tasked to him to find the bug causing the issues and deal with it. He turned on his foot and began walking to his flatbed truck with purpose, a worn beaten hunk of machinery nearly twenty years old.

"What you planning to do? Get some insecticide?"

Franklin reached the side of the truck and reached over to the assortment of items he had on the back of it. "Those fire ants, they ain't fire proof, are they?"

Simon was confused. "'Course not."

Franklin grinned. "Then I got the best goddamned bug-killer right here." He picked up a full can of gas and started walking back to the hills. Twisting off the cap he began splashing the fuel all over the three hills until the can was empty. The ants scattered in panic and confusion, trying to avoid the alien smelling liquid as Franklin doused them. Some of them tried to climb up his boot but were soon knocked off with his hand after he had cleared the mounds.

"Wow, wow, wow, you're going to burn up a whole can of fuel just to kill a few bugs?"

"What's wrong with that?"

Simon scratched the back of his neck. "Just seems like a waste is all.

Franklin laughed. "I wouldn't worry about it. The Boss has drums of the stuff back in the barn." He then reached into his jacket, pulled out a box of matches and lit one. He grinned at Simon who was backing away, not wanting to be so close the inferno Franklin was about to ignite. He struck the match and smiled as he watched the flame dance upon its end. "Like I said, an ant's an ant." He tossed the match and it landed on the closest ant hill. Instantly the hill burst into flames, incinerating the tiny insect bodies that had been moving over its surface mere moments before. "They all burn the same."

CHAPTER 2

Martin Bevaux reclined contently after finishing up his meal his wife, Louise had made for him. Ribs, fries and plenty of slaw, he couldn't honestly decide if there were a better meal available on God's green Earth.

"Honey, that was absolutely delicious, thankyou. I am absolutely stuffed."

"Not too stuffed I hope," Lousie replied as she carried the used dishes to the kitchen sink.

"Well, I reckon I've got room for dessert."

"No way are you having desert after that amount of food. You need to get your appetite back before dinner tomorrow. And I want to have you boys real hungry."

Martin chuckled as he watched Louise's figure in her light, form fitting summer dress. He reached across from where he was sitting at the kitchen table and playfully stroked her behind. "I promise you that my appetite has never failed me yet."

"Stop," Lousie laughed, playfully slapping his hand away.

"C'mon mom, can't we have some chocolate ice cream at least?" chimed the couples' eldest son, Dean.

"Yeah, ice cream at least?" added Teddy, their younger son.

Martin regarded his two boys with pride. Dean was sixteen now and growing into a handsome young man. Although when he complained about wanting ice cream, Martin remembered just how young sixteen really was. Teddy was ten and idolised his older brother, always ready to follow him into any conflict Dean threw himself into. Unfortunately, there weren't many conflicts Dean wasn't prepared to enter. He had been more well behaved in the city. Since they had moved out to the desert his behaviour had deteriorated somewhat.

Martin looked from his boys back to his wife who met his gave with a stare that said *"now look what you have done."* He then looked passed her at the large kitchen counter and the prepared turkey that sat on a roasting tray, ready for the oven first thing in the morning. Behind the turkey were numerous cooking pots, filled with vegetables ready for the boil.

"Now boys, it's Thanksgiving tomorrow and you mom has gone to a lot of trouble to prepare a meal that will be just about the best damned thing you'll eat. All she asks is that we skip dessert this once so we can add some hunger sauce to that meal and make it even nicer. Now personally, I don't think that's a bad deal at all. What do you think, Dean?" He deliberately asked Dean first because whatever he said was undoubtedly the position Teddy would hold too.

The boy looked down at the table and then back up to his father. He looked slightly frustrated with the situation but relented. "I guess," he mumbled.

"That's real good of you, Dean. What do you have to say, Teddy?"

"I guess," responded the younger brother, mimicking the tone and body language of his sibling.

"Thanks boys," Louise smiled as she turned and began rinsing the dishes in the sink before placing them in the dish washer.

"Now, kiss your mother and get out of here," Martin chuckled as he took a sip of his beer. He felt a pride deeper than he would have ever guessed he could feel pre-children as he watched his sons thank their mom before heading off to their respective rooms.

"Thanks for that," Louise said as she continued rinsing dishes.

"No problem at all," Martin smiled as he stood and walked up behind her. He circled her waist with his arms and pulled her against himself, kissing her neck and smelling her perfume.

"And thankyou for such a delicious meal."

Louise lifted a hand and caressed her husband's cheek. "Did you notice how frustrated Dean looked?"

"He's just upset that he didn't get his sweet treat," Martin responded absently, kissing her neck more deeply now.

"He's frustrated because he still remembers the city," Louise stated firmly, causing Martin to withdraw.

"C'mon now, why'd you have to go and say that again? He barely remembers the city."

"Oh, he remembers. How can he not. It's only been three years. It may seem like a lifetime ago but it's really not. The people he talks to most are his old friends from back in New York on his computer. I can't remember the last time he brought home a friend from around these parts. He's bored here. Teddy loves it. Dean, well, he's struggling."

Martin had returned to the table and picked up his half-finished beer. He took a sip has he looked out of the large kitchen window, admiring the open Arizona pastures in all their Godly spectacle as the sun dropped low in the sky, bathing everything in golden rays. It was his own little slice of Heaven, here on Earth. It was hard to believe he owned the sun-stroked land before him, but he did. Even if it was mortgaged, he owned over half of it outright. It was even harder to believe when one took into account that up to three years ago Martin had been a successful trader working on Wall Street. City life had always left him empty, yet he seemed to be good at running the rat race.

He never would have dreamed of moving out into the sticks and buying a working ranch, but that was exactly what he had done. It was his father's death which had done it. It had made him reconsider what was important in life and the daily grind had begun to feel more and more hollow.

It had been a risk and he thought it would have been a hard sell to Louise. How wrong he had been. Louise had grown up an Arizona country girl and she had longed for the chance to one day return to a simpler way of living. When he'd brought up his plans to relocate she'd jumped at the chance of a change of scenery. Before he could even wrap his head around what changes the move would mean to their lives, she'd been searching properties on the internet.

Martin had zero previous experience with farming but when Yellow Hills Ranch came on the market he'd felt an immediate affinity for it. That feeling only increased after they had toured the property. It felt like home, no two ways about it. The property was pricey, fortunately Martin had made a considerable amount of money in New York, and he could afford it. At least in principle. Part of the mortgage agreement was that the ranch would need to remain a working farm and so Martin had been forced to invest in a herd. He was now the proud owner of over four hundred head of cattle; Texas Longhorns to be precise. He knew he wasn't in Texas, but he figured he was close enough. He'd then paid out for the interior of the main house to be gutted and completely refurbished, along with as many modern luxuries as he could afford. When they had first brought it the décor had been dark and wind had whistled as it penetrated the walls. Now the interior was contemporary, complete with hardwood flooring, white, open walls and the best insulation he had ever experienced.

He'd done the math and assuming everything went to plan he would be mortgage free in another five years. Not too bad. He knew the ranch could become a safe investment so long as it was managed correctly, so he'd thrown all his efforts into learning the life of an outdoors man. It was a stark contrast to working in banks, and he was all the richer for it.

He'd employed a number of local hands to help out. Most of them were on leave due to the holiday, though two of them had agreed to work today to help keep things going. Not that there was too much for them to do. The herd had already been round up and taken to the shed where most of their needs were automated. Hence their jobs for the day had consisted of shovelling shit, completing odd jobs around the house and get to the bottom of what was stinging the cattle.

Old man Franklin had worked the ranch before Martin had

brought it and lived in a trailer on the edge of the homestead line. Martin was fine with that, after all his ranch covered nearly three hundred acres. Franklin was a known face about the local town and it was upon his recommendation that he's employed Simon. Martin had done just that and although they both presented as uneducated to him, they always knew exactly what they were doing around the ranch, which was good enough for Martin.

Louise had also thrived in her new role as domestic goddess/country girl and spent most her time at the farm shop and perfecting new recipes for the family. For Teddy, everything seemed like a new adventure. The only person who hadn't immediately settled in was Dean. He'd been devastated when he's learned he'd have to leave all his friends behind and start anew in a new state across the country. Due to the internet, he'd been able to stay in contact with most of his old friends, although Martin had mixed feelings about that. At first it had seemed to be a positive. Now it felt like Dean would be better off cutting ties with them and making new friends, rather than pine after a life he no longer had.

"You think we made a mistake?" Martin asked as he admired the view. Louise left the dishes and approached him. Now it was her turn to hold him close to her. Martin tried to keep his eyes on the idyllic scenery. Try as he might, Louise's piercing emerald green eyes drew him in.

Louise smiled as she thought of the crime rates and horror stories she's heard in New York City. "Oh yeah, big mistake," she mocked gently. "What with all the street gangs and pollution and drugs and guns…"

"Hey, don't knock guns. In New York I had none. Now I have two," Martin retorted in a mock-serious voice as he thought of his firearms, a Glock and an AR-15 rifle, complete with scope. He hadn't wanted to buy them, truth be told, although they felt like a grim necessity. His hesitation wasn't because he was anti-gun or anything like that, merely his inexperience. He always kept them locked up in the cabinet in his bedroom and prayed he would never have need to use either of them.

Louise lent into him, resting her head against his chest. "You've never failed at what you set out to do. And buying this place was the best thing you have ever done. You just need to try with Dean a little more, y'know? And those guns are to protect your investment, not mug some poor sap in an alley. They'll be no profit to be made if coyotes chew up the whole herd."

"Coyotes I can deal with, it's the bugs I'm having trouble with at the moment. You seen some of the welts on those poor longhorn?"

At that moment there was a loud tapping at the backdoor, hard enough that it felt like the door would be knocked off its hinges, and before either Martin or Louise could respond the door swung open and Franklin sauntered in, work boots leaving a dusty trail wherever he went. "Bugs are dealt with," he announced with the pride of a man who had completed a job well done.

Louise grinned at Martin. "And another problem bites the dust." She pecked her husband on the lips before pulling away from the embrace and returned to stacking the dish washer. "Thirsty, Franklin?"

"Is the Pope Catholic?" Franklin laughed as he opened the fridge and helped himself to a nice cold one. It irked Martin a little at just how at home Franklin acted in the homestead. He guessed the previous owner had not minded. Either that of Franklin had been oblivious to any protests that had come his way in the past. Regardless, it was a small price to pay for a reliable labourer.

"You've spent all afternoon running after bugs you still haven't got around to fixing the bathroom door," she chastised him playfully. "It's still sticking closed."

"I fixed that damned door three days ago," Franklin protested.

"Really? Then how come I got stuck in it last night for nearly ten minutes before Martin could force it open?"

Martin shrugged. "Guess it got unfixed. Want me to have a

look at it now? Before your guests get here?"

"That's okay," Martin smiled. "We'll get it sorted in a couple of days. The important thing is that you found those bugs. You think that the bug problem is sorted?" Martin asked as he walked to the fridge and pulled out a beer for himself. He took a swig, savouring the taste.

Franklin burped. "Yup, no problem at all."

"So, what was the culprit that was biting the cattle?"

"Goddamn ants is what. Me and Simon found just about the biggest ant hills you'd ever seen. Must have been over a million of the bastards in it. Big bastards, too."

"Ants? Huh." Martin took another swig. "But you've dealt with them?"

"Yup, set fire to the hills myself."

"Fire? That'll work?"

"Hell, what you think? That them suckers are fireproof? Jobs done. Those bastards are being cremated as we speak. See for yourself." Franklin gestured out the kitchen door and Martin walked to it to see what he was being shown. Sure enough, a column of black smoke rose from the land, about a mile out from the property.

"Jesus, they sure are burning."

"Yep, you don't mess with Franklin," the old man beamed, gulping down his beer noisily.

"You ever had any problems with ants like this before?"

Franklin's self-assured look vanished, replaced by a furrowed brow as he made the effort to search his memories. "Not that I can recall. Simon said they were foreign bugs. Probably hitched a ride on the back of some border-hopper."

Martin chewed over what Franklin had said. He couldn't shake the feeling this issue wasn't over yet, especially if Franklin's assurances on the ants being dealt with held the same weight as his assurances about the sticking door. The last thing he needed was an outbreak of some foreign type of ant. God only knew how that could affect the sale of his herd when they went to market.

A crackling sound filled the air, making the trio jump. "Franklin, you read me, over?"

Franklin pulled a walkie talkie from his belt and put it to his lips. "I hear you, Simon. Over."

"I'm heading off home now. Just thought I'd remind you that you've still got one of the walkies."

"I know, I know," Franklin shot back. "I ain't senile, ya know."

"Yeah, right. Over and out."

Franklin put the walkie down on the side counter picked up his beer. He sipped as the sound of Simon's dirt bike could be heard starting up, leaving the barn before growing quieter as he rode it away from the ranch. "You believe that?" Franklin snorted.

"You are going to put that walkie back in the charging cradle, though? Right?" Martin asked. "I only ask because you have been known, on occasion, to misplace it." Martin's claim was an understatement. He had brought twenty walkie-talkies which were cradled in the barn across the front yard. The barn had become the de facto base for Martin's staff, as well as a storage building. It held copious amounts of hay before it was transferred to the shed for the cattle to feast on, as well as barrels of gas to fuel the various generators they had running. The radios were a resource for the workers to share. Several had gone missing and Franklin was the chief suspect. It wasn't that the older man was being malicious, it was just that he was forgetful. Martin decided to get back to the business at hand.

"In the morning I want you and Simon to search the ranch for any more of those ant hills, just in case that wasn't the only one. The last thing we want is for an infestation to take route. And make sure those hills you burnt really are dead."

"No problem, Boss-Man," Franklin grinned. "Only, not tomorrow, you mean the next day, right?"

"I do? Why? What's happening tomorrow?"

Louise joined the conversation from across the kitchen. "It's Thanksgiving, genius."

"Of course it is. I'm sure I'm going senile in my old age," Martin replied as he turned to his wife, dutifully tending to a kitchen counter full of cut veg and turkey she'd been slaving over it for the last few hours. "We were just talking about it, to boot."

"I swear, when you turn on work-mode, you forgot all about everything else."

"Not everything," Martin chuckled with a wink before turning back to Franklin. "In a couple of days, then. I'm sure those ants can wait one more day. You got any plans tomorrow, Franklin?"

"Nope, just sitting in my trailer. That's a lot of food you've got there, Missus Bee."

"It's for Martin's family, they should be here any minute now," Louise replied. She'd sensed Franklin was probing for an invite and wanted to shut down that line of thinking immediately. It wasn't that she didn't like Franklin, only that he was good in small doses and he would hardly meld well with Martin's brother, Tom. Or his wife for that matter.

"Sorry Franklin, no room at the inn," Martin followed up. He deliberately tried to make the phrase as humorous as possible to soften the blow. He didn't want the old man to take it personally, but he had enough on his plate with out the old, salt of the Earth man thrown into the mix. He felt a little bad for the old man, even though it couldn't be helped.

"No worries, there's some Holiday Special on the teevee I wanted to catch. You guys have a good day, ya hear?" With that Franklin downed the last of his beer, put down the can and made his way to his truck.

As Martin watched the older man leave Louise came up beside him. "Feeling bad for him?" she asked.

"A little," Martin responded. "I just wish he had someone, ya know? He seems lonely."

"I know," Louise sympathised. "Maybe if it all goes well with Tom, Franklin can join us for drinks in the evening."

Martin finished the last of his drink, his eyes once more

returned to the curling black smoke Franklin had said was rising from the ant hills. "Yeah, maybe."

Louise gave him a knowing glance. "Guess ol' Franklin is going senile after all."

"What do you mean?"

She held up the walkie the labourer had discarded on the counter and completely forgotten about.

"Goddamn it," Martin swore.

"You gonna take it over to the barn?"

"Nah, I am officially in holiday mode. A whole twenty-four hours off. I'll cradle it when I'm back on the clock."

Louise laughed. "You're right, your boss is an asshole. I wouldn't do him any favours."

"Less of that talk," Martin laughed as he chased her around the kitchen.

CHAPTER 3

Tom Bevaux squinted his eyes as the low Arizona sun nearly blinded him. He cursed as he struggled to follow the snaking desert road. Six hundred dollars for a pair of sunglasses and they weren't good for shit.

"Christ, this sun is a killer," be complained to his wife Marie, who sat cross armed in the passenger seat, staring out the door window. Her body type was the complete opposite to her husbands'. Whereas she was tall and thin, too thin according to some, her husband was short and fat. Still, what he lacked physically he made up for in his bank balance.

"What did you expect, it's the fucking desert." Tom glanced into the rear-view mirror at his daughter, Cassie. Where Marie was now neurotic and always clawing to regain her lost youth, Cassie was eighteen and already a stunner. She was grown up in more ways than Tom wanted to think. Growing up in New York had made her too damned sophisticated too damn fast. And worse still was that she had developed her mothers' cruel tongue. Everything Cassie said dripped with either sarcasm or distain. Often both.

"Language," Tom warned her. Cassie didn't respond and turned to look out her own door window, her expression a mask impossible to penetrate beneath the large designer sunglasses she wore. Tom shook his head in bemusement.

Marie twisted her head to face her daughter. "Don't be a bitch. Let's make this experience as painless as possible, please."

Tom squirmed uncomfortably at the tension in the brand-new BMW SUV. It wasn't his. New York was far too far to drive. They had flown and the car was a rental. The drive to his brother's ranch still took over six hours through featureless desert and he'd wanted to be comfortable. No amount of luxury seemed enough to dispel the constant discomfort he felt in his wife's and daughter's company.

"Maybe I wouldn't be such a 'bitch' if I wasn't freezing my tits off," Cassie replied.

"It's over a hundred degrees outside, what, do you want me to turn the AC off?" scoffed Marie.

"Maybe if you didn't always have the air con cranked to full you wouldn't be so frigid," tutted Cassie, with a demeanour that stated that trading insults with her mother was so beneath her.

"Are you going to let her talk to me like that?" Marie shot back to her husband.

Here we go again, thought Tom. His wife and daughter were like fighting dogs. Any amount of time within a closed environment and they soon started tearing chunks out of each other. And, as always, he was the one trapped in the middle. He glanced at his gold Rolex, a steal at sixteen grand, and noted the time. "Come on guys, it's nearly half past seven. We're almost at Yellow Hills."

"That's what you said an hour and a half ago," sniped Marie, feeling betrayed Tom hadn't backed her up.

"Aha, we're here," said a triumphant Tom as they approached a sand worn sign saying "YELLOW HILLS." He took the turning and began driving down the long dirt track, passed a barbed wire fence. He whistled, sounding impressed. "Wow, a couple of a million bucks goes a long way out here."

"Yeah, more sand and dirt than you can ever want," groaned Marie. "Who's that? Is that Martin?"

Tom could see the dust trail approaching them from further down the twisting desert road and squinted his eyes until he could make out an old, battered flatbed truck. "Maybe times are harder than we thought," he smirked. As they approached the vehicle, he realised the driver was not his brother, rather an older man, wearing dishevelled clothes with grey hair and a full beard. As the man acknowledged them he flashed his lights, indicating for them to pull over.

"He wants us to stop," Tom stated. "I wonder who he is."

"Dad, if you stop I swear to God you're going to get us all murdered. This is classic Hills Have Eyes shit."

"You're not going to stop, are you?" asked Marie, concern edging into her voice.

"Stop worrying, he's probably one of Martin's hands on the ranch." Tom pulled over and, as did the truck pulled in front of him. With both vehicles parked bumper to bumper, the old man, old, thin and with a short white beard, got out of the truck and walked towards Tom's car door. He stood beside it and knocked on the window when it became apparent Tom wasn't going to wind it down automatically. "Hi, how's it going?" he asked the man, trying and failing to stop his voice from sounding nervous.

The man leant down and scanned the interior of the car. His eyes lingered on Cassie longer than Tom would have liked. He felt he should say something. He didn't. Cassie, more than used to unwanted male attention, ignored him and continued looking out of her window. Eventually the old man's attention returned to Tom. "You Tom?"

"Yes."

"My name is Franklin, it's nice to meet you." He held out a hand and Tom shook it awkwardly. "You're Martin's brother, right?"

"I am."

"And these two pretty things must be your wife and daughter. You sir, are a lucky man."

"Luckier than he realises," Marie said curtly.

Franklin chuckled. "This road is pretty twisted as you get closer to the house. Don't go too fast or you're liable to come off and wreck your vehicle. The boulders out there'll snap your axel like a toothpick. Just keep following it straight and you'll come to the main house."

"Thanks for the advice," Tom replied and gave a polite

wave.

Franklin ran his eyes over each of the car's occupants one last time before standing up straight. "Happy Thanksgiving, guys. Be seeing you." He rapped on the roof of the car and then started walking back to his truck.

"Man, what a weirdo," mumbled Cassie as she lowered her sunglasses to watch the old man climb back into the pickup. "'Be seeing you?' Sounds like some kind of fucked up threat."

"Now Cassie, that's just how people are out here. He was just being friendly. Nothing to worry about."

"If he *had* tried something, what would you have done?" Marie asked accusingly.

"Well, obviously I would have protected you both," Tom responded, hoping he sounded more convincing than he thought he did.

"Right," nodded Marie. She crossed her arms and cocked an eyebrow, unimpressed.

"Well look, I made a judgement call, and nothing bad happened. Can't we leave it at that?"

Franklin pulled away in his truck fast, creating a cloud of dust in his wake. Tom quickly drew up his window to keep from being suffocated by the sand when he heard the ping of a stone striking his windscreen. He looked in horror at the new chip that had been caused by the stone, flung up from the truck's tires.

"God damn it," he cursed, waving his arms in exasperation.

* * *

"They're here," Louise called as she watched the BMW pull up outside the house, between her car and Martin's truck. "Dean, Teddy, get your butts down here."

Martin quickly checked himself in the mirror. "How do I look?" he asked as he straightened his hair the best he could.

"Terrified," Louise laughed.

"It's been four years…" Martin began.

"Martin, he's your brother. Four years ain't gonna change that. If you want to make things up with him, it's never gonna get easier than right now."

Martin opened his mouth to say something, then shut it, nodding in agreement. "Boys," he called.

Teddy came running down the stairs, full of excitement. "They're really here? Awesome."

Dean trailed behind his younger brother, hands in his pockets and looking bored. "Why have I got to come down to meet them? He's your brother."

"And your uncle," Martin shot back. "And don't you want to spend some time with your cousin. You guys used to be thick as thieves growing up."

Dean rolled his eyes.

Martin took a breath to steal his nerves and then opened the door to greet his brother. "Tom, how you doing?" he beamed, walking down the stone steps from the front door down to the dirt driveway. Louise felt he was laying it on a little too thick but hid her feelings behind her own beaming smile.

Martin walked to the hire car and shook his brother's hand. Even though Martin was the older of the two, it was Tom who looked out of shape and aged. He gave Martin a double handed shake back. "It's good to see you, Martin."

"And Marie, as beautiful as ever." He leant in and gave his sister-in-law a hug.

"Always the charmer," grinned Marie, feeding off the compliment. "Hi Louise, you're looking, homely. You certainly are looking the part out here in these rural lands."

Louise felt the intense desire to tell Marie to fuck off and swallowed it down for her husband's sake. "You're looking thin," she smiled. The two women have each other a friendly hug and kiss.

"Cassie, you've certainly grown up," Martin smiled as his niece stepped out of the car.

"Hey uncle Martin," she waved awkwardly.

"You remember Dean and Teddy, of course."

Cassie turned her head towards her two cousins, locked eyes with Dean, which instantly made him blush and look uncomfortable. "Of course," she smiled.

"Let me help you guys with your bags," Martin offered as he walked to the car's trunk and pulled out the two larger suitcases. "What happened to the windscreen?" he asked, noticing the chip, dead centre of the glass.

"Some cowboy who works for you did it when he pulled off passed up just up the road," Tom grumbled. "There goes my deposit."

Martin was irked to learn Franklin had caused the damage, even if it was accidental. He didn't want anything so trivial to ruin his reunion with his brother after so long. "Geez, I'm sorry to hear that, Tom. Do you want me to pay for the damages?"

Tom's face lit up and he grinned. "No, don't worry about it. These things happen," he shrugged. "I must say, your house looks fantastic. When we came over the ridge, the first thing we saw was that house there and I was beginning to regret coming."

Martin laughed, looking over to the building Tom was referring to. "That's the barn. Mainly where I keep hay for the cattle. Fuel for the generators and amenities for the working men. My house may not be a Manhattan penthouse but I assure you it isn't *that* humble." Martin smiled and began walking back to the house with the bags. "Son, won't you help your cousin with her bag?"

Scratching his arm Dean nodded and began walking to the trunk where Cassie was heaving her suitcase onto the ground. He couldn't help but notice how good her ass looked as she moved. "Need a hand?" he asked, heart threatening to break his ribs with the intensity of its beats.

Cassie looked him up and down and smiled. "Thanks. You know, you've grown a lot since I last saw you."

"You too," spluttered Dean as he reached to take her case. As he did his hand brushed against hers and his legs turned to jelly.

"I have," Cassie winked at him.

Red faced, Dean turned and began walking back to the

house. "Let me show you to your room," he mumbled.

Teddy watched his brother in bewilderment. "Hey, Dean, what's wrong?"

"Nothing," Dean glared back.

"Why have you gone all quiet?"

"Shut up."

"Why have you gone bright red?"

"Go to Hell."

Cassie watched the two boys walking into the house and smiled wickedly to herself. *Perhaps this trip won't be as dull as I anticipated,* she thought.

CHAPTER 4

"That was absolutely delicious," smiled Tom, leaning back in his chair and downing his beer.

"Thanks, it was just sandwiches. No big deal," Louise replied humbly as she cleared the table.

"You sell yourself short," Tom insisted. "If you can make beef sandwiches taste that good, I can't wait to see what you do with that turkey."

Louise rolled her eyes, laughing.

"Sounds like you married the wrong person. I can't even cook an egg," said Marie coldly as she sipped her white wine.

Tom laughed nervously, trying to ignore the hostility in his wife's remark. "Well, that's not the reason I love you," he joked.

"What is the reason?" Marie responded, flatly.

Sitting opposite his brother, Martin made wide eyes to Louise, unmistakably a plea for help to stop an argument from breaking out.

"Marie, how would you like me to give you the full tour of the house?" Louise asked in the most inviting, host with the most tone she could muster.

Marie gave a returning smile that didn't quite meet her eyes. "I would absolutely love that," she said with barely concealed boredom. As the two women left the room, Louise made eye contact with her husband once more. The message between them didn't need to be spoken; *'you owe me.'*

Martin gave a slight nod of acknowledgement before turning his attention to the other end of the table, where Cassie picked fussily at her beef sandwich while Teddy chattered to her about coyotes and rattle snakes. Dean sat looking stumped for anything to say. "You don't like the sandwich? You want me to knock something else up for you?"

Cassie's displeasure instantly disappeared, replaced by her best attempt at appearing friendly and child-like. "No thanks, Uncle Martin. Just not hungry, I guess."

"We did stop and get something a few hours back," Tom explained. "And our Cassie isn't the biggest eater. She's always managed to get by eating the bare minimum. Between her and her mother you'd think it was permanently lent or something at our place."

Cassie rolled her eyes and laughed. "Just saving myself for the big event tomorrow." She almost sounded genuine.

Martin smiled. "Hey, Dean. Would you like to give your cousin the tour?"

Dean looked like a startled deer, as if the words were terrifying to him. "What?"

"Your cousin, give her a tour. I'm sure you she'd love to see all the stuff in the games room."

"I certainly would," smiled Cassie. "Please Dean, show me everything." Her enthusiasm seemed to border on mocking as she stood up and grabbed Dean's hand, pulling him behind her as she strode from the room. It looked more like Dean was the one being taken for a tour, but Martin didn't have time to worry about that right now.

"Wait for me," called Teddy as he chased after them.

"Stay in the house," Martin called. "It's getting dark out, leave the outdoor tour until tomorrow." There was no response as the kids chattered around themselves as they left the room. Martin rested back in his chair, finally alone with his brother. He tried to ignore his anxiety as he searched for small talk. He decided it shouldn't be this hard talking to his own brother.

It was Tom who finally broke the awkward silence, albeit with strain in his voice and a desperate smile. "I thought it was only in the city you had to worry about the weirdos who come out at night."

"It's not so much people who we have to worry about out here. Nearest town is twenty-five miles away. I'm more worried about the coyotes and rattle-snakes that Teddy is so taken with."

"I see," nodded Tom, nursing his empty bottle. "Although that Franklin guy on the way in here who looked pretty odd."

"That's our Franklin for you. He's a little bit odd, but otherwise harmless. He works hard for me."

"Where did you find him?"

"Didn't, I kinda inherited him. He worked for the guy who owned the ranch before me. He lives in a trailer at the edge of my land."

"Really? Does he pay rent?"

"Nah. I got enough land, I think I can spare him a tiny corner. Plus, he's worked here a long time. Knows what he is doing. That goes a long way. I think of it as a mutual beneficial arrangement."

Tom laughed. "You always were kind-hearted."

"You know me, kind to a fault."

Tom's face twitched at the comment and Martin wished he hadn't made it. It was too late for that now, however, so he left the words hanging. He decided to leave the silence linger, waiting to see how Tom would respond.

"Look, Martin. I'm sorry," Tom said, scratching the back of his neck and sweating profusely. "It was wrong what I did."

Martin mirrored feelings but managed to keep his physical tells in check. "It was," he said simply.

"I just, I was money blind and wasn't thinking straight. You know what it's like. Everyone has money problems, the only thing that changes is how many zeros are on the end of them. I was going through a rough patch with Marie at the time and, I dunno, I felt the extra money could have really helped me out."

Martin had convinced himself he wouldn't get angry, that what was in the past was in the past. Now, as he was sitting across from his brother who was trying to explain his actions, that rage had returned as if it was yesterday, instead of four years. "You tried to cut me out of a deal worth seven hundred and fifty thousand dollars."

"I know," said Tom, looking down at his hands. "I still don't know what I was thinking. I don't even know if I could have gone through with it."

"The only reason you didn't go through with it was because your secretary was about as discreet as a thousand-volt shock to the balls. Don't you dare deny that you were going to rip me off."

Tom looked utterly deflated without a hint of fight in him. Martin had expected Tom to come out with a million excuses as to how Martin had got the wrong end of the stick, but after nearly four years of silence Tom appeared to have done a lot of soul searching. "I just, I want my brother back. Like it was in the old days."

Martin considered his words carefully, praying Louise was doing a good enough job at keeping Marie busy. He was well aware of the kind of woman Marie was, and the expensive tastes she had. He had little doubt she was the main motivator behind Tom's actions four years ago.

Martin and Tom had both succeeded in the financial markets and formed their own company, Bevaux And Bevaux Investors with the agreement that all profit would be split down the middle. They had worked well together, although not as well as Martin had initially hoped. Upon looking at the books it became apparent he was providing more than seventy percent of the company's income. Meanwhile, Tom's expenses were suspiciously high. Against his better judgement, Martin had ignored the warning signs and got on with his work. He knew Tom wasn't perfect, but they were brothers and it had always felt like the Bevaux boys against the world.

That had changed whilst Martin had been on a long overdue week break and was enjoying some sun with his wife and kids down in Florida. A particularly juicy case Martin had been working on came back early in the affirmative for everything to go ahead. Because Martin hadn't been at the office, Tom took it upon himself to fill out the necessary paperwork. Oh, and also scrub Martin's name off the files and attempt to collect to commission for himself.

To say Martin had felt betrayed had been an understatement and all Tom's excuses and justifications for why he needed the money fell on deaf ears. Whether Marie had known what Tom had been up to or not, he never said, although it wouldn't surprise Martin one iota if the whole thing had been her idea.

Martin had told Tom he had wanted to put the whole thing behind him, and Tom had only been too eager to agree. Once the deal had gone through and Martin got his share of the profit he walked away from the business and his relationship with his brother. It had hurt, the two of them had been close. Tom's betrayal had hurt more. After cutting contact with Tom, Martin had worked in the financial sector intermittently throughout the next several months, although he knew his heart was no longer in it and he was tired of the cutthroat world of New York. It was then that his big plan to relocate and reinvent himself as a rancher solidified.

He'd worried that people would accuse him of having a midlife crisis, and people did. Hell, even he wondered if he was. Never Louise though. She'd backed him all the way and made his dream a reality. It'd taken everything he'd got but he'd made it happen.

He'd been working the ranch for about three years now and although it was hard, he loved it. He'd begun to wonder how different his life would have been if Tom had never tried to rip him off. Perhaps he was getting soft in his old age, but he even wondered if perhaps he should thank his brother for setting him on this new and more fulfilling path.

Martin had called Tom about four months ago after Louise badgered him to make amends. It wasn't that she was particularly fond of Tom and Marie, rather she could see how losing the relationship with his brother had hurt Martin. Initially the conversation was strained. Eventually the small talk became easier and easier. Tom often talked about how well he was doing, and Martin listened and offered his congratulations, even though his bull-shit detector was going off massively. Tom never brought up the incident that had drove them apart and for a while Martin thought maybe that was for the best until he couldn't ignore the feelings building up inside him anymore.

Upon discussing it with Louise he'd decided that to mend his fraternal relationship he would need to mention Tom's indiscretion, although over the phone was not a smart way to do it; there was too much risk of either one of them losing their shit and slamming the phone down, potentially cutting ties forever. Face to face was the way it had to be, and what better time than Thanksgiving?

When Martin had offered hosting Tom and his family at Thanksgiving, he wasn't entirely convinced his brother would take him up on the offer. He did though, and now Tom had bared his soul, the ball was in Martin's court.

Martin took a breath and spoke with each word measured. "It can't be like it was in the old days."

Tom nodded, looking like the saddest man alive.

"I've got a new life here. I'm never going back to the city. We may never be as close as we used to be. That's just me being honest. But I don't want to never see you, either."

"What are you saying, then?"

Martin arose, walked to the fridge and retrieved two cans of beer. He threw one to Tom before cracking his own. "Here's to the future."

Tom smiled. "The future."

*   *   *

Dean opened the twin polished oak doors and walked into the games room. Teddy ran in behind him and jumped onto the couch in the corner.

"This is our, uh, leisure area," Dean said, awkwardly explaining the obvious to Cassie, who followed behind him. She scanned the room. It had a couch, tee-vee and games console in the corner, a dart board, a pool table and even a small bar.

The walls were all polished oak, like the doors and the floor was polished grey stone tiles.

"Cool," remarked Cassie, genuinely impressed.

"You wanna play a game?" asked Teddy, already booting up the system with a controller in his hand.

"I'll pass," she smiled. Her hand traced along the edge of the pool table before pulling one of the balls along. "Do you bring girls down here?" she asked with a wicked grin.

Dean spluttered, unsure how to answer.

"Dean doesn't ever bring girls back to the house," Teddy responded, matter-of-factly, his attention fixed to the tee-vee screen.

"Dude, I swear," Dean warned.

"So, I'm the first?" Cassie teased, enjoying watching Dean squirm.

Dean swallowed, his throat suddenly very dry. "Uh, I mean…"

Cassie picked up a pool cue and leant over the table, lining up a shot. "I used to play pool with my old man all the time when I was younger," she stated before striking the white. With a satisfying tap it hit a red, which rolled directly into the corner pocket.

"Nice," Dean said, watching the shot.

"Nice? You mean the shot or my ass?" said Cassie accusingly, putting the cue down and staring daggers at him.

"No, of course not," Dean protested.

"Because I'm your cousin. That's sick," Cassie continued.

"I wasn't looking at your ass…"

"Because it's not good enough for you?" she took steps towards him, invading his personal space.

"No, it's a great, uh, I swear, I wasn't." Dean was tripping over his own words, unable to formulate a coherent response.

"There are laws against that kind of thing," continued Cassie in outrage, her face inches from her cousin's. "I should tell our dads."

"Please, don't."

Cassie grinned. "Just fucking with ya."

"What?" Dean was in shock.

Cassie laughed and twisted on her heel, walking back past the pool table and checked out the dart board. "I was kidding. Just goofing around. Relax."

"Oh, I see," said Dean, relief flooding his body, his legs turned to jelly. "Uh, good one."

Cassie smiled. "So, you noticed me ass, then?" Dean was once again frozen like a deer in head lights. "You're too easy," Cassie laughed, rolling her eyes and moving on from the dart board. She was having more fun than she'd thought she would. "So, does the bar work? Is it stocked?"

Dean approached, trying to regain his composure and appear cool and collected. "Yeah, totally."

"Pour me a beer?"

Dean hesitated for second. "Sure."

"You're not allowed beer," Teddy warned from his seat on the couch."

"Dude, shut up."

"Is that true? Aren't you allowed?" Cassie asked. "Because I don't want to get you in trouble." She talked to him as if one would talk to a young child.

Dean considered his response in a milli-second. "No trouble. No trouble at all." He poured her a beer and she stood close as he did so. Her perfume was intoxicating. "There you go," he handed the glass to her and she took a sip.

"Tastes good," she smiled, squeezing his arm. "You gonna have some?"

"Sure," Dean smiled, pouring himself a glass and sipping it. The taste was more bitter than he expected and he failed to hide the displeasure from his face as he set the glass down.

Cassie laughed. "You're cute." Dean blushed. She then gave him a sidewards glance, chewing on her bottom lip. "You're not trying to get me drunk, are you?"

"Of course not," Dean protested.

"I'm kidding, chill." Cassie laughed and rested her hand

upon his. Dean wanted the moment to last forever. "What's over there?" she asked, glancing to the back of the games room. The back wall of the room was glass, with a built-in glass door. Whatever lay beyond it was hidden under a cloak of darkness.

"That's the bike garage," Dean said, following behind her.

"Bike garage?" Cassie's voice peaked in delight.

"Yeah, quad bikes." Dean brushed passed her and flicked a switch and the garage was instantly lit, displaying four quad bikes. One of the bikes was smaller than the others, undoubtedly Teddy's. All the bikes looked in pristine condition. Behing them was a roller door which led outside.

"Can I ride one?" Cassie asked as she went to push the door open, only to find it locked.

"Sorry, my dad's a bit safety conscious. We don't really ride them much, and when we do it has to be with him."

Cassie pouted. "That doesn't sound very fun."

"Sorry."

"Can't we go out together, just the two of us."

"My dad keeps the keys in his bedroom. He thinks I don't know where they are, but I know. We can go with him tomorrow."

"Don't you want to have fun with me?" Cassie asked with exaggerated sadness.

"Of course," Dean explained. "But it can be dangerous, what with uneven ground and boulders and stuff."

She took a step towards him and ran her hand down his arm. "I'm sure you know what you're doing, don't you? You can look after me, show me the best position to be in and such while I'm riding?"

Cassie's perfume overwhelmed Dean's senses. "Of course, but the key…"

"You said you know where you dad keeps it?" She edged closer, her open lips so close to his.

"I do…"

"You can get them?"

"I can…"

"You can show me the best positions to be in?"

The double-entendre made Dean blush bright red. His voice failing him, he nodded.

"Great," Cassie beamed, stepping back from Dean and walking back to the bar, her seductive manner instantly erased. "When can we go?"

Dean's head was spinning as he tried to make sense of what had just happened. "We can't go now, it's too dark."

"Spoil sport," Cassie pouted playfully. "All the best things happen in the dark."

"I can get the keys tomorrow, after breakfast. We can head out in the morning for a bit."

Cassie considered his proposal, nodding mischievously. "Excellent, I can't wait." She finished her drink.

* * *

"God, that feels good," Tom sighed with relief as he sat on the edge of his bed and removed his shoes. As he massaged his feet he looked around at the bedroom his brother had provided for them. It was a little smaller than he was used to and homely decorated. He decided he liked it, although he dare not tell that to Marie, who was sat in front of the vanity mirror, applying her skin regime.

"Glad you're having a nice time," she snapped, bitterly. "This desert heat is drying my skin up something chronic. I can't wait until we're back in civilisation."

"It's only a couple of nights," Tom replied as he removed his clothes and climbed into bed. "And this place is nice."

Marie characteristically rolled her eyes. "It's only a façade, dear husband. Did you hear about the downstairs bathroom door?"

"That it keeps sticking? Yeah, so what?"

"Louise was saying that if I want to pee downstairs then I should leave the door open a crack, lest I become trapped all Thanksgiving."

"That was probably just hyperbole."

Marie sighed. "That door is just a glimpse of what this place really is."

"Which is?"

"Rural hell."

Come on, Marie. Even in New York you can get doors that stick on occasion. It's just a problem with the lock not working properly. This place is nice."

"Whatever you have to tell yourself to get through the visit."

"What did you think of that grand old fireplace in the living room? You must admit that looks nice.

Marie gave a sideways smile. "I'll admit, I like the fireplace. It'd make the room cosy, if only it wasn't sweltering outside."

"You want us to get one?"

Marie walked over in her silk negligee and climbed in beside him. Tom took the opportunity to admire his wife's sleek figure before it was hidden beneath the duvet. "That's a discussion for another day. Did you talk to your brother? Really talk, I mean."

"I did."

"And?"

"And I think we're going be okay. We've acknowledged the past and are going to try and put it behind us."

Marie was already lying on her side, her back to him. "Did you apologise?"

Tom hesitated. "I did."

Marie bristled. "Huh, as if you have anything to apologise for. He's the one who left you high and dry."

"Marie…"

"Did he apologise?"

"No…"

"I see."

Tom turned off his lamp and lay down flat, a million thoughts and feelings running though his head.

After a couple of minutes Marie asked; "Did you discuss what you wanted to discuss with him?"

Tom sighed. "He's taking me for a tour of the ranch

tomorrow morning. I'll ask him then.

"See that you do."

CHAPTER 5

After leaving Tom and his family on the dirt track, Franklin had drove the meandering desert dirt roads between the low hills until he eventually reached his tiny slice of heaven. His trailer was old and beat up, but it was his and that made all the difference. It sat at the foot of a lone wooden telephone post, the communication wire above stretching across various other posts as it zig-zagged through the wilderness, connecting Yellow Hills to the rest of the world.

He pulled up outside, his beat-up truck looking at home next to the piles of scrap metal and rubbish he had strewn about the place. The generator made an ear-splitting noise as is burnt through gas and powered his home. The generator was old and wasteful, burning through an entire tank of gas in a couple of hours. This meant that Franklin had to stop by an hour or so before his shift ended each day and top it up, just so he could have cold beer ready for when he came home. Pert of him begrudged his boss, Mister Martin Bevaux for subjecting him to such a lifestyle. Another part knew this was nonsensical, seeing as Franklin had never once mentioned his power arrangements to his employer.

Walking over to the generator, Frankin twisted the cap off and inspected how much fuel was left inside. Seeing there was a quarter of a tank left he picked up one of a number of haphazardly piled fuel cannisters and refilled the generator. He knew people said you shouldn't refill whilst the generator was running, but what the hell did they know? He admitted he probably needed to give the old girl a service, though. The desert sand wasn't kind to mechanisms or technology of any kind.

Once refilled, he tightened the cap and walked into his trailer. The inside looked exactly as someone would imagine from driving past and looking at the exterior; worn, cluttered and dirty; potentially abandoned. Franklin didn't care, it was home, and he was always glad to return. He turned on his radio, always tuned to the best of country music, and opened the fridge to pull out a beer. It was ice cold and felt good going down. Some may call it wasteful to leave a generator burning for hours before his working day ended just so his beers stayed cold. Franklin thought those same people were a bunch of assholes who should mind their own business.

The remaining beer poured down his gullet and Franklin gave a guttural burp before retrieving another one and cracking it open. He drank from it as he pulled down a can of beans from the cupboard. Using an old-fashioned tin-opener, he twisted the top off it and slopped it's contents into a stained saucepan. He ignited the hob and began stirring as he continued drinking and enjoying the music.

By the time the beans were cooked, Franklin was onto his third beer. He walked outside with saucepan in one hand, a large tablespoon resting within it, and a remnants of a six pack in the other. He sat down on an old rocking chair he had rescued from the garbage dump. It creaked noisily as it took his weight and even more so as he begun rocking it back and forwards.

Careful not to burn himself on the metal of the saucepan he began shovelling beans into his face. To hell what other people would say, it saved on washing up.

After finishing his meagre meal, he put the saucepan down and cracked his third beer. He sipped it at a slower pace than the previous cans as he looked up to the sky. The setting sun created a myriad of colours in the sky and casting the landscape in deep reds and purples. Franklin would bet his last buck that every colour in God's palette were used to paint the picture in front of him and it was a view he never tired of. He doubted a more awe-inspiring view existed anywhere in the world. So what if he didn't have much money or a wife of his own? He had all the splendour of God's creation to enjoy. Money couldn't buy that. What else was there to life?

Reaching back behind the rocking chair, Franklin plucked up his phone. The exertion was greater than he liked to admit and he passed wind due to the manoeuvre. He dialled a number and then waited. After three rings, a voice answered.

"Hey Simon, how ya doing?"

"Franklin? I just left you over a couple 'a hours ago. I was good then, I'm good now. Why'd you ask?"

"Can't a man just make conversation?"

Simon sighed. "I guess."

"What you up to tomorrow? Wanna come over for a drink?"

"Man, I already told you, I'm having dinner at Marlene's place with her folks. What's the matter, didn't you get the invite from the Boss-Man?"

"Ahhh, screw him. I saw his brother drive in after you left. Real city-slicker type."

"Like the Boss-Man used to be?"

"Yeah, but worse. You should have seen his wife. She had a face like a bulldog chewing a wasp. I would, though."

"She looked good?"

"Good enough." Franklin paused to use his finger to pick some bean remnants that were stuck against his back tooth. "His daughter, now she was purdy. Just as stuck up as her mom, though. They both had faces made me wonder if I'd trod in dog shit."

"Probably bull shit, more like," Simon laughed. Franklin couldn't help but laugh along with him. He wasn't completely unaware of the impression he gave some people. "Sounds like you dodged a bullet then, not being invited, I mean."

Franklin considered Simon's words as he sipped his beer. "I reckon."

There was a beat of silence that went on too long. "Look man, I'm riding past yours on the way to Marlene's tomorrow. I guess I could stop by for one on the way."

"Well hot-dang, don't do me no favours," Franklin joked.

"But just one, y'hear? If I ride on over to Marlene's stinking of booze, there'll be hell to pay."

Franklin chuckled. "No problem, brother. Just one, scouts honour." He hung up the phone, still chuckling. He knew he'd get Simon to stay for at least a couple, maybe more. He opened another beer and began to drink, enjoying the fading heat on his skin and the warmth from within his belly as the sweet tones of Roy Rogers serenaded his ears.

*   *   *

Franklin awoke himself with his own snoring and took a moment to gain a sense of his surroundings. He had fallen asleep in his rocking chair again and had left himself open to the elements. The cold night air had set in, making him shiver. He didn't know what time it was, but it had to be pretty late as the generator had burnt through its tank of fuel and was sitting silent. It had been a good few hours at least.

Sitting up, the chair creaked. Franklin's mouth felt dry and his head hurt. Fortunately, the clear night sky allowed the stars to illuminate the land so he could make out what he was doing, albeit barely. Reaching down he grasped at a beer can and tried to drink from it. It was empty, aside from a tiny amount of liquid and grit. He cursed and tossed it, spitting the foul mouthful out.

He went to stand up, and that was when he saw it. The ant. A little under an inch, the small creature scurried across the sand in his general direction. Franklin squinted to make it out as it paused, waving its feelers in the air before continuing its zig-zagging path.

"Huh, guess I didn't manage to burn all of you after all," he said, bemused. "I can fix that. He stood up and stamped down on the insect. Grinding it into the dirt, he scrapped his foot back and what was left wasn't even enough to be called an ant. Franklin laughed to himself softly. "Don't worry, I'll get all your friends, too."

He yawned, slowly turned around and through his sleep and alcohol induced haze crouched to reach for his phone from behind his chair. He groped in the shadow, knocking empty beer cans over and muttering to himself. He'd have to kick this habit of falling asleep outside. It was only a matter of time before a coyote or something jumped him. His fingers found his phone and he picked it up.

"Fuck," he yelped, instantly dropping his phone and yanking his hand back. A sharp, piercing pain had struck the back of his hand and he instantly thought he'd been tagged by a rattlesnake. Grimacing he jumped back and looked at his burning hand, expecting to see the twin puncture wounds of a snake. What he did see was another ant, this one with its stinger still imbedded in his skin. The pain was increasing and Franklin reacted without thinking, flicking the attacker off.

"Jesus Christ," he swore. The sting had hurt, a lot. He held his pained hand, expecting the pain to subside. Instead it grew, turning into an intense burning sensation that made him sweat in discomfort. He swore some more and kicked angrily at the rocking chair. The light piece of outdoor furniture flew from the force, crashing into a pile of rusted engine parts and breaking apart.

Franklin's anger grew at the prospect of now having to find a new chair, although the anger didn't last long when he saw what had lurked beneath it. Ants scurried randomly in alarm at having their hiding place knocked away from them. The bastards ranged from normal sized to almost an inch and there had to be thirty of forty of them.

"Jesus," Franklin blasphemed again, backing away from the panicked insects. He instantly felt stone cold sober and could tell he wouldn't be able to crush them without suffering a few more stings; something he desperately wanted to avoid.

Turning to look out at the numerous debris strewn across what he saw as his space, he began picking out more and more movement in the shadow. Ants, everywhere. Over everything.

He thought of running to his truck, jumping in and putting as much distance between him and these fuckers as possible. As soon as he looked at the truck, he knew that was impossible, the ants swarming over it. "Fuck this," he whimpered and turned to run back into his trailer.

That was when he noticed the ants, too numerous to count, crawling over the exterior of his trailer. His fear began to grow as he contemplated his next action. The ants were crawling all over his yard and trailer, but they weren't *in* his trailer, at least, he didn't think they were. The door inside was closed and only a handful of insects scurried over it.

His decision made, he hurried to the door. As he got closer, he noticed several ants clambering over the handle and he quickly knocked them off with his sleeve before opening it and running inside. Franklin closed the door and tried to catch his breath. His hand was hurting like hell, worse than anything he's felt before. He looked at it and already he could tell it was swelling and turning red.

He went to turn on the light switch and nothing happened. Fuck, the generator was out of gas, so obviously, the lights weren't working. His eyes darted from side to side, trying to make out if any of the insects had invaded his home. Everything was in deep darkness, making scrutinising the piles of clutter impossible.

The best option seemed to be any that didn't include stepping out into the swarming insects. Help, he needed help. Franklin reached into his back pocket and swore, remembering his phone had been left outside on the ground. He stepped to the door and looked out the window. He could see his phone on the ground where it had been left, the angry insects scuttling over it. *Shit.*

Franklin grimaced as the pain in his hand flared up and he wracked his brain, realising just how much trouble he was in and trying to figure of a way out of this mess. He had a shotgun under his bed. He didn't know how effective it would be against the hordes of insects, but it was all he had.

Running the five steps from his kitchen to his bedroom, Franklin flung the metal frame of his bed out the way and grabbed the firearm and ammunition: ten shells. Not much.

While trying to load the gun his shaking hand, combined with the pain from the sting, almost made the task beyond his abilities and four of the cartridges dropped to the floor and rolled amongst piles of unwashed clothing and beer cans, lost forever in the concealing shadows.

Six shells were loaded, and he clicked the shotgun closed. "Alright, you bastards, you asked for it," he snorted, fear turning to anger. Picking it an old, discarded vest he wrapped it around his left hand so it would be protected when he went to grab his phone.

Walking back to his door, Franklin considered what his next action would be and almost second guessed himself until he noticed movement on the internal door handle. Looking down he was aghast to see the smaller ants coming in through the keyhole. There was no real choice at all.

Steeling himself, Franklin kicked the door open and ran outside as quick as he could. The ants' numbers had increased dramatically and there were certain items almost entirely obscured by their scuttling bodies. Franklin aimed at the nearest dense cluster and pulled the trigger. The shotgun erupted and the insects were obliterated.

It was a small victory considering the masses, but it made Franklin's fear wane. *No goddamned bug is going to get the better of me,* he thought. He aimed at another cluster and blew them to kingdom come. He then darted to his phone and reached down with his protected hand. The action of brushing the ants on the phone away caused another sharp stabbing pain from the sting and he let out an agonised gasp as he picked the device up.

Despite the pain he succeeded in picking the phone up without any ants clinging to it. His adrenaline pumped at the victory as he tried to focus on anything other than the pain.

And then he screamed as several ants successfully scaled his boots and buried their stingers in the flesh above his ankles.

"Oh, God," Franklin screamed, dropping the phone and falling to one knee. More ants crawled up his jeans and attacked, the burning of their stings overriding all of Franklin's senses with agonising pain. His entire lower body felt on fire, and he screamed in utter despair. "Damn you," he cried, lifting the shotgun. The bastards had got him, but he'd be damned if he didn't go down without a fight.

Through a red haze and gritted teeth, he aimed at the nearest cluster of ants and pulled the trigger. He didn't have time to realise the object the ants had been crawling over was one of his many haphazard gas cannisters. The cannister exploded, creating a chain reaction as other nearby cans also exploded, the force throwing Franking back several feet. The explosion pushed his trailer a good six feet on its pads and disintegrated a good third of it. It also wrecked the telephone post, causing it to fall sideways, the weight of the timber support falling pulled on the cables, snapping them under its weight. Franklin was completely unaware of this as he lay on his back, sobbing, his mind beyond reason, knowing only pain. The exploding gas cans had blinded him, burst his ear drums and ruptured several of his internal organs.

The man could do nothing but draw ragged breaths through blooded, broken teeth and try to shut out the pain as the ants swarmed over him, carrying out their evil work.

CHAPTER 6

Martin studied his full-length mirror as he buttoned up his shirt. Although the shirt was casual, it looked smart, and he decided to wear a tie with it. It felt strangely like the act of a forgotten life as he hooped the silk material of the tie around his neck and knotted it. When he worked in New York he had worn a tie every day. Since he had left, he'd come to associate them with the world he used to live in and almost never wore one, except on the most formal of occasions.

He smoothed out the silk material, studied it in the mirror and decided the knot was incorrect. He huffed and undid the knot before starting to redo it. Again, it didn't look quite right, although he didn't really know why, and so he reached up to undo it again.

"You look fine," sighed Louise, sitting at the vanity mirror across the room, applying her lip stick.

"I didn't realise how much I hated these things until I stopped wearing them," he grumbled. He yanked at the tie, ruining any equilibrium it had, forcing the need to re-tie it.

Louise stood and approached him. "It's nothing, just a bit of material," she smiled, wrapping her arms around his middle from behind and kissing him on the cheek, leaving a red smear. Martin hadn't realised how rigid he'd been standing until he relaxed into Louise's hold.

"Maybe it's the shirt. I should pick another one."

"The shirt's fine, the tie is fine. Stop worrying yourself," she soothed as her hands rose to the tie and she started tying the knot for him.

Martin smiled, watching Louise's face in the mirror as

she concentrated on his necktie. "There, done," she smiled. He reached up and held her hands in his. "You're just a little on edge. But it sounds like you and Tom made a big step towards reconciliation last night. You should be feeling confident. You know how sexy I find a confident man." She gently swayed her hips.

"Thanks, darling," he chuckled. "You're right, last night we hashed a lot of things out. He actually felt like my brother again, y'know?"

"Then what are you so worried about?"

"Dunno. If I'm just setting myself up for a fall, letting him in again. Or maybe it's wondering what that bitch Marie is saying to him, behind my back."

Louise reached down and slapped his backside. "You shouldn't call women 'bitches,'" she warned gently. "You're not a rapper."

Martin turned and wrapped his hands around her waist, laughing softly. "But you call her a 'bitch' all the time."

Louise grinned widely and kissed him. "Well, I'm allowed, on account of two things."

"Which are?"

"First, I'm a woman, so it's a woman's prerogative."

"Okay, that makes absolutely zero sense. And the second reason?"

"She's a total bitch." The couple laughed and embraced, their kiss long and with meaning. After they pulled away Louise cupped his cheek with one of her hands. "You probably wouldn't be overthinking this if you'd gotten a good night's sleep."

"Well, I've got Franklin to thank for that."

Louise rolled her eyes. "Of all the nights for him to decide to start firing off that damn shotgun of his."

"Well, he was probably scaring off coyotes and protecting my investment, so I can't be too hard on him."

Louise smiled and kissed her husband again. "My man, always trying to see the best in people."

Martin pulled her close to him again. "So, it was my

compassion that got me into your panties?" he suggestively smiled.

"Among over things."

Martin's hand moved below her waist, squeezing her butt. "So, right now, you must be super turned on, then?"

"I can see where this is going," Louise giggled. "And no, not now. Later."

"Why not now?" he gently pushed his stirring member against her.

Louise looked like she was wrestling with her desires and unfortunately for Martin, her rational self won the battle. "Because your brother and his wife are already up and milling about downstairs."

"Yeah, but…"

"And you're hoping to delay going down there by seducing me and buying yourself an extra five minutes up here."

"Only five minutes? Ouch," Martin pretended to have his feelings hurt. "It'd be the best five minutes of your life, though."

"I have no doubt of that, but no. You go down there and be the best host you can be." She broke away from the embrace and returned to the vanity mirror.

Martin relented. "Okay, okay, you win."

"Don't I always?"

"Every time."

"I just need to reapply my lipstick; I'll be down in a minute myself. And rub those lip marks off your face."

"Yes ma'am," said Martin, using a tissue to wipe away the evidence of his wife's affections. He tossed the crumpled tissue in the small trash can and walked to the door.

"Oh, and Martin?"

"Yeah?"

"Tonight I'll be looking forward to the best damn five minutes of my life."

Martin blushed, amazed his wife could still make his heart beat so fast after twenty years glorious years together. "Yes, ma'am," he grinned.

* * *

Walking into the well-lit open kitchen, Martin said his good mornings to Tom and Marie, who were already sat at the breakfast bar. The comforting smell of freshly brewed coffee drifted slowly through the air. He walked over to the coffee machine and poured himself a cup.

"How'd you guys sleep?" he asked.

Tom, wearing a silk off white shirt with wide, grey tie smiled eagerly. "Great thanks, slept like a baby. Must be that country air. I was really knocked out."

"It was either the country air or the beers you consumed," sighed Marie, keeping her eyes on Tom as she sipped her coffee. "Your wi-fi's down, by the way. And I can't get a signal on my phone anywhere."

"Really?" Martin checked his own cell and saw the Marie was right. "Weird. Hopefully it'll sort itself out in a couple of hours."

"Hopefully, otherwise I'll be stuck with Tom's half-baked opinions for conversation."

"Good one," Tom laughed, as if it were a joke. It didn't sound like a joke to Martin.

"How did you sleep, Marie?" asked Martin. He really didn't want to ask the question, but etiquette and a desire to change the path of the conversation seemed to dictate he should.

Marie's eyes flicked towards her brother in-law, and she put down her drink as if she were about to say something he should probably sit down for. "To be honest, I slept terribly." Tom looked down, suddenly finding the black liquid in his cup very interesting indeed.

It hurt Martin to keep his composure when he just wanted to tell Marie where to go. He smiled through gritted teeth. "Really, I'm sorry to hear that."

"It's not all your fault," Marie bemoaned sullenly. "I mean, true, the bed was hard and the sheets are hardly the quality I'm used to. I can hardly blame you for this oath's snoring though, can I?" she gestured to her husband, who remained impassive.

Martin faked a laugh, although he could tell the comment was meant more as a barbed jab than a jest.

"I guess the real problem was all that shooting in the night. Are you sure we're safe here?"

"You're quite safe, I assure you," Martin insisted. "I can pretty much guarantee that those shots you heard last night came from Franklin."

"That man who chipped our windscreen, yesterday? He has access to firearms?"

"He does and I hear him let them off from time to time. He scares the coyotes and such away from the land. He's even bagged a few since I've been here."

Marie considered his words. "And you are sure it was him doing the shooting?"

"Positive, I've heard his old shotgun go off a number of times. I'd know it anywhere."

Marie looked back at her husband. "I can't believe that man is allowed to carry guns."

Before Tom could respond, Martin beat him to it. "I'm afraid that, although we are safe, the same isn't always true for the cattle. We have to be ready to defend them from predators from time to time."

"Predators? Really?" Marie scoffed.

"Really. You ever seen what a pack of hungry coyotes looks like when not in a zoo? I don't like to shoot animals, but all those misgivings go out the window when you see how aggressive they can be and there are no bars between you and them."

"You shoot them, too?" asked Tom, interested in what Martin had to say. He had never owned a gun, though they fascinated him.

"No, I've never had to."

"But you've got guns?"

"Yep. Two of them. A Glock and an AR-15 rifle. That's a

mean bit of kit."

Tom whistled, impressed. "Sounds like it. Can I see?"

"Maybe later," Martin replied.

"Isn't that dangerous?" sneered Marie with distaste. "Having guns in the house? Especially around young boys."

Martin countered. "I've taught both my boys never to touch guns and to always treat them with the utmost respect."

Marie rolled her eyes. "But boys will be boys."

Martin struggled not to lose his temper. "Besides, the guns are kept locked in a cabinet in my bedroom and the boys don't know where the keys are. I assure you, it's one hundred percent safe having the guns in the house." He thought Marie was going to push further and was relieved when she appeared convinced and took a sip of her coffee.

"Guess I'll have to pack ear-plugs if ever we come back here," she muttered to herself.

"Good morning, how ya'll doing today?" beamed Louise with her most welcoming smile as she entered the room and to Martin's rescue. Martin loved her more in that instant than he ever had before.

"Fine," Marie replied curtly.

Tom was much more enthusiastic. "Hey Louise, good morning. Can I pour you a coffee?"

"No, please, stay seated. I'm supposed to be the hostess, after all." She walked to the counter and poured herself a drink. "Kids up, yet?"

"Yeah, they're up and getting along famously. They've already ate their croissants and are hanging out in the games room," Tom said.

"I'm glad to hear that they're getting along," Louise beamed. "Have you two eaten, yet?"

Marie rolled her eyes before Tom spoke. Clearly, she had heard what he was going to say already. Tom spoke with a conspiring edge. "To be honest, the croissant didn't even touch the sides, Lou. Do you reckon there's any chance of you frying up some bacon and eggs, real quick?"

Louise gave mock outrage. "Tom, we told you it would be just croissants this morning. We don't want you ruining your appetite for the big dinner I'm going to be slaving over all morning, do we?"

The tone in her voice reminded Martin of how she explained things to their sons, like an adult talking to a child, and he hoped Tom didn't take offense.

If Tom was irked, he didn't show it. Martin decided his brother was probably used to being talked down to like a child, considering who he was married to. "I know, I know. It's just, I thought that advice was more for the kids. To be honest, I could eat a horse."

"You can *one* extra croissant; we have some more in the pantry. And that's your lot until dinner. Okay?" Louise jovially bartered.

"You drive a hard bargain," laughed Tom has he jumped up and eagerly made his way to the pantry. He offered a second croissant to his wife, which she declined out of hand.

"Morning Uncle Mart, Aunt Lou," said Cassie as she walked in wearing denim shorts and a tank top. "Did my parents tell you the internet is down?" She walked to the fridge and helped herself to a glass of fresh juice.

"They did. Sorry Cas, it's never happened before. Hopefully it rights itself soon."

"I hope so, I haven't got any signal at all. If I don't update my socials soon my friends will all think I'm dead."

"Welcome to the wilderness," Marie sighed, sounding bored. "We can both be dead together."

"Looks like you'll have to make your own fun," Marty said to Cassie. "I remember back when I was young, I used to always be outside, having adventures and such. These days kids are too addicted to their screens."

Cassie smiled in a way Martin couldn't decipher as friendly or patronising. "Don't worry, I'm an expert at making my own fun." With that she walked off down the hallway, back towards the games room.

"Kids," Tom laughed between chews.

"Say, Tom, after you've eaten that, what say I take you for the tour outside? I'll show you what a working ranch is like."

Tom nodded as he chewed a mouthful, washed it down with a glug of coffee. "Sure, I'd love that," he smiled.

"While the boys are doing that, do you want to give me a hand preparing dinner?" Louise asked Marie, trying to make the offer as enticing as possible. "It'll be nice to have a good catch up. You know, I've lost contact with a lot of people since moving down here. Perhaps you can catch me up on everything going on in the Big Apple."

"No problem," Marie said, dryly. "Although I'm not really much use in the kitchen."

"That's okay. Its more a case of gossiping and keeping me company, to be honest. I just wasn't going to tell the men that."

Marie chuckled and Martin half expected her face to crack. "As long as it's not too early for a drink or two."

Louise hid her surprise as best she could with amusement. "No, sure, I'll get the wine."

*   *   *

"It's still not working," Teddy complained as he tried to get his games console to connect online for what had to be the fiftieth time.

"That's what you get for moving to the middle of butt-fuck nowhere," sighed Cassie, perched on the side of the pool table, sipping her drink. "At least you have a pretty sweet pad, if nothing else."

"We didn't choose to move here," Dean grumbled, throwing darts.

"Well, why would you?" Cassie teased.

Dean went to respond when he heard Uncle Tom call to them from down the hallway. "Hey, Cas, Uncle Martin's going to give me a tour of the ranch. You want to come see?"

Cassie locked eyes with Dean and rolled them at the

absurdity of the suggestion. "No dad, I'm good thanks." Her voice gave a sense of enthusiasm and sweetness her face did not match. She listened to her dad and Uncle Martin put their boots on and leave via the front door, then shook her head and said; "Can you believe my dad? Why on Earth would I want to see a bunch of rusty outhouses and a bunch of cows?"

"I know, right?" Dean agreed, clearly because it was what he thought Cassie wanted to hear. He turned away and threw a couple more darts, then went to collect them. "Wanna throw?"

A devious smile spread over Cassie's face. "Oh, I can think of something a lot more fun than darts that we can do," she said suggestively.

Dean went red and his body language betrayed how uncomfortable he was feeling. He quickly glanced at Teddy to make sure he wasn't listening. He still looked like he was fiddling around with the settings of his console. "Like what?" he coughed, his throat dry.

Cassie giggled and lowered her voice. "Can you get the keys to the quads?"

Dean's awkwardness suddenly turned to panic and he again checked his younger brother wasn't eavesdropping. He took a step towards Cassie and his voice lowered. "You're serious about that?"

Cassie acted coy. "Come on, you said you knew where your dad kept them."

Dean did indeed know where the keys were kept; in a metal tin in the bottom drawer besides his dad's bed. That was also his dad's hiding place for the keys to the gun cabinet. Dean decided he wasn't going to share that information with Cassie, fearing she would want him to take a gun for target practice or something. "My dad will kill me. There's no way he won't find out."

"Don't you want to have fun with me?"

"Sure. I'll tell you what, I'll speak with my dad and…"

Cassie reached for Dean and squeezed his forearm. "We can't have as much fun with your dad along for the ride."

Dean chewed his lip, the internal dilemma in his mind taking over his entire thought process. "I dunno."

"I was so looking forward to having a ride. I was thinking about it all last night."

Dean gulped at the seductive tone and the conflict in his head was instantly resolved. "Okay, no problem. I'll be back in a few minutes."

"Oooh, really?" Cassie exclaimed excitedly, and it instantly felt to Dean the idea had been his all along. "I'm so excited."

Dean gave Teddy a cursory glance before leaving the room. Cassie began humming happily to herself as she studied numerous photos of Dean and his family on the walls. As her vision slowly moved around the room, her eyes set on Teddy, who was staring back at her. "What?" she barked harshly. The ten-year-old immediately turned back to the television in shock at his cousin's scorn.

Pleased with Teddy's reaction, Cassie returned to studying the various pictures. One picture caught her attention. It was of Dean and his father wearing fishing gear and standing nearly hip deep in a river. They looked to be having fun and Cassie felt a pang of jealousy as she tried and failed to conjure any memory of having fun with her own dad. She'd lied the night before when she'd claimed she'd played pool with her dad. The truth was she'd learnt to play alone, in their large, impeccably decorated and furnished, empty house. She reacted to the tiny pain the memory created the same way she always did; by turning her heart cold.

"What a bunch of yokels," she said quietly to herself, careful to make sure Teddy couldn't hear. Dean re-entered the room, looking like the guiltiest man alive. Cassie's eyes lit up at her victory; she'd learned at a young age that she could make men perform for her, like puppets on a string. Dean was only a boy, making the manipulation almost too easy. "You got the keys? Seriously?" she added an incredulous tone which she did not feel. Of course he had got them for her, she could almost see her strings on him.

"Yeah, no sweat," Dean responded, sounding as nervous as ever. He strode to the glass doors at the far end of the games room and slid the correct key into the slick lock. "Our dads have gone up to the cattle shed in the truck, if we're gonna go, now's our shot."

Cassie stepped beside him, squeezing his arm. "Ooooh, I like this side of you, Dean. Didn't know you were such a bad boy."

Dean smiled with newly discovered confidence and was about to reply when Teddy spoke up from the sofa. "You shouldn't be doing that, Dean. Dad will be mad."

Dean glanced at Cassie before responding. "Don't worry about it, Teddy. Dad will never know. We're just taking them out for a quick spin."

"But what if you hurt yourself?"

Cassie scoffed.

"I know what I'm doing. I've gone out with dad loads of times before. You've just got to avoid the uneasy ground." Dean unlocked the door and opened it into the garage area.

Cassie walked in, checking out the four quad bikes before sitting on the one that had 'LOUISE' stencilled on the engine with fancy lettering. "This is so cool," she chirped, becoming genuinely excited.

Dean walked past her and unlocked the shutter before pulling it up, exposing the garage to the hot open air from outside. Harsh sunlight poured in.

"You know how to ride one of these?" Dean asked his cousin.

"I'm a quick learner, just show me the basics." Dean did so before sitting on his own quad and starting the engine. He looked back and spotted Teddy, now standing at the glass door. He looked torn. "It's no big deal, Teddy. Do you want to come with us?"

"Can I?"

"If it'll stop you freaking out, then sure."

Cassie rolled her eyes. "He's scared."

"Am not," Teddy protested.

"He's not scared. Are you, Ted?"

"No way."

"Then come on, let's ride."

Teddy laughed in the affirmative and jumped onto his own quad, starting the ignition as if it were instinct to him.

Dean was happier than he realised seeing Teddy look like he was now on a mission to have fun.

Teddy grinned as he pulled on the small quad's throttle. "Let's ride."

CHAPTER 7

The heat of the day began to bake the earth and sand as the morning went on. To the ants, nature dictated that as the sun approached its zenith they would hide in cool, dark tunnels. There they would wait in safely, among their own kind. That was the natural way. It was a behaviour that they now abandoned.

The ants had been attacked by an enemy they could neither conceive nor understand. All they recognised was that they had encountered a threat to their existence. They didn't comprehend its nature, nor did they desire to. This new threat had the power to kill them all. The workers, the larvae, the queen. The response was singular; the threat must be destroyed.

The creature responsible for burning so many of their kin had been killed, and its body had been used to feed the nest. Yet it was just one of its kind. Others were nearby. More threats to be eliminated.

And so, the ants marched on, staying in the shadows if possible, scuttling across open ground when shade wasn't an option. Their goal was singular. All enemies of the nest must be destroyed.

*   *   *

Upon leaving the house, Martin had led Tom down the stone steps to the flat driveway and walked across to show him the large, weather battered barn.

"You really thought this was where I'd be living?" joked Martin as they both stood inside the dark building. Against the backwall were hay bales, piled haphazardly almost to the height of the roof.

"Well, we were pretty far off," Tom shrugged. "It could have been a house, from a distance."

"It's mainly used the storage. The hay we feed the herd is stored here until it's used to replenish the stocks in the shed. And there you can see my fuel depot," he indicated a number of barrels stored to one side of the barn.

"They're all filled with gas?" Tom asked. "Isn't that a bit of a fire hazard?"

"Don't worry about it. We have a strict 'no smoking' policy." He pointed to a sign on the wall which said as much. "It takes a lot of fuel to keep the lights on here, not to mention all the machinery. There are various generators that have to be kept topped up. We're off the main grid out here. I can't make the drive to the gas station every day."

"I guess," shrugged Tom. "And what about that area over there?" He thumbed towards a small table and chairs, along with a tee vee, battered and stained fridge and a few worn, grimy desks covered with various tools and miscellaneous items. "Is that where you live when you and the missus have a falling out?"

Martin laughed. "No, that's just a little rec room for the workers. They also work and store bits and pieces there." His light mood suddenly darkened. "God damn it," he swore.

"What's up?"

Martin nodded to the radio cradle, lined with charging walkie-talkies. "Franklin left his walkie in the house yesterday evening. I was meant to bring it out here."

"You want to do it now?"

"Nah, that's okay. I'll get 'round to it later. Now, let's hop in the truck and I'll drive you up to the shed.

*   *   *

Martin's herd, four hundred head of longhorn cattle, stood in their pens, chewing the straw that had been provided. The cow shed was the most modern available and Martin had spent a small fortune on it. Separated into pens of five, the cows were fed at four-hour intervals by an automated feeder belt that ensured none went hungry. Their drinking troughs were also kept full automatically.

Although costly, it would pay for itself in labour costs in about ten years, so Martin didn't mind. He was in farming for the long haul now, and he'd learnt in his city life that investing early always paid dividends in the end. Go big or go home.

He walked amongst the enclosures, explaining how the animals were fed and watered by the machines.

"Too bad they don't clean up the shit as well. Christ, it stinks to high heaven in here," Tom complained, holding his nose.

Although Martin was a little irked that his younger brother appeared completely unimpressed, he wasn't without sympathy. When he'd begun farming the smell of the animals had overwhelmed him, too. It wasn't the shit so much as the urine. The stench of ammonia hung heavy in the air, even with the shed's extraction fans humming on full power.

"I know, right?" he laughed. Tom laughed and it felt good to Martin that they were getting along like they used to. "The longhorn are pretty well spaced out so they don't need mucking out every day when necessary. Normally the shed is cleaned out every day, whilst the cattle are out on the range, but it allows me to have the odd day off here and there. It's still pretty full on, though."

Tom rested a foot on the bars of one of the five foot pen fences and draped his arms over the top. "Could they get out of their pens?"

"If they really wanted, probably."

"Then why don't they?"

"Why would they? They got all they need. Food, water. Remember they're not usually in here. Most the time they're out on the plains, as nature intended."

Tom rolled his eyes. "You always knew how to romanticise a business venture."

"It's more than just a business venture, Tom. This is my life now. Shovelling shit and all."

"And you're happy? Really?"

Martin thought about the question, probably more so than his brother intended. "I am. I actually am."

Any poignancy Martin had intended for the moment was lost when Tom wretched. "Listen, bro, I gotta get out of here." He nodded towards the mooing cattle. "*They* definitely smell better barbequed with some butter."

Martin laughed, patting his brother on the back in sympathy and leading him back out into the bright sunlight. "I'll admit it is a little riper in here than I am used to. Must be the heat."

"I bet they usually smell like potpourri," Tom laughed, dragging his shoes against the ground to scrape off any clinging odour once they were outside. He then looked out at the view before them. The Arizonan desert in all its harsh beauty. It was hard not to fall in love with the view. About half a mile down hill was the main house. Already Tom started feeling hungry, thinking about the dinner Louise and Marie were prepping. "Four million certainly buys you a lot out here," he said, filling his nostrils with fresh air.

Martin eyed his brother warily as he pulled the sliding door closed behind them. The fact his brother had just stated a dollar attachment to what he had just referred to as his happiness didn't sit right. "It does," he agreed. He could tell Tom wanted to say something and was struggling with the words.

"Martin, can I ask you something?"

"Shoot."

"I wanted to do you a favour. A big favour, to make up for..." he chewed over his words. "... past indiscretions."

Martin couldn't shake the sinking feeling which had developed in his belly. "Okay..."

Tom opened his mouth, and it were as if he no longer needed to pause for air. "Well, long story short, this great opportunity has literally landed in my lap. You remember Casey?

Casey Burns? Of course you do. Well, he was at this very elite club in Soho a few weeks back. I've been there before, very elitist clientele. And he met the one and only Hans Mickle. You know, from Goldman and Sachs. Top trader. And anyway, he's let Casey into his confidence about this company, Hydrodyne. They specialise in cleaning the oceans and waterways and shit. Anyhow, they've engineered a bacteria that breaks down plastics and oil spills like that." He clicked his fingers to emphasise his point.

He continued. "I know, no way, right? Too good to be true, right? This could be the end of all the pollution woes people have been worried about for ages. Imagine a future without plastic floating in the seas, clogging up the dolphins. Fucking amazing. Well, the reason I am telling you this is because the bacteria, or whatever it is, hasn't been made public yet. Nobody is any the wiser."

"That sounds great, but why are you telling me all this?" Marty asked.

"Because shares in Hydrodyne are currently estimated at five dollars apiece. In three months, the information about the bacteria is being announced, and when it does, well, I don't need to tell you. The sky's the limit with this one."

"Okay," said Martin, fearing where this conversation would lead. "Thanks for the information. Maybe I'll pick a few shares up."

"That's the catch. Remember I said 'estimated'?"

"I remember."

"The company hasn't gone public yet. It floats a week before the information about the bacteria is published."

"That sounds suspect."

"Come on, Marty. Don't be naïve. You know how these things work. The information is being held back so the stocks can be sold to the right people at the right price. You know Casey's got friends in high places. He's been let into the buy-in and he's offered me a chance, too. Only those with connections are being given this chance. The general public aren't even getting a look in."

"Well, that sounds like a good opportunity for you." Martin wanted to break away from the conversation as quickly as possible. The sinking feeling in his stomach had been replaced. First with disappointment and now with anger.

"The thing is, the minimum buy-in is pretty steep."

"Really?"

"Yeah. I mean, obviously it would be. Seeing as a man could quadruple his money in a couple of weeks, obviously he'd need to throw down a fair bit of cheese first."

"How much?"

"Seven hundred and fifty grand."

"Jesus."

"I know. A bargain. Right?"

"Listen, Tom, thanks for giving me this," he paused, carefully choosing his words, "opportunity. I'm going to have to pass. I haven't got that amount of money to gamble."

"Hardly a gamble," Tom continued. "And that's what I was coming up to next."

"What was?"

Tom looked around to make sure nobody was in earshot, which was ridiculous as they were over half a mile from the house and aside from Franklin over at his trailer, nobody was within fifteen miles of the ranch. "I was going to ask if you wanted to go halves with me. You know, three-seventy-five each."

"I see."

"Like I said, only select people are allowed in on this. I'm in, but since you left the game people aren't too sure about giving you a shot. As your brother, I'll let you in on half of my buy-in. As a way of apologising."

Martin had just about heard enough. He couldn't even look at his brother as he spoke, for fear he would punch his lights out. "So, your way of apologising to me is by asking for three hundred and seventy-five thousand dollars."

Tom was in full salesman mode, either ignoring or not

recognising the look of fury on his brother's face. "No, I'm apologising by offering you the chance to get rich. I mean really rich. Rich enough that it doesn't matter if your ranch is a success or not, because either way you'll be set for life. Obviously, the funds and shares will have to move through my accounts, for admin reasons. As soon as I'm allowed to move the shares to you, I would do so."

"Thanks, but no thanks." Martin started walking to his truck. The desire to get away from his brother was palpable.

Tom jogged up behind him. "Hey, this is the golden ticket. If not for yourself, think about it for Lou and your kids' sake." He put his hand on Martin's shoulder. Martin swung around and hurled his fist square into Tom's face.

* * *

In the shed the longhorns went about their business, mooing, eating and creating waste. The machines chimed, a noise deliberately created to let the animals know that fresh food was on its way. In her pen of five, cow number One-Oh-One grunted in excitement as she pulled away from the water trough. She had just slackened her thirst and now her stomach demanded the near constant intake of food the cows desired.

Pushing passed the four other bovines in her pen, One-Oh-One hurriedly trotted to the conveyer belt and pushed her nose into the heaps of hay. Contented, she started grazing.

Inside the dried hay, the ants stirred angrily. Their numbers were many. The individuals had marched into the cow shed, sensing the presence of many mammalian bodies. Bodies they saw as enemies to be conquered. As One-Oh-One pushed deeper into the hay and fed, she engulfed and devoured hundreds of the tiny invertebrates, infuriating those that remained.

One-Oh-One pulled her head up and out of the hay in alarm as the insects in her mouth that hadn't been chewed to pulp began to sting her tongue and upper pallet. The pain caused the animal to panic, and she shook her head desperately from side to side. Other members of the herd backed away from her, their kin's defensive behaviour spreading alarm among them.

Even as One-Oh-One shook her head more and more violently and rearing up onto her rear legs in pain and confusion, the same thing was occurring in numerous other holding pens throughout the shed. Members of the herd panicked and thrashed their bodies as the ants emerged from the hay they had been feeding on. Many suffered the insects' numerous stings on their faces as the ants found and attacked the sensitive areas in the cattle's noses, ears and upon their eyes.

Vocalising their alarm and distress, cows stamped their hoofs and threw their bodies against the pen barriers. The stainless-steel bars bent from the forces of the heavy animals, desperate to escape the stinging attackers. The desperate animal struggles further enraged the invertebrates who managed to cling to the beasts' legs and sting the tender areas where hoof met flesh.

Within a couple of minutes the entire shed had descended into chaos, as the cows hurled their bodies at the pens. Ribs and legs were broken. One cow, in her thrashing, caught her long curved horns in the gut of her sister and split her open. Lashes of blood spilled out across the concrete floor and the wounded cow responded with an attack in turn.

The desperation of the animals increased and increased, creating utter pandemonium as more and more of the ants emerged from the hay and various other shadows, cracks and holes. Their number seemingly endless, the ants swarmed the defenceless animals.

* * *

"Jesus Christ, you punched me," exclaimed Tom. He was sat on the ground, where he had been knocked down, pinching his bloodied nose. Blood leaked freely and stained his shirt. "What the hell is wrong with you?"

"What the hell is wrong with me?" shouted Martin. "What the hell is wrong with you?"

"What are you talking about."

Martin laughed in disbelief of Tom's self-pitying behaviour and his own roller coaster emotions. "You know, I was so happy when you agreed to come down here for Thanksgiving. So fucking happy. I thought, just maybe, that we could put the past behind us, let bygones be bygones, and move on. Maybe not quite as close as before, but we could have been brothers again. I really hoped."

"Well you have a funny way of showing it," bemoaned Tom, raising his head to try and stop the nose bleed.

"And now I find out that you're really here for a business opportunity. You're not interested in me. You're only interested in getting me to invest in some lofty, too good to be true, can't lose shares that Casey has dangled in front of you like a carrot, treating you like the fucking donkey that you are."

Tom's incredulousness began turning to anger as he got to his feet. "Now just a minute, I'm giving you an opportunity here. I'm trying to help you out."

"Oh really?" Martin couldn't believe his ears. "I've just been telling you that I'm happy here. That I'm living the life I want to lead. How the fuck are you helping me?"

"It's a good deal."

"You're fucking stupid and you're fucking greedy. And they both inform the other. You are actually unbelievable, Tom. You know that?"

"At least I don't hit people. And I don't run away from my problems and buy a ranch in the middle of fucking nowhere."

Martin went to punch his brother again. He stopped when he saw his brother put up his hands in self-defence. "You're my fucking problem, Tom. To think I would trust you with one dollar of my money is surreal to me. If this Casey deal is so fucking good, you invest the money, give me a call when you're next passing over on a private jet. I'll wave from down here as you fly over."

"Fuck this, I'm going home." Tom started storming over to the truck.

It was then that Martin realised the truth. "You can't afford it, can you?"

"You going to drive me, or should I walk back to the house?"

"You can't afford to raise the seven-fifty alone. Can you"

Tom looked like he was going to say something but the words didn't come out. His eyes were becoming watery, as if he were holding back tears. "Just drive us back to the house," he demanded.

Martin sighed. "Whatever happened to you, man?"

"She's going to leave me," Tom shouted, the sheer emotion in his voice made him sound like a completely different man than the one Martin knew.

Martin tried to comprehend what Tom had said. "What?" He sounded as dumbstruck as he felt.

Tom leant his back against the truck and slid back down into a seating position on the ground. He kept is gaze downwards. "Marie. She's going to leave me."

"Why? She doesn't love you, anymore?"

Tom looked up as if he were being talked down to. "Don't act like I'm thick."

"What do you mean?"

Tom gave a bitter, short laugh. "You think she ever loved me?"

"Well, you've been together over twenty years."

"And how long do you think she'd have stayed if the money ever dried up?"

Martin didn't answer. He walked up to Tom and slid down beside him. "Man, I'm sorry, Tom."

"She's got meaner. Talks to me like I'm a piece of shit all the time and fucking around behind my back."

"You think she's having an affair?"

Tom gave a knowing look. "An affair? Try multiple. She was cheating on me before we were even married. Truth be told, sometimes I stay awake all night, terrified in case it ever comes to light that Cassie isn't my kid."

"Jesus. I had no idea."

"It's not your fault. She seems good at hiding her liaisons and rendezvous' from everyone except me. Part of me thinks that is deliberate, you know? Another way of saying, 'hey, Tom, fuck you.' The joke of it is, I still love her. I've always loved her. I will always love her."

"So why is she leaving you now?"

"Why do you think? Money."

"But you're certainly not poor, Tom. You've got a good business head on you."

"Thanks for the flattery," Tom said, genuinely smiling. "But we both know that you were always the smart one in our business."

"We both made it work."

"Since you left, it hasn't been the same. More mistakes, more bad calls. I've kept it going, but like a coma patient on life support, just waiting for someone to pull the plug."

Martin put his hand on his younger brother's shoulder. "I had no idea it was so bad."

"I got a fine about a year ago, for not filing the correct tax work on this big deal I had going through at the time. Word's got out just how fucking useless I am. And now Marie has begun to realise it, too. Unless I get a big win, I'm going to lose everything. I'm going to lose Marie. Cassie. The house. The business. Everything. Everything I've worked so hard to achieve. And I'm fucking terrified. I've lied, begged, borrowed and cheated to raise funds for this Hydrodyne thing, but I just can't make the money on my own. I'm sorry Martin. For everything. We've already lost Mom and Dad. I don't want to lose contact with you. I'm sorry, for everything."

The two men sat in silence for a while. "And I'm sorry, too."

Tom looked at Martin, confused. "Sorry about what?"

"Sorry about slugging you in the nose."

Tom chuckled. "That was a cheap shot. You're lucky I didn't decide to put you on your ass for that. I've been learning karate, don't you know?" They both laughed gently.

"Tom, I'm sorry about your troubles. I really am. But I'm not lending you the money. I can't jeopardise what I've built here."

Tom looked wholly sad. "I understand. It was wrong of me to ask."

Martin nodded. "It was. But I'm still your brother. And I still want us to *be* brothers when all is said and done."

Tom smiled. "We did have some good times, back when we were young city boys, didn't we?"

Martin chuckled. "We sure did." They laughed some more before Martin's expression became earnest. "Please don't go home yet. The girls are cooking us a delicious dinner as we speak. It'd be a shame to let it go to waste."

Tom smiled and looked down at his blood-stained shirt. "You're buying me a new shirt, tomorrow."

Martin roared with laughter. "Okay, you win. To be honest, I probably did you a favour." They both laughed until Martin asked Tom to quiet down, suddenly dead serious.

"What's wrong?" Tom asked.

"You hear that?"

Tom listened. At first he couldn't pick up on what his brother was listening too. Then he heard it. The unmistakable, guttural sounds of animals in harrowing distress. As they listened, the noise grew like a crescendo, along with the sounds of the heavy beasts banging and crashing against the pens within their shed. "The hell? Is that normal?"

Martin slowly stood, focussing on the sounds that were becoming more and more like a wall of noise which blotted everything else out. "I've never heard anything like it." Slowly he began to approach the shed doors. He moved cautiously, aware that something was very wrong but not knowing what. Could it be a fire? It seemed the most probable reason for the animals to panic, even though he had no idea how a fire could have occurred.

Tom was now standing alongside his brother. He followed Martin at a distance, although where his brother was cautious and curious, Tom felt no desire to solve the mystery of why the animals were acting up. "Maybe we shouldn't open that door 'til they calm down," he suggested. "They sound pretty riled up in there."

"Tom, they're my investment. If anything happens to the herd, I'm high and dry." Martin said, licking his lips as he summoned his courage and approached the main shed door. The noises from the animals were now even more intense and Martin couldn't guess what had happened to cause such stress. As he reached for the door a loud bang startled him and the entire side of the shed shook from the impact. Clearly a cow had escaped its pen and had charged at the corrugated metal.

The bang was followed by a second, then a third. Then multiple impacts shook the shed wall over and over. The metal dented and bent, looking ready to give at any moment.

Martin very slowly reached for the shed door and froze as a heavy impact shook the doors on their tracks. They were left distorted and it was obvious a few more impacts of that magnitude would force the doors open.

Martin reconsidered his options. There sounded like a lot of angry cattle in the shed, and if they wanted out, he was standing between them and freedom.

Another bang, the doors bulged and stayed that way. "You know, I'm thinking I'm not going to open the door," Martin called back to his brother.

"Amen on that," Tom uttered under his breath.

Martin slowly backed away from the shed.

Bang, bang. Two more impacts rocked the shed exterior. The average cow weighed in at fifteen hundred pounds. It didn't take a physics major to understand just how much damage one could do whilst charging. The shed walls were now so distorted that it was no longer a case of if they collapsed, but when.

Martin turned and started jogging away from the threat

within the shed, and not a moment too soon as with an almighty crash the doors flew off their tracks and the beasts inside bolted for freedom. They were moving faster than Martin had ever seen before and were acting completely wild.

The animals bellowed as they charged. Martin couldn't tell if the animals had even registered his presence, so blind was their panic and so strong was their apparent desperation to escape their confines.

"Run," he called to Tom as his jog turned to a sprint. A particularly large longhorn overtook him on his right as it galloped for freedom. Another overtook him to his left. This one was so close it almost managed to lean its body weight into him and he had to jump away from it to avoid falling beneath its hooves and being trampled. Behind him he heard the calls of the beasts as they stampeded, their many hooves thundering down on the ground. Martin knew that if he fell he would certainly be killed.

Tom reacted as anyone would upon seeing over a hundred head of cattle charging towards him. He turned and ran. It didn't take long for the herd to reach the truck where he had just been standing and numerous animals charged full speed into the truck. Some of the cows went down, the muscle in their necks tearing from the fierce impact. The two-ton flatbed truck caught the impacts on its side and flipped from the combined force of multiple animals.

Tom looked behind himself and cried out in terror as the truck came down on top of him.

Martin called his brother's name, the thundering of the stampede drowning out his calls. He'd watched in horror as he ran, cows passing him left and right, as the truck up ended and landed on Tom. And then, to add to the sickening assault, members of the herd started jumping up and trampling over the truck to get past it.

Praying his brother wasn't dead, Martin searched for shelter of any kind. It was a miracle he hadn't been flattened already and he knew he couldn't rely on luck forever.

Struggling to see through the thick dust cloud that was being kicked up, Martin felt almost blind. The deafening noise left him feeling more vulnerable than he had ever felt before. To his left he managed to spot a dried tree log, discarded on the side of the track. It wasn't much but it was better than nothing. Breaking off to the left towards the log, Martin kept an eye on cows as they hurtled past him. He had to stop mid-stride as a cow trampled the ground in front of him. As soon as it had overtaken him, he continued his weaving to the left until he reached the log.

Making a jump for the relative refuge, Martin jumped behind the log and hugged the ground, praying that none of the animals made the same jump and crushed him under hoof. The ground shook violently from the herds stampede and Martin could only cover his head and hope the madness would be over soon.

CHAPTER 8

"It's not much of a view, is it?" Cassie sighed as she studied the selfie she'd just taken of herself, the vast, open Arizona wilderness behind her.

"I guess not," Dean grumbled quietly. He tried to hide his embarrassment. Once he had stolen the keys to the quad garage, he had led the charge, promising Cassie views that would wow her socks off. And perhaps other things would be wowed off also, his teen addled brain had whispered to him. Although the thought was semi-ridiculous, he was at the age where even a million to one chance seemed like a bet he'd go all in on.

Using his knowledge of his father's land, he'd managed to pick a route that would avoid their respective dads attentions. Knowing that their dads had driven over to the cow shed, Dean had led Cassie and Teddy on a trail that remained on low ground. A ridge between their low trail and the higher trail to the cattle shed had kept their misdeed hidden until they made enough ground that various other rocky outcrops hid them. He'd thought the view from atop a particularly elevated rocky ridge was phenomenal. Okay, Arizona may appear bleak to some, mainly flat and peppered with harsh rock elevations, but to the keen eye it could be viewed for what it was; a harsh beauty that offered the kind of views one couldn't find anywhere else in the world.

At least, that's what he *had* thought, before hearing Cassie's blunt criticism. He'd told her that the view from the ridge was amazing and had waxed lyrical about it, his passion for the surrounding country growing as Cassie seemed to become excited at the prospect of seeing it for herself. Now that she had seen it and given the view a "five and a half out of ten," Dean felt silly. Apparently, the view just could not compete with the New York skyline.

"Well, I like it," said Teddy, defending the land he called home.

Cassie looked down at him as she posed for another selfie, trying to stop the sun glare from ruining the shot. "Of course you do." She rolled her eyes.

"Shut up, Ted," Dean snapped, using Teddy to vent his frustrations. He turned to Cassie. "You're right, not really much to see here, to be honest. Not like home." He hadn't used the word 'home' to describe New York for a long time and saying it now almost felt like a betrayal to his father and the life he now had. Regardless, Cassie was *very* hot and he decided he could live with himself. He was almost certain that cousins were legal, at least in the southern states, so his path was set. "I wish we'd never moved here. I hate it"

Cassie looked down at him as she pocketed her phone. One eyebrow was raised in amusement, as if she found it funny that Dean wasn't defending his dad's ranch. "Oh really, you hate it, huh? That's not what you said to me while you were leading me up here."

God she was beautiful, Dean thought. Did she have to be sarcastic about everything, though? It was really starting to fuck with his head. "I know, I was just hoping it wouldn't be as shit this time." He was well aware of how painfully lame his mutterings made him sound. He looked over at Teddy, who was busying himself turning over rocks, no doubt looking for lizards.

Cassie put her hands on her hips, eyebrow still cocked. "Why did you bring me up here in the first place, then? Perhaps we should go back. It feels like this is a waste of time, to be honest."

Dean suddenly felt alarm that all the promise and cool points his act of rebellion had gained him had been squandered. "You can't go back yet," he said, trying and failing to hide his desperation.

Cassie took exception to that. "Oh, can't I?" Now she seemed pissed and Dean couldn't bring himself to look her in the eye. He stared off into the distance, hiding his anger at the situation. "And *why* can't I?"

"We can still have fun."

"How can we have 'fun', exactly?" There was an accusatory note in her words.

Dean wracked his brain, trying to think of how to impress her. What was it, girls liked? Flowers? Maybe he could find an exotic desert flower to give her? No, that was a stupid, pathetic idea. It was too revealing of his thoughts. Plus, it was doubtless that no matter what he found, it wouldn't be able to compete with what could be found in Manhattan's florist shops.

Bad boys, that's what girls liked. Cool guys and bad boys. She'd been impressed when he's stolen the quad keys. He just needed to show her how cool he could be.

Lightning struck as he hit on the answer. Extreme sports were cool. "Want to see me do some stunts on the quad?"

Cassie couldn't hide her intrigue. "Stunts? Like what?"

"Yeah, like what?" asked Teddy, also curious where Dean was going with all this.

Dean scanned the local vicinity and spotted two elevations of rock some five foot apart. They were shaped in such a way he could ride his bike up one and down the other. The drop between them wasn't much, maybe four feet, but it was enough. "Wanna see me jump that?"

Cassie looked over at where he was pointing. "Sure, that could be cool," she smiled.

"Are you sure?" Teddy asked with concern.

"Nothing to it," Dean responded with faux bravado and climbed onto his bike.

Cassie walked up beside him as he turned the ignition and began revving the bike and put her hand on his back. "Good luck, Eval Knievel."

Dean nodded, eyes fixed on the jump and then accelerated towards the jump. He had to hit a certain speed to make the jump which meant he had to pull off a number of twists and turns, following the contours of the rock they were on as well as avoiding a number of small boulders which littered the ground. Confident he could pull the manoeuvres off, Dean sped towards the target, swerved left, then right, then opened her up fully as he hit the incline and flew off the edge. He felt a moment of cold dread upon realising nothing was beneath him and then he hit the rock on the other side with a thud and juddered to lower revs as he circled back around to where Cassie and Teddy stood watching them.

"Wow, awesome," Teddy said in awe.

Cassie grinned, nodding in agreement. "I've got to admit, that was pretty cool."

"Weren't nothing to it," Dean smirked, enjoying the moment.

"Really? Reckon you could do another one, then?" She gestured to another crevice that looked suitable to jump. This jump was wider and deeper. The width was around eight feet and if he failed, he would probably end up falling around seven feet. It was leagues more dangerous than the first jump. The ride up to it was possible, although would also be trickier.

"That one?" Dean confirmed. He hoped he sounded confident, even if a pang of fear had returned.

Cassie stood closer so she could be heard over the quad's engine. "Yeah, if you could jump that, I'd be super impressed." She chewed on her bottom lip, looking coy as she rested her hand on Dean's upper thigh and gave a squeeze. "Reckon you can?"

"No sweat," Dean replied. In truth, he hadn't even properly sized the jump up. He was too busy thinking about how gorgeous Cassie was when she looked shy, along with the fact her squeeze of his thigh had caused his blood to flow somewhere far from his brain.

"That's a pretty scary jump, Dean. Maybe you shouldn't."

At that moment Dean saw Teddy as nothing more than an obstacle between him and Cassie's incredible body. "If you didn't want to have fun, you shouldn't have come," he snapped. "Go back to looking for lizards, or whatever."

Teddy looked hurt and returned to turning over rocks, the hurt on his face apparent. If Dean hadn't been on to a sure thing, he would have felt regret for hurting his brother's feelings. As it was, he decided apologies could come later.

Cassie looked to be loving the promise of the second jump. "Get to it, cowboy."

Nodding, Dean finally focused properly on the jump's trajectory and imagined the path he would need to take and the speed he would need to make to cover the gap. He realised how the jump was several magnitudes more difficult than the first, but there was no way he was going to express his doubts now. The ground was more uneven and treacherous and would require all his skills. He'd spent many hours riding with his family all over the ranch, he was sure this was within his skill limit.

Releasing the throttle, he began speeding towards the jump, only slightly aware of Cassie cheering him on. He swerved around one boulder, then another, picking up more speed. He had to release the accelerator to swerve around a third, then immediately pressed on it again to keep his speed from dropping, only too aware of what could happen if he wasn't going fast enough. His speed increased as he hit the incline. The rocky ground was more slanted, and it took supreme effort not to slide off the required path. He hit the jump and then he was sailing through the air, the bouncing off the rough ground replaced by a sense of calm.

His front tires hit the other side with a thud that jarred his back, yet he kept the throttle fully open, worried his back tires weren't going to land. His heart skipped a beat as he was sure he hadn't cleared the gap, hadn't had enough speed, and knew that what happened next would hurt, a lot. His fears were alleviated a second later when they too landed and he sped down the descent, releasing the accelerator and rolling back to Cassie.

Cassie was jumping up and down, hooping and cheering and Dean felt utter elation though his heavy beating heart and the adrenaline in his veins as he watched the gorgeous girl's breasts bounce in her tank top.

"That was fucking incredible," she screamed in glee as she rushed over to him, flung her arms around him and kissed him on the lips. Dean's head spun as if he were in a dream as he placed his hands on her hips and enjoyed the moment. He opened his lips and his tongue searched for hers. She opened her mouth in reciprocation and their tongues met. She tasted so good; Dean wanted the moment to last forever. Cassie had other ideas and broke the kiss off after a couple of seconds, although she remained in the embrace. "Cool your jets, hotshot," she laughed.

At first Dean was going to protest, feeling she was somehow making fun of him again. When he saw the genuine, fun filled wide smile she had he couldn't help but laugh along with her, all insecurities dropping away, if only for the moment. He glanced over to Teddy, who, upon realisation that he'd been caught watching them busied himself very quickly with turning over rocks again.

"Wanna see me do it again?" Dean beamed at Cassie.

The girl thought for a moment, then grinned. "I want to try."

Hesitancy flashed across Dean's face. "You want to try?"

"Sure, why not?" she giggled. "What's the matter? You don't think I'm up to it?"

"It's not that, just that, well, I've got more experience with these bikes than you. You could get hurt. If it goes wrong, I mean."

Cassie pulled out of his arms, hands once again firmly on her hips. "Stop being a pussy. Nothing will go wrong. And it's not like I want to try the big jump or anything. Just the smaller one."

Dean considered this, although his train of thought was broken when Teddy gave an alarmed yelp that turned into a cry. Both teenagers turned to see what had happened. Teddy was sitting on the ground, knees pulled up to his chest and holding his right hand up at a distance.

"You okay?" Dean asked, leaping off the bike and rushing over. Cassie rolled her eyes and followed at a slower walking pace.

"Ow, ow, ow," Teddy cried, tears running down his cheeks. "It hurts."

"What's wrong?" Dean looked down at what Teddy was presenting to him. On the back of his outstretched hand were several ants. The tiny creatures, slightly larger than average, had Teddy's skin pinched in their jaws and had sunk their stings into his flesh. Dean's first thought was that Teddy must have disturbed a nest while using his hand he brushed the insects off. "There, they're gone. Okay, now?" Dean snapped. His tolerance level for any distractions breaking the flow of his experience with Cassie sat exceedingly low.

"It hurts, it hurts, it hurts," Teddy sobbed, holding his wounded hand. Vicious red welts were already appearing in the locations he had been stung. He then cried out in a more alarmed scream as one of the ants managed to crawl over his shoe and sting the bare flesh just above his ankle, creating another jab of searing pain. He quickly batted the insect away and jumped to his feet, scrabbling away from the tiny attackers.

"For fuck sake," Dean cursed, pulling his brother away from where he was standing, spotting a number of the insects scrabbling around, looking for attackers in the dirt.

"I'm stung, it hurts, really badly," Teddy sobbed, not sure what to do with himself.

Dean glanced quickly over at Cassie, who looked bored by the entire situation. "Well, what do you expect if you go sit in an ant nest?" he said, harshly.

Teddy kept crying as Dean led him away from the offending insects. "It hurts, Dean. I want to go home."

"You can't go home by yourself, and we're not ready to go home either," Dean stated. "Can you just hold on for a bit? Please?"

"Maybe we should go back," Cassie teased. "Poor little Teddy has been stung by the big, bad ants. He needs his mommy to kiss it better." She made an exaggerated pout.

"Back off'a him," Dean snapped at her and Cassie's

exaggerated pout turned into a real one. She crossed her arms and begun walking away, unaware of the tiny insect clinging to her sneaker.

"Whatever," she huffed.

Dean turned back to his brother and spoke softer. "Look, Cassie really wants to do this jump. We're all having a great time. We're having fun. You can stay out, a little bit longer, can't you?"

Teddy sniffed back tears, his nose full of snot. "It hurts, Dean."

Dean studded Teddy's hand again. He had to admit the stings looked painful, but what was the worst that could happen? Nobody ever died from ant stings, did they? "Just give us a little bit longer, okay? And then you can play any of my games when we get back home. Okay?"

Teddy searched his brother's face, picking up on the pleading nature Dean's request had taken. He was also excited at having free reign on his older brother's games library. "Any game?"

"Any game."

"Will you play it with me?"

"Sure, no problem."

"Promise?"

"Promise."

Teddy thought about it for a moment. "Okay," he sullenly agreed.

*   *   *

"Release the throttle as you turn, hold it as soon as you are back on a straight, and keep you head down," Dean explained to Cassie. She was sat on her commandeered quad, the engine running as she focused on Dean's words.

He stood close to her, leaning in and speaking into her ear to combat the sound of the engine thrumming. He was closer to her than he needed to be as he explained how she should go about pulling off the jump. Cassie either didn't mind or didn't notice. Either way, Dean was enjoying the close proximity, the smell of her perfume and the sensation whenever a gust of wind would sweep her stray hairs against his skin.

"Remember, the key is to keep your speed high so that you clear the gap. Too slow and you won't make it." Upon saying the words out loud, Dean suddenly felt a sense of hesitancy. A niggling thought in the back of his head said *'perhaps this isn't such a good idea.'* "You're sure you want to try this?"

Cassie picked up on his concern and her intense, concentrating face gave way to a relaxed look of amusement. "Of course I am, it's cool. And with your tuition, what can go wrong?"

Dean smiled, even though the uneasy feeling he had remained. "Okay, if you're sure."

"Of course." Her smile turned into a wide grin. "It's sweet that you're worried about me. Can I let you into a little secret?"

"Sure, shoot."

She glanced over at Teddy, who was perched on a boulder, inspecting his wounded arm and looking glum. Satisfied he wasn't listening, she leant into Dean's ear, her lips almost touching it, and said: "I'm so fucking wet right now."

Dean went bright red and gave a spluttered laugh. "I, uh, I see," he laughed, not sure where to look.

"You can check for yourself, later," she winked.

Dean choked again, trying to keep his composure and yet not sure how to respond. "Will do," he grinned.

"You're cute," Cassie smiled, pecking him on the cheek before refocussing on the task at hand. Her voice went from flirty to very serious. "So around that boulder, right around that one, and full throttle?"

"As simple as that," Dean said, the stupid grin still remaining, his mind on things other than the stunt at hand.

"Okay, nothing to it," Cassie said, steeling her nerves as she revved the bike.

Taking her cue, Dean walked over and sat next to his brother on the boulder. "You okay, dude?" he asked.

"Don't feel well," mumbled Teddy, holding his arm. Dean only half listened, concentrating on Cassie.

Cassie revved the bike a few more times, visualising her path to the jump. Her heart was racing, and she felt a small quiver of fear in her belly. It felt good. For all her life, things had seemed to come to her so easily, it got boring. It felt exhilarating to actually challenge herself and put herself in danger. She may not be wet, as she'd said to Dean, but she couldn't lie, she was excited as hell.

Releasing the brake, the quad bike roared forward and Cassie held on tight and kept her body low to reduce drag as she manoeuvred as Dean had shown her. Accelerating as fast as possible, releasing the throttle to avoid hurtling off the track, twisting to avoid uneven ground, left around one boulder, right around another, down on the throttle again to gain full speed. She hit the incline fast and kept accelerating as she hit the gap.

The moment the wheels of the bike left solid ground she knew she had easily made the jump. She was going way faster than Dean had managed, and she was lighter. It was a no brainer. Not so hard after all, she thought, congratulating her own abilities. If felt to her like everything was moving in slow motion as the quad bike covered the gap and landed with a thump, back on solid ground. The moment the bike landed; time sped up again. She felt a tiny tickling on her thigh. That's when everything went wrong. The tickle turned into the sensation of a burning needle piecing her skin.

Dean looked on in horror as Cassie cleared the gap, landed and started to wobble. He realised instantly that she had lost control. He wondered if it was his fault, having spent too long focussing on the incline, he hadn't even thought to mention the decline, which was just as treacherous, if not more so.

Cassie swerved, the two left hand wheels arose from the ground and Dean thought she was going to barrel roll. By some miracle Cassie managed to right herself and the two offending wheels slammed back onto the ground. It was a victory, but she wasn't slowing down. Why wasn't she slowing down? What had happened? He saw her look of panic as she clumsily veered around one boulder, only to hit another, full on. The smash of crumpling metal was sickening, and Dean wished he could turn away as the bike flipped, Cassie's light frame hurling off it. She crashed down to earth, rolling and bouncing off rocks, carried by her own velocity until the numerous impacts slowed her down.

The quad bike cartwheeled over her, crashing and breaking, completely destroyed and reduced to a ruined heap of metal. It missed Cassie's slight form by the narrowest of margins before coming to a rest.

"Fuck, Cassie," Dean yelled in abject horror as he sprinted towards her. *Fuck, fuck, fuck, this is bad.* Before he could even allow himself to comprehend what had happened, he was beside her, crouching down and viewing the damage.

Cassie was hurt, and hurt bad. Her scant clothing was torn, failing to offer much in the way of protection. Large gashes and scratches covered her limbs, as well as half her face. Her lips were split, and her teeth were covered in blood. If she'd bit her tongue or if teeth were broken, he didn't know. One of her arms were bent at an odd angle above the wrist, clearly broken. Most horrifying of all, her shinbone had snapped and had broken through the skin, glistening white bone protruding from a bloodied wound.

"Oh shit, oh shit, oh Jesus. Cassie, can you hear me?" Dean cried. This was all so stupid. How could he have been so fucking stupid?

Cassie's eyes flicked open and fixed on his. Her face was screwed up in debilitating pain, eyes filled with pain. "Dean... hurts..." she managed to say, coughing up blood.

Dean's heart was racing. He was no fool, he knew this was bad, but he had enough sense to realise Cassie being awake was a very good sign. "Cassie, are you okay?" *Fucking stupid question*, he chastised himself. "How does it feel? Where does it hurt."

"Everything... cold," she grimaced, clearly in agony.

"You're going to be okay," he sobbed. "I'm going to get help. Don't move."

"Something inside… broken," she squeaked. Her voice seemed so small, so frightened. Nothing at all like the self-assured young woman she had been just moments ago. "Hurts to breath."

"You're going to be okay; I just need to get our parents out here. They'll get you to a hospital." Through tears he checked his phone and swore upon realising there was no signal. There never was, out here.

"Something… stung… leg… Is it okay?" she croaked.

Dean couldn't even comprehend her question. If something had stung her leg, that was the least of her problems now. He needed to get help, and fast. He clasped the hand of her none-broken arm and stoked it, hoping to sooth her in some way. "I need to get help. I won't be long, okay?" he stuttered as he spoke and realised his own body was shaking violently in panic and shock.

"Don't leave… scared…" Cassie whispered through gasps of pain.

"Teddy," Dean called. "Teddy, I need your help." He turned and saw his brother stumbling towards him. Something looked wrong. He still held his wounded hand, which now looked swollen and sore. His face was white as a ghost and covered in a slick layer of sweat. Teddy's eyes looked dull, as if he hadn't even acknowledged the tragedy that he had just witnessed.

"I don't feel well," he muttered weakly before dropping to his knees and falling onto his front.

CHAPTER 9

The sound of the stampeding herd was all encompassing, as was the sight of heavy bovine bodies thundering past him. Martin closed his eyes tight, covered his head tight with his arms and drew his legs into his body and waited. The dust being kicked up made him feel like he was being smothered and he held his breath, only breathing when it couldn't be helped.

The herd felt too numerous to comprehend, even though logic dictated there were only two hundred head of cattle within it. He didn't want to think of the damage that could be caused if just one longhorn brought its weight to bear, and a crushing hoof came down upon him. There was no way he could actively avoid that fate now. He could only lay in the foetal behind the brittle, dried log he's chosen as shelter, curled up as tight as possible and pray.

Soon enough, although it felt like a lifetime to Martin, the herd thinned out, the thundering hooves grew more distant and the kicked-up dust and dirt began to settle. Warily, he opened his eyes and watched as the herd headed off into the flats of the ranch. For a moment he feared they would stampede by the house, potentially endangering the women and children. He breathed a sigh of relief upon realising that wasn't the case.

When satisfied he could hear no other animals running in his direction, Martin peaked his head out from behind the ruined log and surveyed the track where he had just been talking with his brother.

The dust was still dense in the air, though already the gentle breeze was disbursing it. Several longhorn that had fallen and were trampled by their sisters lay still and broken.

The ruined cattle shed stood ominous and foreboding. Inside the sounds of cows could still be heard, mooing in distress. No longer the defiant, deafening, shocked noises that had pre-empted the stampede, the remaining animals sounded more wounded and without hope, weak and resigned to a fate Martin couldn't understand.

There was still no evidence of fire or anything of that nature and Martin wandered if perhaps a predator such as a coyote or wolf had stumbled inside and caused the panic. If so, the animal showed no sign of making itself known to him.

In a daze, Martin surveyed the carnage until his eyes rested on the remnants of his truck, now mangled and ruined. The numbness that shock had shrouded him in lifted as he suddenly remembered that Tom had dove beneath the truck in hope of shelter.

"Tom?" he called as he ran to the iron heap that had once been his truck. A cow had evidently ran full force into the side of it and broken its neck, the beast laying dead beside it with red froth oozing from its mouth. "Tom, you okay man? Speak to me?"

"Martin, I'm here," his brother called back, and Martin had never been happier to hear the son of a bitch's voice.

"Tom, man, I'm coming." Martin ran around the hunk of scrap and discovered his brother, sheltered beneath the upside-down flatbed. "Give me your hand," he said and when Tom obliged he pulled him out.

Tom gasped in pain as he was pulled free of the wreckage. He was dishevelled, his clothes ripped and covered in cuts and bruises. His worst injury appeared to be his ankle. Tom insisted it was broken while Martin was pretty sure it was just sprained, albeit badly.

Tom gasped as he fought the pain. "What the hell caused that?" he groaned between grimaces. "Jesus Christ, we could have both been killed. I should sue your ass."

"I've never seen anything like it before," Martin replied. He looked out at the ranch flats, squinting in the brilliant sunlight. The herd seemed to have stopped a mile or so out and had dispersed, wandering aimlessly. He had no doubt Louise would have noticed the cattle and would be wondering what was going on.

He checked his phone in case she had a missed call. It usually didn't have any signal at the best of times and now a large crack from corner to corner rendered the device unusable.

"This is going to be a nightmare to put right," Martin grumbled to his brother.

Tom laughed bitterly whilst massaging his swollen ankle. "Hah, we nearly get flattened and you're worried about some cows."

"They're more than that," Martin replied, irritably. "They're my investment. I could be in real trouble here. I could lose the ranch if I can't get a handle on this. I would have thought you could at least understand that."

Tom nodded glumly, scanning the horizon. "Yeah. I can."

"What I want to know is what spooked them in the first place." He looked over towards the shed. "We're going to have to walk back. Think you're going to be okay with that ankle?"

"What choice have I got?" Tom lamented.

"Okay, well you're pretty shook up. Take five. Catch your breath."

"Where are you going?"

"I'm going to find out what's at the bottom of this."

Tom nodded grimly and leant back against the truck. Martin had hoped Tom would volunteer to investigate with him, although wasn't surprised that no offer was given.

Gingerly Martin approached the shed. As he got closer he examined it with a more critical eye. All the sheet metal that made up the sides was heavily distorted by the panicked animals and would need replacing. He wondered if his insurance would cover it.

Edging towards the open doorway, the interior appeared darker than ever and the shadows seemed to hide malicious intent. The inside of the shed stunk even worse than usual and looked like a bomb site. Twisted, deformed and broken metal and bars abounded. The automated feeding system was destroyed. Practically everything was severely damaged and would need replacing. Where the animals had been going wild they had damaged themselves on the sharp edges of broken metalwork. Copious amounts of blood dripped from razor sharp edges and the forms several longhorn lay dead or dying. One of the dead animals appeared to have ripped itself open on broken pen bars and lay still, its intestines glistening wetly in a pile leaking from its bowels. Another animal was still alive and sorrowfully mooing, its legs caught up and bleeding in tangled chicken wire.

No threat could be visually detected, although anything could have been hiding in the gloom. The thought of some blood thirsty predator watching him from the shadows unnerved him more than he liked to admit.

Martin cautiously approached the living cow tangled in wire, holding up his hands to show her he wasn't a threat. The pitiful creature looked afraid by his presence, yet there was no fight in her to try and back away from him.

"Calm down, girl. Calm down," he soothed the cow as his hand gently rested on her head. He stroked her gently so as not to spook the animal. As he soothed the animal he took in the surrounding carnage, still unable to identify what had caused the stampede.

Something crawled over the back of his hand, and he quickly withdrew it in shock. He checked for what had crawled over him but whatever had been on his hand had evidently fallen off when he'd jerked his hand away. He almost dismissed the culprit as likely a fly when he spotted something scuttling over the concrete floor towards him. It looked like an ant, although it was larger than an ant should be, almost an inch in length.

Watching where he stood, he watched the tiny creature. He remembered what Franklin had told him yesterday evening, about the large nest he and Simon had discovered.

He watched it curiously as the ant scurried around various blades of straw, seemingly on a path towards him. It didn't seem to be acting like a normal ant at all. Instead of the meandering common in such creatures, this one seemed to be making a deliberate bee line towards him.

Remembering the stings and sores he'd previously found on his cattle; he decided this bug was one of the culprits. With grim resolution he crushed the creature beneath his heel. It was then he spotted movement in the surrounding darkness. He squinted his eyes to make out exactly what he was seeing but it was hard to discern in the shrouding shadows.

Reaching into his pocket, Martin pulled out his broken phone. Although the screen was damaged the torch function was bound to a physical button on the side of the device. He flicked it on and illuminated the nearby environment. What he saw made him shudder.

Ants. Lots and lots of ants.

The interior of the shed was alive with the tiny invaders. They ran up and down the metal work, scurried across the floor and amongst the hay, and covered the wounded cow. He shuddered as he could see hundreds of the insects biting and stinging the longhorn, whilst the beast could only protest pitifully, resigned to its painful fate.

Stepping away from the swarming bugs he swept the light from his phone further and more ants seemed to emerge from dark hidey-holes, disturbed and irritated by his presence. He even spotted the six-legged things squirming and swarming in the red pool of intestines and offal leaking from the gutted animal. Were they eating it? Impossible, he told himself.

Much like the lone attacker he had just crushed, the insects all seemed to move towards him, like a wave of death. The longer he observed, the more numerous and densely packed they appeared to become.

A sudden tickling on his head made him reach up and swipe at his hair. He saw the half inch long ant he knocked fall to the ground. In horror he looked up and saw even more insects scurrying over the roof of the shed overhead. There had to be millions, and as they began to drop he realised just how much danger he was in.

Turning around, Martin broke into a mad dash for the shed's exit as the insects rained down around him. Covering his head as he ran, he crushed ants indiscriminately underfoot as he headed for daylight. He dare not stop, for he knew that if he did the ants would be upon him.

Escaping the shed, Martin didn't stop running until he reached Tom. Tom looked up at his brother with a look of bewilderment as Martin feverishly brushed and swiped and his hair and clothes over and over.

"Are any on me?" Martin cried out in alarm.

"Any what?" asked Tom, confused as he pulled himself up, checking Martin over.

"Ants. Are there any ants on me?" Martin demanded.

"Ants?"

"Yes, ants. Fucking ants. Can you see any?"

"No, no ants. Are you okay? What's going on."

Martin tried to calm himself down, still swiping and itching at imagined attackers clinging to his body. "In the shed. Ants. Millions of the fucking things. Big bastards."

Tom's confusion turned to annoyance. "You're telling me ants attacked your herd?"

"You're fucking right I am."

"You're serious?"

"Deadly fucking serious."

"Come on, man. Ants?"

"We've had a problem with something stinging the cattle the last few weeks. Franklin found a nest of these big bastard ants yesterday. Said he killed the fuckers. Clearly, he missed some."

Tom limped a couple of steps towards the shed, scanning it. "Jesus, missed some is right."

Martin turned to look, and dread gripped his insides. The shed he had just been in was now covered by the angry insects.

He couldn't believe he had been inside there mere moments ago and realised just how lucky he was to get out unscathed.

"No wonder your cows wanted out," Tom shuddered. "Is that normal around here?"

"No," said Martin, bluntly. "No it is not." Watching the ants, he noticed a number of them crawling over the ground around the entrance to the shed. They were coming for them. "Look, on the ground. Looks like they're pissed."

"Jesus, man. You need to call an exterminator or something."

"Believe me, I intend to. Come on, we need to head back to the house. Now."

Tom nodded in agreement. "No arguments here." He turned and started hobbling away from the shed and realised just how painful his ankle truly was. "God damn it, that smarts."

"Here, put your arm around me," Martin said, coming up beside him. He wrapped his arm around Tom's waist and Tom reached his arm over Martin's shoulders. Tom rested his weight upon his brother and Martin grunted. "Damn, you ever heard of jogging?"

"Hey, I eat when I'm stressed, okay? I'm seeing a shrink about it."

"Right," Martin mumbled. The house was only about half a mile away, down the trail. It looked much further.

CHAPTER 10

Louise stared out of the window is desperation as she held her phone to her ear, listening to it dial Martin's number for the fifth time, immediately followed by the "no signal" tone.

She watched from the kitchen window as a longhorn hastily trotted by, a few hundred yards out. Surrounding her were all the makings of a feast, Thanksgiving dinner with all the trimmings. All morning the dinner had felt like one of the most important things in the world. Now it was a forgotten, hollow periphery. That cow troubled her more than she wanted to admit.

Marie finished off her glass of wine, her third since their husbands had left on Martin's grand tour. She walked over to the wine fridge, checked a couple of bottles before choosing her favourite one and twisting the cap off without asking Louise if she was allowed to. She poured herself a large glass.

"So, some cows have gotten out. Big deal," she scoffed as she gulped a mouthful.

Louise ignored her. Marie clearly couldn't grasp how fundamentally wrong it was that the cattle were trotting across the ranch when they were supposed to be locked up. Something had happened, she could feel it in the depths of her soul. Something bad.

"Back in New York you should see the size of the rats that scurry about at night. If we're talking about problematic animals, now they're something to worry about," Marie droned on inanely, too caught up in her own little world to understand anything else.

"What are you even talking about?" Louise snapped, her

patience wearing thin.

"I'm just saying, cows on the loose aren't that big a deal. You'll just have your guys round them up tomorrow. You let them roam free most the time anyway, right? Or is that just something you say so you can stick a 'free range' sticker on them and charge an extra thirty percent?"

Louise tried Martin's phone again. Again, there was no signal. "I'm trying the land line," she informed Marie. "Can you check on the kids? Tell them to stay inside. Cattle can be dangerous, especially if they're riled up, which I think they are."

Marie glared daggers as if she couldn't believe she'd been so inconvenience but walked out down the hallway without saying another word. Louise was grateful. She was sick with worry for Martin and didn't know what she might say if Marie started giving her attitude. They had worked so hard to try and repair their relationship with Tom and his wife, it'd be a shame to blow it now, even with a crisis on their hands.

She picked up the housephone, put it to her ear and started dialling. It took her a moment to register that it was completely dead, with not so much as a dialling tone. She looked at the handset, as if it bore the most troubling message she could have heard. She'd been made aware that the internet was down and had dutifully unplugged the modem and then turned it on again. When that hadn't worked she had shrugged, having exhausted her knowledge in the realms of tech-support, marked it up as an inconvenience and gone back to her tasks at hand. She knew the recipes and timings for all the food she was preparing and the tee vee was still working so it was a problem to be worried about later. It wasn't the first time it had happened, and didn't these things usually sort themselves out in the end?

Living in such a rural area, internet connection issues had reared their head. Never, though, had the phone lines gone down. She struggled to think up why that could have happened. There hadn't been any warnings from the phone company regarding work being carried out. Nor had there been any extreme weather. As far as she knew, no trees had the potential of causing damage to the wires, given the arid nature of the landscape.

It was a perplexing mystery, one that wouldn't have troubled her nearly as much if not for the fact that some, if not all their herd of cattle were now wandering the ranch, when they should have been contained. Was this foul play? Had someone cut the phone lines and released the animals?

She shook her head, trying her best to lose the uneasy thoughts. She had to be jumping to conclusions. Once she heard from Martin everything would be okay. Probably some failsafe in the shed had failed, releasing the animals. They'd still have an issue on their hands, but it would be a rational, explainable one.

"I'm going to take my SUV up to the shed, see if Martin and Tom are okay," she called to Marie.

"They're gone," Marie shouted back with alarm, from somewhere beyond the hallway.

"What?" called back Louise, hurrying from the kitchen. "What do you mean? They can't be gone." She strode into the games room, where Marie could be seen standing in the open glass door, looking out of the quad garage's open roller door.

"Boys," Louise called, brushing past her, trying to keep her growing alarm down as she noticed three of the four quad bikes missing and walked to the roller door. The heat of the desert coming in was in stark contrast to the pleasant, cool, air-conditioned interior of the house. She scanned the immediate vicinity and the horizon. No trace of the kids could be seen.

"Where have your boys taken Cassie?" Marie snarled, giving an accusatory glare.

"I don't understand it," Louise responded, unable to hide her bewilderment. "We keep the garage locked and the keys hidden."

"Well clearly someone knew where to get the keys."

Louise blinked, trying to piece together the possibilities of how the quad bikes had been taken. "We keep the keys in the bottom drawer of the bedside table, along with the gun cabinet keys." Her heart dropped at the thought.

"You mean to say those boys could be riding around with my Cassie, armed to the teeth?" Marie was furious at the prospect, laying all blame firmly at Louise's feet.

Louise wanted to defend her boys, but at that moment it seemed like the least of her priorities. Not rising to Marie's accusations, Louise ran upstairs and checked all the bedrooms, calling to her sons and Cassie, in the vain hope that they were in the house.

Marie followed her from room to room, looking triumphant when Louise's search came up empty and asking for clarification just how unruly her sons were. Louise then marched into her bedroom and checked Martin's bedside cabinet to confirm her suspicions and, sure enough, the keys to the garage were missing. Fortunately the keys to the gun cabinet were still there. Louise even unlocked the cabinet to confirm the firearms were still where they should be. The Glock and AR-15 were both present, much to Louise's relief. She relocked the cabinet and returned the key to the tin box in the drawer.

"And did your boys know that was where the keys were kept?" Marie demanded, her face glowering as she gulped down more wine.

"I don't know. I don't think so. Maybe."

"Too damned trusting, that's your problem," Marie spat.

Rage washed over Louise like a tidal wave, and she decided she'd had enough of Marie's bullshit. "You know what, Marie, you're right. I am too damned trusting. And that's a trait I share with Martin, I'm afraid. That's why we've let you and your husband back into our lives after you both tried to backstab him the first chance opportunity knocked."

Marie was outraged at the accusation. "How dare you?" she roared. "Whatever business dealings Tom and Martin had going on was nothing to do with me."

Louise gave a bitter laugh. Of course Marie would defend herself whist leaving Tom spinning in the wind. "Do you think we're stupid, Marie? Do you think we can't see your strings controlling Tom like a puppet?"

"This weekend was a mistake," Marie hissed. I want you to find my daughter and we are leaving."

"That's fine with me," Louise yelled, brushing by the infuriating woman and heading back downstairs.

Marie followed close behind her, ranting and raving as she continued gulping her drink. "You and Martin aren't holy than thou, you know. You think we can't notice when you're talking down to us? Like we're the shit on your shoe?"

Louise spun around. "I've been nothing but courteous and welcoming."

"It broke Tom's heart when Martin left the business. It broke him even more when Martin left New York."

"Oh, so now you're worried about Tom's heart? Don't worry, I'm sure he has life insurance. You've probably even got a few policies on him he doesn't even know about."

"What are you implying, that I'm some kind of gold-digger?"

Louise suddenly grew weary of the entire conversation and turned away, heading back to the kitchen and to where the key hooks were. "If Tom valued his brother so much, perhaps he shouldn't have tried to rip him off." She felt bad about exploding at Marie and hoped she hadn't cause irreparable damage to Martin and Tom's relationship. Martin had tried so hard to get his brother back and she hoped she hadn't ruined his chances by losing her temper.

"What are you doing?" Marie demanded.

"Somethings clearly wrong. I'm driving up to the shed. Then we're finding our kids and tanning their hides. I can't drive cross country in my SUV, we need Martin's truck. Those longhorn can be dangerous when spooked. The quads might make them angry so the sooner we find the kids, the better."

Marie nodded and downed the last of her drink. "I'm coming with you."

Louise wanted to protest, although she couldn't think of a good reason why she should go alone, except for her intense dislike for the woman. She was about to speak when she saw something out the window that made the point moot. She opened the back door to get a better look.

"What are you looking at?" Marie said, walking beside her and looking up the trail.

Coming over the hill were Martin and Tom. *Why are they walking?* Louise thought. A number of reasons flashed across her mind. None of them were good.

"Something's wrong with Tom," Marie said, placing her empty glass down and rushing out the door towards the two men. Louise could have sworn there was a genuine hint of concern in Marie's words and actions and followed after her. Marie was right. Both men looked like they had been roughed up, with dirty, torn cloths and numerous scratches, cuts and bruises. Had they been in a fight? If so, was it a fight between each other or had they been jumped by criminals of some description?

She decided an accident was more likely. Clearly, whatever they had endured, Tom had been the worst off for it. He'd been bleeding a lot from his nose and he was limping painfully. She doubted he would have been able to walk far without having Martin to support his weight,

"Oh my God, what happened?" she called as Marie and herself closed the gap between them.

"Stampede," Martin replied grimly, as Marie fussed over Tom, asking if her was okay and frantically checking over his injuries. "Let's get Tom in the house, his ankle is badly twisted."

Louise looked at him questioningly. "The kids are gone," she blurted out, unsure how else to lead into the conversation.

"What?"

"They took the quads."

"Took the quads? How could they have done that? I keep the keys hidden."

"Evidently not hidden well enough," sneered Marie as she took some of Tom's weight and they headed slowly to the house.

* * *

Tom groaned in relief as he was gently lowered onto the plush living room sofa. The clean material was instantly dirtied by the sand and earth on his clothes, but nothing was further from Louise's mind at the moment.

Louise rushed to get water for both men while Marie got some wet wipes and begun wiping away the dried, clotted blood from Tom's nose to help him breath better.

"How'd you do this to your nose?" she asked as she gently dabbed.

Tom glanced at Martin before shrugging. "I got knocked about pretty bad."

Martin nodded a silent thanks. The last thing they needed right now was added drama.

Louise gave them a glass of water each and both men eagerly downed their glasses. She had also brought in the first aid kit from beneath the kitchen sink and popped it open before placing it besides Tom.

"Thank you," Tom managed, with heart-felt sincerity.

"No problem," smiled Louise.

Marie didn't make eye contact with Louise, instead she had knelt on the roll out red rug and was busy sorting through the first aid kit and pulling out the antiseptic, cotton balls and plasters. After tending some of Tom's more superficial scrapes and cuts she looked down and touched Tom's swollen ankle and he grimaced in pain. "We've got to get you to a hospital, Tom. This looks broken to me."

"I think it's just a sprain," Tom winced.

"What happened?" Louise enquired again.

"Ants," stated Martin.

"Ants?"

"Yeah. Big ones, like Franklin said he saw yesterday. There were millions of the bastards, all over the herd in the shed. Made them go wild."

"Jesus."

"The cattle made a break for it. Can't blame them, really.

Unfortunately, we were in their way at the time. They damn well nearly killed us. We're lucky to have survived."

"The truck?"

"It's clean written off. A number of cows were killed, also."

Louise felt numb, trying to comprehend the gravity of the situation. The herd was their livelihood. If they weren't fit for market when the time came, they could lose the farm. "Where on Earth did they come from?"

"Fuck knows. They'll have to be exterminated professionally as soon as possible."

"Are they dangerous to people?" asked Marie. The question was far more poignant than any of them realised until they heard the words out loud.

Martin and Tom exchanged looks. "You went into the cow shed. What do you think?" Tom pushed.

Martin made a discomforted face, remembering the hordes of insects running towards him, dropping from the ceiling and making a mess of the remaining longhorn. "They're definitely aggressive," he confirmed. "We need to find the kids as soon as possible and get out of here."

"There's something we can all agree on," Tom forced a smile. Nobody reciprocated.

"Any idea where they went?" he asked Louise and Marie.

"No idea. We didn't realise they were gone until just before you two returned."

"I see." Martin thought for a moment. "We didn't notice them so they can't have headed north or east of the house. That was probably a deliberate decision on their part."

"Cassie wouldn't have known to do that," Marie barked, the fight in her returning. "Obviously your boys are to blame for this." She shot Louise a dirty look.

"Marie, not now," Tom said meekly.

"What? I'm just saying. If anything has happened to our daughter, I'll be holding you two and your boys fully responsible."

Martin sighed. The last thing they needed was Marie's

antagonistic nature right now. "I promise you, those boys will be severely punished for doing something so reckless. That's something we'll deal with after they are found. Right now, we need to concentrate on finding them. Now, to avoid Tom and I seeing them, they must have headed out southwest, into the rockier part of the ranch. There's no way we can use the SUV or your rental to search that area. The terrain is so rough, it'll vibrate those cars apart."

"Without the truck, what other option is there?" asked Tom.

* * *

In his bedroom's ensuite Martin splashed water over his face before pulling on a t-shirt and light denim jacket. He looked up at Louise, who was watching him from the door. She was chewing on a strand of her hair. It was a habit she'd developed whenever she was scared. She hadn't done it in years.

"Are you okay?" she asked him.

He gave her a half smile. "I don't know what I am at the moment. This is one hell of a situation."

"Worried about the herd?"

"I'm worried about the kids. You didn't see those ants. They're dangerous. Scared cattle; they're dangerous too. Perhaps more so. That's not even considering the usual dangers associated with riding those bikes. I hope they're being careful."

Louise nodded silently and Martin noticed how pale she was and how watery her eyes were becoming. She was clearly distraught and trying to keep it together. Martin walked over and held her. As he did, he felt her rigid body relax and almost thought she was going to collapse. She started to sob into his chest.

Martin kissed her forehead and stroked her hair. "Hey, hey, it's okay," he comforted her.

"Oh Martin, I'm so scared," she wept, her body trembling. "This is awful. Just awful."

"I know. I know. Don't worry. I'm going to find them. Chances are I'll find them goofing around, give them an earful and be back before you know it."

CHAPTER 11

"Teddy, Teddy, can you hear me?" Dean desperately shook his younger brother's shoulders, trying to wake him up. Teddy's skin was slick, pale and hot to the touch. Certainly not good signs. The sun was now high in the sky as midday was approaching and the heat was reaching nearly unbearable levels. It was hot, especially for this time of the year.

Dean chastised himself for not having the fore thought to bring any bottled water along. His dad had always tried to engrain in him a healthy respect for the desert. He'd heard stories of how early settlers had perished, back in the old days, before technology appeared to make man invincible. His dad had taught him never to become complacent. Despite civilisations' cocoon of safety the desert was just as cruel, uncaring and dangerous as ever. Those who ventured into it unwarily would pay the price.

All those lessons had been ignored and wasted. And why? Because he was chasing pussy? How insanely stupid. Now he was paying the price, alongside his brother and cousin.

Not too far away was a long mesquite tree growing from the rocky ground. Its canvas was fairly broad and its branches fairly low, beginning around six feet from the ground at the trunk. It would provide shelter from the blazing sun for him and Teddy. He wasn't sure if he should move Cassie. Her body was badly torn up and he'd heard that accident victims shouldn't be moved for a variety of reasons, mainly boiling down to causing even more damage than was already present.

Cassie still lay where she had fallen, on her back, torn and twisted and barely breathing between quiet half sobs and gurgles. She had to be in so much pain. Her condition terrified Dean. She might die, even if paramedics arrived. And it was all his fault.

He could barely manage to comprehend how to best react and help Cassie when Teddy had passed out, leaving him feeling more alone and out of his depth than he could imagine. He'd thought he was acting like a man. Now he felt tiny, like a child, lost and with no hope of finding his parents.

He had failed to wake Teddy, despite his best efforts. Rolling his brother over so he was laying on his back, Dean had returned to Cassie. All the while, tears streamed down his cheeks.

Cassie tried to focus on him as he approached, although one of her eyes seemed to struggle following him. She gasped in pain through each breath and the fingers on her none-broken hand flexed. The message was clear, she wanted him to hold her hand.

Dean obliged, unsure what to do. "Can you hear me, Cassie? You're going to be alright, ya hear?"

She clenched her bloodied, broken teeth in what looked like agony. "It hurts, Dean. It hurts so, so much."

Dean looked her over quickly, the site of her mangled form breaking his heart. He couldn't bring himself to look at her leg and the gleaming white bone sticking out of her shin like a spike. He wanted to be brave. He wanted to comfort her. "I, I don't know what to do," he wept.

Cassie remained unchanged, her expression a mask of pain and fear. A deep, bloodied graze obscured most of her features down one side. He wondered if she even had and features beneath the graze or if they'd been ground off. Regardless, she would never look so effortlessly beautiful again.

A sudden coughing from Teddy drew his attention and he turned in time to see his younger brother turn his head to the side and vomit. Releasing Cassie's hand, he ran back to Teddy, using fingers to hook out any vomit still in his mouth for fear he could choke. He then tried to rouse his brother again, without much luck.

Dean decided to pull his brother's limp form across the

ground to the shelter of the tree. He felt so much heavier than Dean remembered, as he hooked a hand beneath each armpit and pulled.

His back burnt from the effort and he cursed himself for his weakness. He'd thought he was grown up. A young man, wise and ready to take on the world. What a fool he had been.

By the side of the wrecked quad bike, Cassie rasped wetly as she felt the need to draw faster and shallower breaths. A pressure was building, similar to when she'd held her breath in the spa swimming pool. She coughed and hacked up blood which dribbled from her mouth, down her cheek and puddled on the dry, coarse ground. It was thick and sticky and she wanted to brush the wetness away.

She struggled to move slightly, succeeding only in a slight wiggle, like a worm baking on hot concrete. Everything hurt, more than she'd realised it ever could. As she breathed she could feel something hard grinding in her chest. She didn't want to think about it. She tried to wiggle again and the severe pain running down her back turned white hot as she gasped at the overwhelming nature of it.

Tears streamed from her eyes as she couldn't help but wonder why this had happened to her. She'd thought she was untouchable. She had every privilege possible; she was beautiful, smart, rich. The world dropped at her feet. This shouldn't be the way it ended. She knew she could be a bitch, but surely she didn't deserve this wretched death, did she?

Cassie couldn't be brave, no matter how much she wished she could be. She was scared, and she wanted her mommy and her daddy. She was cold. Even in the Arizona heat, she was cold, and that only scared her all the more.

Dean managed to pull Teddy into the shade of the tree and leant him in a sitting position against the trunk. He shook him again. "Teddy, can you hear me?" He didn't expect any response, which was why he was taken aback when his brother's eyes flicked open. "Teddy, you're awake," he exclaimed, almost joyously.

Teddy took a moment to focus on Dean. He looked out of it and groggy. "Dean? What's happening? Head hurts... hand hurts..."

"Ted, you've been stung by some ant. You're having a reaction or something." He looked down at Teddy's hand, it had swollen to twice its size and looked dark and bruised. The welts where the insects had stung him were raised and bright red.

"Thirsty... hot... burning..." Teddy was mumbling, looking like he was going to pass out at any moment.

"Stay awake, Ted," Dean shouted and slapped him on the shoulder. Surprisingly it seemed to work, Teddy's half-closed eyes went wide and he suddenly seemed a lot more lucid. He refocussed past Dean, at Cassie, laying in a heap on the ground. "There was an accident." Dean began to explain. "Cassie's hurt. She's hurt real bad. I don't know what to do."

Teddy's eyes returned to his brother. "We gotta get Mom and Dad," he whimpered.

It was such a child-like response, thought Dean. It was also the only course of action available. He nodded, determined. "You're right. We do." He looked down at the ground for a second. "Do you think you can ride your quad?"

Teddy looked afraid and his head dipped for a second before raising again. "Don't know. I think so."

Dean eyed him critically and placed a hand on Teddy's forehead. His brother was burning up, bad. The stings had clearly brought on a fever or something and he was struggling to stay awake. Dean wished that he could trust Teddy riding back to the house. The evidence before his eyes told him that was not the case. He doubted Teddy could even walk in a straight line, much less ride a quad.

Yet more cold dread heaped upon him, but he knew he had to use his brains, rather than follow his gut. If he let Teddy ride his bike, there was a good chance he would have an accident and end up like Cassie. He couldn't even trust Teddy to hold on to him whilst he rode.

Moving Cassie was simply not an option. She was too badly

hurt. They'd need a helicopter or something to come get her. So, he was left with two options. Either wait with them both until they were found, or otherwise jump on his quad and ride back to the house. Waiting felt more right, the idea of leaving them both in the wilderness, alone and defenceless felt fundamentally wrong.

Yet he knew that any time lost waiting could be critical for both of them. Teddy needed anti-toxin or something and Cassie needed, well, a lot of attention. Fast. She'd lost a lot of blood, was no doubt internally bleeding also and there was no telling how damaged her insides were. He didn't really understand how shock came into play, but he knew people could die from it and it was hard to imagine Cassie wouldn't go into shock, considering her injuries.

Dean made up his mind.

"Teddy? Teddy, listen to me. I need to go get Dad. You'll be okay here while I'm gone. The house is only about fifteen minutes away. I won't be long at all. I'll come back with Dad in his truck. Okay?"

Teddy nodded, his face looking terrified at the prospect at being left alone. "What if a coyote comes?"

"No coyotes will come in the day. You've just got to stay here and we'll come get you. Understand?"

Teddy nodded again, his fear still very present, although he showed no intention of fighting Dean's decision. It made Dean feel like a fraud as he realised that while Teddy was afraid, he trusted his older brother with his life. It was a trust Dean didn't feel like he'd earned and he swore to God that after this he would never take his younger brother for granted again.

"Just stay here," he ordered again, before standing and trotting over to Cassie.

Cassie was still laying in the same position she had been in before, her breathing even more laboured and now she was shivering as she gasped. Crouching beside her, a lump in his throat, Dean gently slipped his hand into hers again. He talked more gently to her, his authoritarian persona for Teddy wiped away in an instant, replaced with deep feelings of culpability and regret. His voice broke several times as he spoke, informing her of his plan.

"Please… don't… leave me," Cassie cried. "I'm cold. Scared. It hurts." She paused and then gave a deep wail that turned Dean's legs to jelly. She then coughed and more thick, sticky blood oozed from her mouth. "I don't want… to die here. Scared."

"You're not going to die," said Dean, trying to convince himself more than Cassie. "I'm going to get help. You're going to be okay. I've got to go now." He gently pulled his hand out of hers. She feebly tried to hold on, though she was too weak.
Wiping away tears, Dean reached down and brushed some of Cassie's hair, matted with dark blood, out of her eyes.

He yelped and withdrew his hand in panic as he recognised what was an ant under her hair, scurrying over her face. It wasn't just any ant, it was clearly similar to the ones that had stung Teddy's hand, only bigger. The insects' body was nearly an inch long, far larger than an ant should be, and it moved far more deliberately and with a purpose he wouldn't have ascribed to other bugs.

He took a couple of steps back, unsure what to do. He wanted to brush it off of her. The thought of what its sting could do to him made him hesitate, icy fear slithering up from deep inside him. Cassie's eyes remained locked onto his, her pained expression now taking on a deeper fear. She struggled taking deep, gasping breaths and her eyes were imploring him to explain what was going on.

Before Dean could comprehend what he was seeing, another ant appeared, scurrying over Cassie's face. Then another. And another. Looking beyond her, Dean noticed for the first time that thousands of the insects were swarming over Cassie's overturned quad bike and were now crawling all over her.

Cassie's laboured breathing became panicked and loud, like the gasping breaths of someone with who smoked sixty a day as she ants began to bite and sting her. She wriggled pitifully in an attempt to escape the onslaught. Dean prayed she was beyond pain, although he feared she was only beyond the ability of verbalise it as her gasping increased and the insects covered her. Dean watched helplessly as her now covered form gave a slight wiggle, Cassie's final, futile attempt at defying the horrific fate she had been dealt.

Dean turned to run, not wanting to wait, not wanting the knowledge of knowing how long it would take Cassie to die under the bodies of thousands of vicious, stinging insects. Scanning the ground surrounding him he realised there weren't just thousands of the red, attacking ants. There were millions. The ground was now alive with them and they were closing in on him, fast and with singular purpose. He knew at that moment they were deliberately aiming to kill him.

Dean directed himself towards the two intact quad bikes. The ground around them was crawling with the insects, but they were still sparsely spaced out compared to where Cassie had fell. He was fairly confident he could run and leap onto the bike and get it started before the ants got to him. It was no guarantee, yet what other choice was there?

And leave Teddy to die? A voice inside his head cried out.

Fuck, in his desperation to escape this impossible situation he'd almost completely forgotten about his little brother. Teddy was still sitting on the ground, back leaning against the mesquite tree. He seemed to be awake, though completely unaware of the army of rampaging insects that surrounded them. There was no doubt that if he went for the quad bike, Teddy would die.

"Ted," he yelled as he sprinted over to him.

Teddy looked up in confusion.

"Those ants, they're everywhere. We need to get up into the tree. Now."

Teddy surveyed the ground behind Dean, his vision hazy and making it hard to discern details. His brain struggled to make sense of what his older brother was telling him. Then his eyes fell onto Cassie, almost wholly covered in a blanket of the stinging insects and he cried out in alarm and fear. He turned away, looking for an escape from the hordes, only to see millions more scurrying over the ground in all directions. Even his fever addled brain could realise the hopelessness of the situation. He then searched out the quad bikes, his distress growing as he watched hundreds of insects climbing up the wheels of the bikes.

Dean reached his brother and yanked him to his feet. "We've got to climb, Teddy. Before they get us."

Teddy looked from the ants to his brother, to the lower tree branches and back to the ants again. "The branches are too high, Dean. I can't reach them." Dean could tell his brother was on the edge of hysteria. Teddy's need to be protected gave Dean something to focus on. If he had been trapped alone, he didn't know how well he'd be able to make a coherent thought. Because his brother's wellbeing was at stake, his will to protect allowed him to concentrate on the necessity of the task at hand.

"If I bump you up, do you think you'll be able to climb?" Teddy just gave an apprehensive look at him before again staring at the ants, drawing ever closer. "Teddy, don't look at the ants. Look at me. Good. Now, you need to climb Teddy, you always were the better climber. You need to climb now."

Teddy nodded and Dean assumed the position, the fingers of his hands locked in place. Cautiously Teddy supported himself with a hand on the trunk of the tree and stepped up onto Dean's hand. Dean glanced at the insects. They were only about twelve feet away and closing the gap, fast.

"Ready?" Teddy nodded and Dean heaved his brother's small frame upwards into the branches. Teddy reached up with his good hand and managed to grab hold. He tried to grab with his swollen hand and cried out in pain.

"It hurts, it hurts, it hurts," he screamed out.

The ants were only nine feet away from Dean's feet.

"You've got to climb, Teddy. You've got to. They're almost on me."

Pulling with all his might, Teddy managed to lift himself up enough to hook his other arm around the tree branch, careful not to knock his swollen hand. He then hoisted himself up from Dean's hands.

Dean looked back to the ground, the ants only six feet away. He jumped for the branch. He missed.

Fuck, is it too high for me to reach?

The ants were three feet from him, their eagerness in reaching their prey growing.

Dean jumped again, knowing that if he missed he would land back down amongst the teeming insects. He likely wouldn't get another attempt.

His hands grabbed at the rough bark and with an almighty effort he pulled himself up into the branches. He looked down to see the ground where he had been standing moments before engulfed in the furious insects. He felt they were enraged at being denied their prey.

"Look," cried Teddy, pointing to the tree trunk. Dean followed his brother's finger and he lamented the situation as he saw the ants begin to climb up the trunk in numerous columns. They were far from safe.

"We've got to climb higher," Dean said and Teddy nodded. He knew it was only a tactic to buy time, but what other actions could they take? It felt like the ants were a force of nature and escape was impossible.

The boys climbed a couple of branches before Dean realised that they would be able to get more distance between themselves and the insect army if they climbed outwards, away from the trunk. He ordered Teddy to do just that, and the young boy nodded. Dean could see the pain on his brother's face as he navigated the twisted branches, trying his very best not to knock his bloated hand.

They managed to reach the outermost reaches of the branches and stopped, having run out of places to flee to. If they climbed any further, either up or out from this position the branches would be too thin to take their weight and likely would break. The ground beneath them wasn't as densely covered in the ants as it had been previously. The larger numbers of ants were gathered either around the trunk of the tree or around and over the body of Cassie.

The ants were fanning out along the tree's branches now, running between leaves and twigs. Their numbers and locations impossible to decipher. It wouldn't take more than a minute for the insects to reach them, followed by thousands of burning stings.

Dean tried to imagine jumping down and running through the insects beneath him. There was less of them, although the ground was still alive with the things. Would he be able to hit the ground running and avoid being stung? He dismissed the idea, almost certain the creatures would overwhelm him. And what of Teddy? There was no way he would make it on the ground and if left in the tree, he would be condemned to a lonesome, horrific death.

At least they wouldn't die alone, Dean thought, realising they were out of options. He had brought them a minute longer. That would have to do. He wrapped his arms protectively around his brother and held him tight.

"Dean, I'm scared," Teddy cried.

"I know. Me too."

Dean closed his eyes and waited a few seconds before he opened them again to the sound of a quad bike horn going off. Both boys twisted and watched in amazement as a quad bike thundered towards them, with their dad in the bike seat.

*   *   *

Martin couldn't believe what he was seeing. The ants were swarming in their millions, all over the quad bikes the kids had taken. One of the bikes was upside down and wrecked, barely visible under a coat of the vicious insects. Shit, where were the kids. He scanned the scene in desperation as he approached. The ants' numbers were incalculable and he had no doubt they would be capable of killing people. He'd heard that fire ants could kill young children if they managed to overwhelm them. That was normal fire ants, these bastards were far from normal, and bigger too.

He almost swerved away, praying the kids had escaped on foot when he looked over at the nearby mesquite tree. The ants' numbers were greater at the foot of the tree and when he looked up he felt a great elation. His boys were sitting precariously in the branches, holding each other for dear life. He realised the ants were among the branches, chasing them and they had run out of places to go. But they were alive, and Martin thanked God for that.

He honked the loud horn of the quad numerous times to get the boys attention and both of his sons were soon whooping and waving at him in desperation.

The ants were moving fast and would be upon his sons in moments. The ground below the boys was alive with the hostile insects, so they wouldn't be able to escape on foot.   He accelerated towards the tree, calling over the engine. "I'm going to pull up beneath you. You're going to have to jump down. And be quick, I can't stop for more than a moment, otherwise the ants will manage to crawl up the bike wheels.

Dean and Teddy looked at each other and nodded with apprehension. "Hurry dad, they're nearly on us," cried Dean. He drew in his feet and dared to move slightly further out from the branches as the ants approached. The branch he was on began bending.

Martin sped through the insects, trying to ignore them as he pulled up below his sons. He straightened his legs into a standing posture, his feet on the quad footrests, and reached up. Dean quickly lowered Teddy down. As soon as Martin's hand gripped Teddy's legs he yanked him down hard.

Teddy clung tight to his father's chest, burying his face as if to deny the reality they were experiencing. "Now jump, quickly," Martin shouted. He noticed the ants had started climbing the tires of the bike. If they managed to reach the bike's chassis being stung would become a certainty.

Dean expertly swung out of the tree, landing on the seat

behind his dad. "Hold on," Martin ordered and opened up on the throttle. The bike wheels spun, kicking up dust and sending ants flying as it took off with speed.

"You okay?" Martin called behind him as he pulled out from beneath the tree as quickly as possible. Even now ants were dropping from its branches, back onto the ground. They were clearly aware that the prey they had been pursuing had escaped them.

"Ted's hurt. They stung his hand and his leg."

Martin nodded affirmation. He kept his eyes on the track. He'd have to examine Teddy once they got back to safety. "Where's Cassie? Is she still up in the tree?"

Dean blinked away tears upon hearing Cassie's name and the joy he felt at being rescued was replaced by the true horrific weight of what he had just experienced. He couldn't bring himself to say the words, so he pointed instead. "There," he said, not even looking, trying to spare himself the anguish.

Martin looked where Dean had indicated, saw the heaps of ants, like a moving carpet, swarming over the overturned quad and something else beside it. He realised with horror and numbness what the irregular shape beneath the insects was.

"I see," was all he could managed as he kept riding, putting as much distance between them and the hostile insects as he could.

CHAPTER 12

Louise stood by the window, looking outside, praying for any sign of Martin returning with the kids. Not only did scanning the horizon help her avoid the need to make conversation with Tom and Marie, but it also helped stop her from losing her mind. There really wasn't anything else to be done.

Marie and Tom were constantly trying to call and send messages in the hope something would get through. As it stood, their attempts had been fruitless. After struggling to get himself changed and cleaned up, Tom had returned to the living room sofa. His ankle had swollen dramatically and Louise had provided him with the strongest pain killers she had to try and keep him comfortable.

Marie had marched from room to room, hoping to stumble across somewhere where a slither of phone reception could be found. So far unsuccessful, she'd hung the phone out of windows and walked around the house's perimeter in her mission.

Louise was glad Marie had something to occupy her. Every time they were in the same room together the woman had stared accusatory glares at her and Louise was getting worked up enough to lose her composure again. For whatever reason, Marie hadn't told Tom about their argument. She doubted it was because Marie was going to let it go. More likely she wanted to tell him when Louise wasn't present. That way she could paint the conversation as she saw fit. That was just fine with Louise. As long as it kept her from having another square off with the woman, Marie could curse her to high heaven behind her back.

Martin's plan had been simple. There was one quad left in

the garage; his. Since the truck had been totalled the quad was the only vehicle they had that was capable of navigating the ranch's rough terrain. He knew the kids must have left the house to the southeast and so he would commit himself to searching that area. The ranch may have been large, but it wasn't so large that people could disappear and not be found again. Fencing ran the property border so the boys wouldn't be able to leave their land accept by the main gateway. They knew there was nothing for a good fifteen miles except desert in any direction so there was no reason why they would leave.

The area to the southeast was more uneven and rocky than the pastures to the north, so finding them would take a little more time, but nothing Martin felt he couldn't handle.

He's been gone nearly forty-five minutes now and with every passing minute Louise's anxiety was increasing. The hostile environment inside the house was getting to her. Marie's snide comments were grating worst and worst, and she knew why. She was genuinely worried for her children.

The desert was dangerous at the best of times. The heat could dehydrate a person fast, and the uneven ground could be treacherous if one wasn't careful where they took the quad bikes. In the past it had always been insisted upon that the bikes only be taken out with either her or Martin present. Neither Dean nor Teddy had seemed to question that rule, which made her feel Cassie had to be somewhat to blame. She'd noticed how Dean had been looking at his cousin and she'd noted Cassie was very aware of the effect she was having on him, even if she had tried to hide it from the adults. It was pointless to begin pointing fingers and placing blame, though. That was Marie's game, not hers. Not to mention Cassie was undoubtedly the person most at risk if something did go wrong. She was a city girl with zero experience in the wilderness. At least Dean and Teddy had some idea what they were dealing with.

As if the land itself didn't present a big enough danger, to be treated with the utmost respect, there was also the snakes, spiders and coyotes. Any unexpected run ins could be tragic.

Now she had spooked longhorns and rampaging ants to add to the mix.

The cattle were one thing, at least she understood the threat they represented. The ants were an unknown entity. She was no expert, but she had never heard of ants acting the way Martin had described. Maybe they were army ants from South America? But even then, it seemed unusual.

The nest Franklin had discovered had been a good couple of miles from the shed, so did that mean the insects were on the march? Or were there more nests than the one they had already discovered? If they could harm several cattle, they could almost certainly hurt a human. She turned and looked up the track towards the shed. It felt ominous and unknowable, as if harbouring dark secrets she couldn't guess at. It was only half a mile down the road. Too damned close. Martin had said the ants had begun chasing him and Tom. Would they follow the trail all the way down? If so, they would surely find the house.

As soon Martin returned with the kids, she would insist they leave the property. Franklin, Simon and some other workers could round up the cattle, Louise decided. There was no way she would let any of her family set foot back on the property until the ants had been investigated and destroyed by qualified people or the government.

She apathetically looked down at her phone and pressed the call button to try and reach Dean. As expected, the call could not be connected. She kept trying, simply because there was nothing else to do.

Looking up, she spotted Martin approaching through the hills in his quad. She was happy to see him return, yet she was troubled that he seemed to be riding alone. Squinting, she realised Dean and Teddy were riding on his quad with him. In that moment Louise knew something had gone horribly wrong. Cassie's absence was alarming.

She ran down the stairs. "Martin's coming back," she called.

"Thank God," sighed Tom with relief, squeezing Marie's knee in enthusiasm. She was sat beside him, looking up from her phone, looking relieved by the news. "Has he got the kids?" Tom asked.

Louise hesitated, unsure how to explain what she had seen. "He's got Dean and Teddy with him." It was the simplest statement she could think of. Just the facts and nothing more.

"What about Cassie?" Marie asked abruptly. Louise could see the fear growing on Marie's face as the situation suddenly morphed from three kids disobeying the rules to something far more ominous.

"I don't know," Louise said. She felt relief and guilt upon seeing Dean and Teddy. Relief that her boys had been found. Guilt because, for whatever reason, Cassie wasn't returning with them.

"Louise, what about Cassie?" Marie pushed, standing up.

"I said 'I don't know'," Louise repeated, turning to leave the room. She didn't want her own fears to show and feed Marie's. She felt afraid for the woman, even if Marie was a first-class bitch. Fear for one's child was the most palpable and she wouldn't wish it on any mother.

Marie followed a step behind Louise, firing unanswerable questions at her while Louise opened the front door as Martin pulled up on the quad. He leapt from the bike, Teddy in his arms. Dean followed behind him. Louise's heart sank further still. Teddy, her baby, was hurt.

"Martin, what happened?" she cried out.

"We need to get inside. Quick. He's been stung."

"The ants?"

Martin nodded as he rushed in.

"Martin, what about Cassie?" Marie demanded. He ignored her, all energies focussed on his son.

"Clear the table," Martin ordered, and Louise obeyed, with one hand sweeping the cutlery and fruit bowl onto the floor. The fruit bowl broke and she couldn't have cared less. She held onto Teddy's hand and started stroking his head as Martin gently set him down. He was unconscious, clammy and hot to the touch.

"He's burning up," Louise cried, tears welling up in her eyes.

"God, his hand," she gasped as she noticed his other hand. It was swollen, engorged with blood and looked pulpy to touch. Several sting sites on it was blatantly present, raised and red, their presence deforming the shape of his hand further, making it resemble a gnarled club more than anything else.

"Those fucking ants," Martin cursed. "He's got a sting on his leg, too."

Louise turned and begun fussing over Dean. "Are you okay, baby? Are you stung?"

"I'm alright mom," he said, looking at his feet.

"Get the anti-venom kit," Martin ordered. Louise nodded and rushed to the upstairs bathroom.

"Where's Cassie?" Marie frantically shouted, on the verge of losing it.

Dean looked away, unable to look at her. He begun crying softly.

"Martin, where's Cassie?" she asked again.

Martin wet his lips. He rested his weight upon the table, trying to voice the worse news he'd ever had to tell. Louise came rushing back in with the anti-venom kit.

"Where is my fucking daughter?" Marie shrieked at the top of her lungs. Everything happening in the kitchen stopped dead, as if time stood still.

Louise looked from Marie to Martin, imploringly.

Martin shielded his eyes, wiping away evidence of tears. He was shaking and didn't want to give voice to what he had seen. He knew once he said the words, they would change everybody's world, forever.

"She's dead," wept Dean weakly. He broke down in tears.

Marie stared at him, open mouthed. A million emotions flashed over her face and died. She held onto her stomach, as if she had just been punched in the gut. "Why would you say that?" she uttered. Dean looked at her, puzzled. "Why would you fucking say that?" she roared and launched herself at him, grabbing his hair and shaking him in blind fury, shouting the same question again and again.

Martin and Louise jumped onto Marie and pulled her off their son, as she spat and cursed and tried to claw at him. "Why would you say that?" She demanded. "Why? Take it back. Take it back. Why would you say that?"

"It's true, isn't it?" said Tom calmly. He had managed to limp down the hallway to join them. At the sound of his words, all the fight in Marie dissipated and she went almost completely limp.

"Say it's not true," Marie bawled, completely distraught. Martin and Louise released her, feeling her pain, her wound. "Say it's not true, she's not dead. She's not dead. She can't be."

Tom kept his eyes fixed on Martin's. "It's true. Isn't it?" Each word was evenly measured and deathly calm.

Martin held his brothers gaze, frozen in place. "It is," he said, pitifully.

Marie bawled harder and louder than before; her whole frame wracked with grief. She slid to the floor, surrendering to her despair.

Tom's bottom lip began trembling. He took a deep breath as he struggled to maintain his emotions. He blinked away tears and tried his best to remain calm, although a wavering tone had entered his speech. "How... how did it happen?"

"The ants. The ants got her."

Tom tried to comprehend the absurdness of Martin's words. "You're telling me... Cassie was killed... by ants...?"

Martin nodded slowly. "Like the ones in the cattle shed. Tom, there was so many. They nearly got my boys. She was already gone by the time I found them."

"And you left her out there?"

"Tom, there was nothing I could do. If I'd tried to get her we would have all been killed."

Marie was rocking back and forwards, wailing as if her soul had been wrenched from her. "You did this," she cried, looking at Dean. "This is all your fault. You did this."

Dean wept. He did not defend yourself.

"Marie," Tom croaked. She kept wailing at Dean and Martin prepared himself in case she attacked his son again.

"Marie," Tom barked loudly and this time she fell silent, looking at him.

"Our baby's dead," she sobbed. The anger had left her suddenly, replaced by a deep sorrow that everyone in the room felt. Louise wiped at the tears streaming down her face.

Tom swallowed hard. "I know. I know. Help me into the living room."

Marie looked at him as if she were going to protest. She then nodded, pulled herself up and helped Tom walk back down the hallway and into the living room in silence. Tom shut the door behind them and crying could be heard emanating from beyond.

"Oh, Martin," Louise cried and stepped into Martin's waiting embrace. They squeezed each other, some of the tension melting away. "This is horrible. Just horrible."

"I know," he agreed, stroking her hair. He looked up at Dean, who numbly stood in the corner. He looked zoned out, as if he were reliving his recent experiences in his head. "Dean, you okay?"

Dean looked up and nodded, but he didn't look okay. Louise broke out of the hold with Martin and went and comforted him.

"I'm sorry," Dean uttered. "I'm sorry."

"This isn't your fault," Louise soothed. "Nobody could have predicted this."

Martin glanced back at Teddy, lying still on the table. His breathing was regular at least, although the fever seemed to be showing no signs of slowing down. Teddy made faces, as if the pain were still affecting him, even in his unconscious state. "Lou, the bag," he said and she quickly passed it to him before returning to calming and stroking Teddy.

Martin unzipped the anti-venom bag, a piece of kit anybody who lived in a rural environment owned, and pulled out the various medicines and syringes. He checked the bottles. Some were for various spiders, others for snakes. One was marked wasps/hornets and he picked it up. It was the closest to ants stings he could see and so he filled the syringe and gave Teddy a shot.

"I doubt it'll completely negate the stings, but with a little luck it should help. We need to get him to the hospital as soon as possible."

Louise nodded. "There's been no luck reaching anybody. Even the landline is down. We can't call an ambulance."

"It'll be quicker driving him to town ourselves, rather than waiting for the phones to find service. We all should go. The authorities need to come sort this out. Those ants, I've never seen anything like them before. We aren't safe here."

"Agreed," said Louise. She walked to the key hook and picked up the SUV. "I can't tell you how much I want to get out of here." She glanced at all the food, prepped and waiting for the big meal she was making. Sighing she turned off the oven which was currently slow roasting the turkey. "Some Thanksgiving," she said, bitterly.

A loud shriek came from the living room, startling them all. Louise made wide eyes at Martin. "Stay here, make sure the kids are safe," he said before running down the hallway.

"Martin, get in here," Tom called urgently as Martin burst through the door.

"What's wrong?" he said, taking in the scene. Tom was standing in the middle of the room, Marie was on the sofa, curled up and still distraught. There was a new emotion on her face alongside the sorrow: fear. "Tom?"

"Look out the window," Tom said with a hint of revulsion.

Feeling like he was suddenly falling, Martin stepped to the large bay window and peered out. At first he didn't see them. Then he noticed the movement. The more he noticed, the more impossible it was to overlook. Ants, everywhere, scurrying all over the driveway and surrounding land, crawling over the cars, the plants, his quad bike. There had to be tens of millions of them.

"Jesus, there's so many." Martin struggled to compute what he was seeing, trying to understand how it was possible.

"They can't have followed me from where I found the boys. It's too far away. There's no way they could have followed me so fast."

"They've had enough time to follow you two from the shed though, haven't they?" Marie declared.

Martin and Tom exchanged glances. "She's right," Tom said. "They've had over an hour. While we've been sitting here, they've been coming for us."

Martin wanted to say that it was a ridiculous notion, but he knew they were right. He peered back out the window, looking at the cars. "We're trapped," he stated.

"What are we going to do?" Tom asked, feeling helpless.

Martin moved closer to the window, peering out at the masses of angry insects. He jumped back, startled, as one of the offending inch long insects crawled over the pane of glass, inches from his face. Its stinger looked cruel, as sharp as any syringe, and its mandibles opened and shut eagerly. The insect's feelers rapidly moved over the glass, searching for a way to get inside as it scurried left and right. "They're on the house," he said in alarm. "They're all over."

Louise screamed from the kitchen, the sound shaking the very core of Martin's being. He called her name as he ran back down the hallway to the kitchen.

Louise stood between the back door and the table Teddy was resting on, brandishing a kitchen knife. Dean remained in the corner, frozen in terror. Martin followed both their gazes and could see several of the large ants clambering over the back door glass.

"Martin, the ants..."

"I know. They're all over the front drive."

"Can we get to the cars?"

"Not a chance." He walked up beside her and gently pulled the knife from her grip. She'd obviously grabbed it and rushed to protect Teddy from the insects, despite it being an impractical weapon given the nature of their foes. Still, he was proud of her fighting spirit.

"Oh Martin, what are we going to do? We need to get Teddy to a hospital."

"I know," said Martin. "We'll get him there. I just need time to think. What we need to do it make sure none of these fuckers can get inside."

Louise nodded and turned, to see Marie and Tom enter the kitchen.

"This is bad, Martin. Real bad," Tom said, his voice beyond tense.

"Don't I know it," Martin said, darkly. "At least the windows and doors are all PVC so they close tight. And the fact the interior of the house is fairly new, this place should be damned bear watertight. With any luck we are locked up tight." The group nodded. "Due to the heat, we left all the windows closed so the air-con could do its thing. I assume that's still the case?"

"It is," said Louise.

"Maybe not," said Marie. Everyone turned to look at her. "I opened some of the upstairs windows when I was trying to get a signal earlier."

"Okay, and did you close them?" Martin asked.

Marie chewed on her bottom lip. "I can't recall."

CHAPTER 13

So far, Simon's Thanksgiving Day had been off to a good start. He'd been woken early, due to the noisy cockerel three door down, and felt a little worse for wear after a night of drinking down at the local bar. Normally this would have been a crummy start to the day, except for one thing. He hadn't woken up alone.

Beside him was Skylar, a particularly fine piece of ass he had been trying to score with for a few months now. After a number of attempts, pulling out his best crude jokes and sending photos of his dick at the slightest provocation, she had eventually agreed to go back to his.

She lived with her dad, and from what he had heard about her father, that wasn't something that she would be thankful for. He guessed the holidays made some people feel the need to make a connection and he would absolutely be that shoulder to cry on, so long as it got him some pie when all was said and done.

Skylar certainly made the time he'd put into pursuing her worthwhile. She was certainly experienced, although he supposed that from what she had confided in him, she'd started learning the language of love from a young age.

He watched her sleeping for a while as he tried to recall the nights' events. Drinking, coke, fried chicken, pussy. He smiled to himself. I had been an awesome night. He guessed he had Franklin to thank for that, at least in part.

Since he had started working at Yellow Hills Ranch, he hadn't been short of cash. Mister Bevaux had come from New York and, even though he had lived around these parts for nearly three years now, he hadn't quite grasped how much he should expect to pay the locals. Either that or he was a generous man.

God bless city-slickers. Still, Simon worked hard for the man and didn't feel he was ripping him off. Far from it, he worked his ass off, most days at least. Admittedly there were the odd days he's turn up still drunk or off his face on ketamine, but those days were few a far between. And when they did happen, Franklin would cover for him and keep Simon's face to face time with the boss down to a minimum.

Good ol' Franklin. He was a one in a million, and he always seemed to look out for Simon. It was him who had got Simon the job in the first place and they mostly worked side to side. Some of the guys down at the bar would rib him, saying that the reason Franklin was so nice to him was because Simon's mom was a whore who gave him extras in return.

Simon ignored such rumours. Not the ones about his mom being a whore. Although she had worked as a striper in her youth and was now a barmaid, he had no doubt she did extra things in exchange for a few extra dollars. It was the rumour of Franklin being one of her Johns he didn't think was true. If it was, he felt Franklin would have let it slip by now. He supposed he didn't really care, either way. It was certainly nothing to risk knocking the apple cart over for. If he was reaping the benefits his mom had given him by laying on her back and playing hide the salami with old man Franklin, then surely it was his job as her son to oblige. It would actually be disrespectful not to, come to think of it.

"Hey, you awake?" he said softly, running his hand over Skylar's soft, warm body. Her eyes opened and met his. She smiled and stretched.

"Hey baby, good morning." Her voice was slightly croaky from too many cigarettes and her breath smelt a little stale.

"All the better for waking up next to you."

She smiled and they kissed. Her hands began exploring his body, finding his manhood and started pulling at it. He became hard at her touch and kissed deeper, squeezing her breasts as he rolled onto her, parting her legs. As they kissed he reached down to stroke her, smiled as he felt her slick wetness. He entered her and then thrusted for a good two minutes until he reached climax. He then rolled off, satisfied.

He couldn't help but smile. In the bar she had been insistent on him wearing a condom. Once he'd got her home, all talk of protection had vanished, and he certainly wasn't going to remind her. As he lit two cigarettes and handed one to her, he couldn't help feeling a little cheated. She'd been a solid seven easy, when he'd brought her home. Now she was a five at best. *Women used makeup to make them look like somebody else, then accused men of being the liars. Fucking hypocrites,* he thought.

"What are you up to for the rest of the day?" she asked casually.

Simon's body stiffened up as he jumped out of bed and started pulling his clothes on. "I told you, I got work today."

Skylar pouted playfully. "All day? Can't we spend the day together? I'll make it worth your while." She ran her hand over her body seductively.

"Sorry sweetheart, work comes first. Now finish your smoke and get dressed, I'll take you home."

Skylar wasn't happy about being dismissed so out of hand and she vocalised the fact while getting dressed. Simon ignored her for the most part, taking a shower and checking his socials. When she was ready he gave her a lift on the back of his scrambler, dropped her off down the road from her place, then returned home.

His mom was in the kitchen, having pulled herself out of bed and wearing an oversized t-shirt as she scrambled some eggs and poured him a freshly brewed coffee. The smells of the cooked breakfast were enough to revitalise Simon and he dug in as soon as the plate was in front of him.

His mom sat down opposite him on the small kitchen table. She took a drag of her cigarette before sipping her own coffee. "You're a fucker, just like your dad was, you know that?"

Simon grinned. "I've only got your word to go on regarding that, haven't I?"

"Smart ass," she kicked him under the table. "What time are

you leaving for Marlene's?"

"Marlene and her folks are sitting down for dinner around one. I'll get to hers maybe half an hour before."

"Reckon you'll be home tonight?"

"Not likely."

"Well, I won't be back until late tonight so don't wait up if you are."

Simon thought it was a little unfair his mom had to work the late shift at the bar on Thanksgiving, though he understood it was necessary. A lot of folks got lonely and needed a place to sing their sorrows. "Ok, mom." He finished his eggs and got up to leave.

"Why you leaving now? It only takes you an hour to get to Marlene's."

"I know. I'm stopping in on Franklin on the way there."

"Franklin? Really?"

"Yeah, he kinda begged me too. Guess he ain't got no one else. He hoped to get an invite at the Boss Man's table, but it never happened."

"What a shocker," his mom sighed. "You're all heart, Simon. Send Franklin my love, ya hear?"

"Will do." He picked up his jacket and left. Getting back on his scrambler, he took the main roads out of the small town and as soon as he hit the highway, he let her rip. There were few pleasures in the world that beat racing down the open highway. He was fairly certain the pigs wouldn't be watching the roads today so he pushed the top speed a little higher than he normally did.

It would take about thirty minutes on the highway to reach Franklin's, just inside Yellow Hills Ranch. He had time for a few beers before he headed on to Marlene's. He knew he couldn't be too drunk for dinner. It was his first time meeting her uncle, who she apparently idolised.

He'd been going out with Marlene for just over seven months now and for the most part it was going well. She probably wouldn't be too impressed if she found out about

Skylar, but who was going to tell her? That was the beauty of having a girlfriend in another town. No complications.

Pulling off the highway, Simon started navigating the dirt tracks around the hills until he reached Franklin's trailer. He stopped the bike in shock at what he saw.

It looked like someone had thrown a grenade at Franklin's trailer. Something had exploded, and it had caused a lot of damage. Burnt shrapnel was spread around the site and the trailer was partially burnt out. It looked like it had burnt through most of the night.

The explosion had also toppled the wooden pylon, pulling the telephone cables with it. As he slowly approached on foot, Simon was wary of touching anything that may be electrified by the cables.

Looking amongst the carnage, it was hard to distinguish what damage had been caused by the explosion and what had been junk dumped by Franklin. The man was a well-known hoarder and not famous for being the tidiest of people.

"Franklin?" he called, approaching the trailer. "Franklin, you in there, brother? What the hell happened?" He reached the door to the trailer and checked inside. The interior looked just how he had imagined it; partially burnt out and in disarray.

Simon had no desire to thoroughly search the trailer. Even if everything had been normal, he didn't want to think of the grotty discoveries he might make. A chill ran up his back as he started to grow concerned.

He decided to head back to his bike. He'd ride up to the Boss Man's house and see if he knew what had happened. Chances were Franklin would be there already. He wouldn't put it past the old fool to burn down his trailer just so he'd have an excuse to spend the day eating Louise's Thanksgiving turkey and drinking the boss' beer. The trailer was a shit hole, anyway. Burning for it was probably for the best.

As he was walking towards his bike, he spotted Franklin's boots, sticking out from behind an old, rusted engine. "Hey Franklin? You okay, man?" he called as he approached. The scrap metal obscured Frankin's body until Simon got close. He already felt he knew what he was going to find.

He covered his mouth and nose as the approached Franklin's corpse. His body was charred and bloodied, his skin looked like it and flaked off pretty much all over save the face and the flesh underneath was severely blistered and deformed. Simon gagged and nearly brought up his breakfast.

Poor old fool, he thought. He knew Franklin had an abundance of gas and propane laying about the site. Clearly something had happened that had caused an explosion. It was probably Franklin's own damned fault. Still, he hadn't deserved to die like this.

The expression on Franklin's face was one of agony, frozen in place and Simon knew he'd see that face whenever he closed his eyes for the rest of his life. Thick blood, now dried and crusty, had oozed from his mouth, nose, ears and eye sockets.

The most horrific aspect of all was Franklin's eyes, or rather, their absence. His sockets were void of anything, just black, ragged pits. Simon swallowed hard. Had they been blasted out from the explosion? Was that even possible? Or had they been picked out by some animal afterwards? Like a bird or something? That seemed more probable, and it filled Simon with revulsion. The gruesome find made him shiver.

Turning his back, he pulled out his phone to call nine-one-one. He cursed when there was no signal. There never was in this shit hole. Franklin had the only phone that ever seemed to work, a beat-up Nokia about twenty years old. Looking at the scattered debris surrounding him, he doubted he would find it.

Simon decided the best thing to do was drive to the boss' house and inform him. Hopefully he had a way of phoning out. Before he left, Simon decided to cover Franklin with his jacket. It seemed like the respectful thing to do.

Taking his jacket off, he crouched beside the corpse of his friend and covered his body with it. He looked at the twisted face, a horrific final image of a man who had been a good friend.

"Sorry this happened to you, man. It ain't the way you

should 'a gone out. You deserved better. You were a good friend. Rest in peace, Franklin." He went to pull the jacket up over his dead friend's face, then yelled in alarm and jumped back. "What the fuck?"

He'd seen movement in the hollows of Franklin's eyes. Movement. He could'a sworn it. Edging forwards, he craned his head to get another look. Although it felt disrespectful, his morbid curiosity called upon him to turn on the torch on his phone a shine it into the dead man's head.

The light hit the ragged, raw meat within the eye socked and disturbed whatever was nestled within. Simon cursed in disgust as he saw some kind of insect crawling around before climbing out. It was an ant, the same kind as the ones they had burnt the day before. It was a big fucker, easily over an inch long and carried a tiny piece of glistening wet flesh between its mandibles.

"Goddam," he swore. He guessed he shouldn't be surprised bugs had found poor Franklin's body. All the more reason to get the authorities to collect him as quickly as possible. Bugs weren't the only thing out here. He could only imagine what would happen if coyotes found his dead friend out in the open like this.

The ant crawled onto what was left of Franklin's ruined cheek, its head turning from left to right as its feelers waved in the air, examining the surroundings.

"Horrible thing," Simon muttered as he went to pull the coat over Franklin's head. At least he could give him a little dignity, even if he were being eaten by bugs.

The ants wavering moments stopped and the insect focussed its attentions on the movement. Clearly it could sense Simon crouching beside it. It freaked out Simon more than he wanted to admit, as the insect began marching straight for him.

Simon dropped the jacket and pulled his hands away. He had never seen an ant act like that before. Normally they appeared to be blissfully unaware of humans. Not this one, though, it knew he was there. And it was coming for him.

Simon stood and backed away, even as he noticed another

ant emerge from the eye socket. *The hell?* Another ant crawled from the other eye. Then another. And another. Soon columns of ants were crawling from both eyes. There had to be fifty, no, a hundred of the morbid things.

Then they started crawling from Franklins nostrils. Then from his ears. Simon was in shock, the old man's head had to be filled with the damned things. Movement caught his eye and he watched as even more ants emerged from beneath Franklin's clothing. Simon's heart was beating out of his chest as he felt he had wandered into a nightmare.

In Simon's peripheral he caught more movement and he turned to see hundreds, if not thousands of ants emerging from the multiple piles of trash scattered around Franklin's site. They acted just as the initial ant had; first they swayed their head, checking their environment. Then they made a beeline straight for him.

Suddenly Simon was calling the cause of Franklin's death into question. *Had the ants been the cause of Franklin's death? Was this some kind of revenge?* The thought seemed ridiculous, yet the ants certainly looked capable of committing harm.

Looking around him he realised their numbers were increasing rapidly, the ground now practically alive with the marching insects. If he lingered much longer, they'd be upon him.

Simon looked towards his scrambler. It wasn't too far away and there weren't too many marauding insects between him and it. "Fuck this," he yelled and sprinted to the bike. There was no way he was going to end up like poor Franklin. He made exaggerated steps to avoid denser patches of the bugs and leapt onto the scrambler. He turned the ignition and pulled on the throttle. The engine whined as he turned the bike and peeled off, away from the waking nightmare he had just experienced.

He had to get to the main house, warn the family about what was on their ranch. He only hoped they would believe him.

Back at the trailer site, the ants sensed their prey had escaped them. They weren't disappointed, for disappointment was a concept completely alien to them. They merely adapted to the circumstances at hand. There would be more prey. There was always more prey. For now, they would return to the task at hand. The insects returned to their evil work, making their way back to what remained of Franklin.

CHAPTER 14

Martin ran to the cupboard under the kitchen sink and opened it, hastily pulling out can after can, looking for anything that could be weaponised.

"What are you doing?" Louise queried. The knife she'd welded was back in her hand and Martin wouldn't deny her the semblance of protection she felt it gave her, even if that semblance was a lie.

"Those things are all over the house. If there's a window open, they'll have found it already. They'll already be in here."

"Can't we just close the bedroom doors if they have got in?"

"We can, but the bedroom doors are wooden. I wouldn't like to rely on them protecting us like the external windows and their plastic seals."

"But if there are too many…?"

Martin grabbed a can of ant spray. He guessed he couldn't have found a more suitable weapon, plus it was mostly full which boosted his confidence facing the invading insects. Beside it was a can of wasp spray, a can of fly spray and two cans of ant powder. The powder wasn't the most offensive item, though it would be useful to deter the ants from finding their way in. He held on to the ant spray and one of the ant powders and went to pass the wasp spray to Dean. "You up for joining me upstairs?"

Dean looked at the can, as if it was the most frightening thing in the world. "I, I don't know if I can," he stuttered.

Martin cursed inwardly. Dean was firmly in fear's grip. He supposed he shouldn't have been surprised. He'd witnessed Cassie be killed by the ants and had only narrowly avoided a similar fate for himself and his brother. He was drained both emotionally and physically.

"I can go," Louise said, her motherly instincts compelling her to protect Dean from the confrontation.

Martin thought it over. He'd rather Dean come with him and Louise stay downstairs. That said, if Dean wasn't feeling up to it then he may end up being more of a liability than a help. If he froze at the wrong time the results could be disastrous.

"Dean, you take the ant powder and sprinkle it over the rims of all external doors, windows and any other places these bastards might try to use to squeeze in here. Hopefully it'll slow them down if it doesn't deter them completely. Can you do that, son?" He held out the second can of powder.

Dean nodded, taking the poison. "I can do that." He looked scared but his willingness to try to help aid their survival was a good sign. Martin knew idleness could be a man's worst enemy when in tight spots.

Martin smiled and squeezed his son's shoulder before turning back to Louise. "I'll go upstairs alone," he said.

"The hell you will, I'm coming with you." Martin and Louise turned in surprise as Marie stormed into the room and picked up the can of wasp spray. Her face was streaked with mascara from where she's been crying. Now her expression was set, hard and cold.

"You sure?" asked Martin.

"Those fuckers took my daughter. If some of them have got in, I'll enjoy a little payback."

Tom limped into the kitchen after her. "It should be me. I should go with Martin."

Marie looked at him as if he had said something ridiculous. "Don't be foolish, Tom. You can barely walk. Louise needs to stay with Teddy. I'm the logical choice."

Tom wanted to argue but couldn't fault his wife's argument. "Be careful," he said.

Marie turned back to Martin. "Let's do this."

* * *

The stairs gave a slight creak as Martin and Marie ascended. Martin was armed with the ant spray and a steak tenderising mallet, as well as the ant powder in his back pocket. Marie had the wasp spray as well as another of their steak mallets.

They walked slowly, backs pushed against the wall as they kept their eyes on the floor and walls, looking for any signs of movement. The floors were hardwood and thus an ant standing still would be slightly harder to spot than one on the walls, which were painted cream.

Tom hovered at the bottom of the stairs, watching them anxiously. Louise remained in the kitchen with Teddy, whilst Dean went from room to room, covering every possible ant sized entrance with ant powder.

Tom reached the top of the stairs and looked in both directions. There were five rooms that had to be checked: four bedrooms and a bathroom, plus two ensuites. The house wasn't massive, but it was large enough.

"We'll go this way first," Martin indicated. "We'll check the master room, the bathroom and," he hesitated, the other room was the one Cassie had been staying in. "The guest bedroom."

Marie nodded, wiping away a tear that betrayed the inner turmoil beneath her calm exterior. Martin and Louise's bedroom door was ajar and they pushed it open. The window was locked and they breathed a sigh of relief.

"Remember, just because the windows are closed, still keep your wits about you. God knows how many other ways these bastards may find to get in."

"I'm not stupid," Marie hissed.

Martin nodded and checked his ensuite. The window was also closed.

Next they had to check the guest bedroom and main bathroom. The windows of the guest bedroom were locked and secure. Martin couldn't help noticing that the ants were running across the glass of the windows, clearly searching for a way in. There seemed to be more of them than before. He thought about sharing the observation with Marie, then discarded the idea. She didn't need him voicing the obvious. The sound of their feet tapping across the glass was a constant reminder, even if one wasn't looking at them.

Marie couldn't help letting out a whimper as they checked the window in the guest bedroom, her eyes lingering on Cassie's belongings and clothes, half unpacked and scattered, as teenagers were prone to do.

"I'll check the bathroom," he said softly, leaving her some time to be alone amongst her daughter's things.

Walking into the bathroom he checked the windows were closed tight, which they were. The glass on them was frosted, leaving the ants as ominous, dark, shapeless shadows whenever they scuttled over it.

A hollow, echoing scratching sound caught Martin's ear and he turned, following the sound. He listened intently, trying to focus on its source. He walked over to the sink, trying to ascertain the noise's origin. Was it coming from the basin? There appeared to be nothing in it.

He moved his face closer, listening.

"What's wrong?" said Marie, now standing at the bathroom door. Her sudden presence had made him jump.

"I think I can hear something," he said.

"Those things are all I can hear," she responded, looking at the dark shapes behind the frosted glass with disgust.

Martin moved his face closer to the basin again. "No, something else."

Movement made him yell in shock and he jumped back as the red ant emerged from plug hole, feelers waving in the air.

"Oh my God," Marie shrieked as more ants became climbing out of the hole.

Acting with deliberate movements, Martin rushed forward and turned on the faucet. The water blasted down, swirling around the basin before draining down the plug hole, washing the ants down with it. "They're coming up the God damned pipes," he exclaimed.

He ran past Marie and called downstairs. "Lou, Tom, Dean, they're coming up the pipes in the washbasins."

"What?" Louise cried out in fear and confusion.

"You're kidding," moaned Tom, limping into view from the living room, where he had returned to rest his ankle.

"Every plug hole in every basin is a way for these fuckers to get in. I want you to turn on the faucets, let some water wash away any ants that may be coming up. Then plug them and fill the basins up with water. And find something to block the overflow inlets."

"On it," said Tom, limping into the downstairs bathroom.

"Okay," called up Louise from the kitchen.

"Got it," confirmed Dean as he went to help his mother.

Martin waited until he was satisfied, hearing both Tom and Louise turn on the taps and following his instructions. Marie had followed the same advice, filling up the basin with water and jamming a sponge into the overflow. She also ran the bath and pushed in the plug before racing to the master bedroom and doing the same to the ensuite shower and wash basin.

Martin continued up the landing. There were three bedrooms to go, Dean's, Teddy's and the larger guest room, where Tom and Marie had slept. The doors to Dean's and the guest room were closed. Teddy's was ajar.

First, he checked Dean's room. The window was tight and sealed. Then he checked Teddy's. The chaotic nature of his room, with various clothes and toys scattered across the floor made for a million hiding places for any of the attacking insects to evade being spotted. The window was closed but not sealed, though it appeared the window was tight enough that no ants had managed to squeeze inside. He sealed and locked the window, trying not to look at the ants outside. They were now obscuring much of the view, their numbers becoming denser and denser.

Martin couldn't think of a happy ending to what was happening. If the ants were tenacious enough, how long could they be kept out?

Closing Teddy's door, Marie re-joined him on the landing.

"You were a while," Martin commented, out of hand. "Everything okay?" He instantly regretted his words. Of course everything wasn't okay, far from it.

Marie stared daggers at him. "I wanted to make sure I'd blocked off all the pipes the best as I could. It's not my house, remember? I don't automatically know where everything is."

"Okay, okay, I'm sorry. I shouldn't have said that." Martin apologised.

The last room to check was the large guest bedroom. A feeling of dread overcame Martin as they approached it. Slowly he put his ear to the door and tried to listen for the scurrying of tiny, chitinous bodies.

"You think you closed the window in here?"

Marie took a defensive pose, mallet and wasp spray at the ready. Her pose told him all he needed to know. "I know I opened it. I don't remember closing it."

Martin nodded, prepared the ant spray to fire and opened the door. The second it was open a crack he knew he had made a mistake as dozens of ants came spilling out. They came crawling across the floor as well as along the wall and ceiling. "Fuck," Martin cried. He wanted to jump back yet had the forethought to slam the door closed again before he did so.

The half second he needed to pull the door closed was a half second too long, as an ant darted onto the back of his hand. As he fell back, Martin shook his hand violently, filled with revulsion and terror. The ant flew from his hand before it could deliver its deadly sting, bouncing off the wall and landing on the hard-wood floor. It immediately began scurrying back towards its intended victim.

"Die, you fuckers," Marie screamed in a berserker rage as she held her finger down on the wasp spray, dousing the insects in the poisonous nerve agent from as close as she would dare.

Martin followed her lead and sprayed alongside her, the insecticide knocking the insects from the walls the ceiling. Ants landed on the floor, writhing and wriggling, their bodies twisting up as they succumbed to the poison.

He noticed more of the ants squeezing through from beneath the door. As Marie delivered death upon them Martin darted to the bathroom and returned with a towel. Reaching into his back pocket he pulled out the ant powder. He sprinkled copious amounts of the poisonous dust at the foot of the door before pushing the towel up against it, bocking the ants' path. He sprinkled more dust over the towel as Marie doused everything else in the wasp spray. The directions said to use the spray in an open environment, though Martin decided death by cancer in forty years was preferable to death by ant.

They both sprayed and brought their mallets into play until all the fifty or so ants that managed to breech the hallway were either shrivelled up or crushed to pulp. Despite Marie's bug spray claiming it was specially formulated to kill wasps and hornets, it was no less effective on the invading ants they now faced.

Finally confident that the ants were all dead, Martin and Marie stopped and caught their breath, stepping back and coughing due to the bug spray fumes.

"You guys okay up there?" Tom called from downstairs.

"Yeah, we're okay," Martin called back down to him. "They're in the large guest room. We've contained them for now."

"They're in," Marie said to Martin and coughed. "Now what?"

"Hopefully that door will hold them off." Already they could hear a low, crackling sound through the door. The ants had begun to chew their way through.

"We need to get out of here. We can't last forever, like this."

Martin thought of Teddy, lying on the table with his high fever. "I know."

Then the screaming downstairs begun.

* * *

Tom leant on the basin, watching as it filled with water. He turned the faucet off as the water reached the top and then shoved as much toilet tissue into the overspill as he could. It felt like enough to stop normal ants, he could only hope that it would stop these monsters.

Limping out of the downstairs bathroom, he took a right turn and entered the kitchen, where Louise was busy filling the kitchen sink. She acknowledged him as he entered before continuing with the task at hand. He limped over to the table and ran his hand through Teddy's hair. The boy seemed to be asleep, the look of pain he had displayed earlier was gone. He hoped that meant the anti-venom was doing its job. An overwhelming sense of loss hit him as he thought of his child, how she was gone, and nothing he did would be able to bring her back.

"This is madness," he muttered.

Louise turned off the water flow and slowly walked over to him. "I'm sorry for your loss, Tom." She didn't know what else to say. She reached up and squeezed his arm.

Tom nodded silently and reached up, wiping away fresh tears. "It, uh, it doesn't feel real. You know? Listen, I know I've made mistakes. I know that. But Cassie didn't deserve to be taken from us like that. She didn't." He was caught slightly off guard when he looked up and saw Dean, sat on the floor in the corner of the room, his knees drawn up to his chest. He was looking down, refusing to take part in the terrible reality he found himself in now that his brief task of sprinkling ant killer had been completed. "You were there? When it happened?"

Dean looked up, looking like a cornered animal due to the sudden attention Tom was giving him. Louise's body suddenly stiffened, ready to intervene and protect if Dean was attacked again.

"I was," Dean said.

More tears forced Tom to wipe his eyes profusely. "Did it… did it hurt? Was she in pain?"

Dean looked back down, hiding his face. He was unable to answer, the pain of reliving Cassie's death too traumatic to verbalise.

"Was she scared?"

Dean's shoulders started rising and falling as the boy wept. Louise put her hand on Tom's shoulder to soothe him, eager to stop the heart-breaking questions he was asking. "You should sit back down, rest your leg," she said softly.

Tom looked her in the eyes. He looked helpless and hollow, as if a part of him was missing and he'd never be able to find it again. He nodded. "Okay, okay. You're right."

Louise helped him walk back down the hallway and into the living room. He let out a groan of exertion as he lowered himself back down onto the sofa. "Can I... may I have a glass of water?"

"Sure thing," Louise forced a smile before leaving the room.

Alone with his thoughts, Ted took deep breaths as he watched the ants scurrying across the large bay windows. He hated them. He hated them with more hate than he thought he was capable of. He wanted to kill them. Kill them all.

Louise came back with the glass of water. Before she could hand it to him, she spun around in panic as she heard Martin yell from the second-floor landing, followed by Marie screaming "die, you fuckers," at the top of her lungs.

Louise looked desperately to Tom as he pulled himself back up, his ankle sending jolts of pain up his leg in protest, making him clench his teeth. He pulled a fire poke from the metal pot by the fireplace. Like Louise's kitchen knife she had welded earlier, it may not have been the most practical weapon, considering the nature of their enemy, but some primal need to hold something heavy and deadly was fulfilled and gave the slightest slither of security. Louise was clearly looking for direction of some kind, looking from Tom to the stairs, to the kitchen and back again.

"Go stay with the kids," he ordered. Louise nodded and

rushed back to the kitchen.

Tom limped to the bottom of the stairs. He could hear banging and cursing, along with the hiss of the insecticides and the thundering of footsteps.

"You guys okay up there?" he called up.

"Yeah, we're okay," Martin called back down to him. "They're in the large guest room. We've contained them for now." Martin and Marie then begun a hushed conversation. Tom wasn't a fool, he knew things were likely even worse than they appeared. Keeping the ants out of the house would be a near impossible task.

He went to put the fire poke back in the metal bucket by the fireplace and froze. Hundreds of ants were crawling out of the fireplace. They crawled across the carpet, along the walls and up the brickwork mantelpiece.

"Oh sweet Jesus," he wheezed, realising the hoards of stinging insects had found the chimney. The fireplace was open, the glass doors hung open, as Martin said they were left for most of the year. He realised in an instant that he had to close those doors before thousands of the insects flowed into the living room. The ants would kill them all.

Adrenaline made the pain in his ankle vanish as he leapt across the room, into the mass of crawling insects, dropped quickly to one knee and slammed shut the glass doors, dropping the hook between them to keep them locked.

As he did do, hundreds of ants immediately fell from higher up in the chimney, filling the fireplace as if were some obscene terraria. They desperately searched for a way in, to join their hundreds of sisters who had managed to slip inside before their entrance had been barred.

The angry ants that had managed to get through swarmed over Tom and he cried out at the severe burning he felt as the inch long insects began biting and stinging him without mercy. He writhed in pain on the carpet, clawing at his own body. All semblance of objective thought had gone from his mind. He felt he was on fire, his body contorting in agony as each sting compounded his pain even more.

"Tom," called Martin as he and Marie ran over to him.

"He's covered in the fucking things," Marie screamed as she batted the insects off her husband, stamping on them as soon as they were knocked onto the carpet.

Tom's body was spasming in pain, as if he were suffering a fit. Martin grabbed him by the ankles and dragged him out into the hallway, away from the fireplace, now utterly filled with the eager, monstrous ants.

"Marie, take care of him," he shouted as he ran back into the living room, ant spray at the ready. He did his very best at killing every ant he could see while Marie concentrated on killing those that had managed to climb onto Tom and now scurried about the hallway. Louise joined her sister-in-law, batting insects off the besieged man and crushing them underfoot.

In the living room, Martin was having a hard time ensuring he killed all the ants that had broken into their sanctuary. The patterns on the carpet and rug made them hard to spot and they could easily have darted behind ornaments and furniture. He pulled items off shelves and moved furniture, killing every ant he could find, yet he knew there was no way he could guarantee he'd killed them all.

When he could see no more, he dashed back out into the hallway, where Tom lay shaking violently, crushed ants surrounding him. Louise inspected Tom's clothes and the floor, her concentration like that of a hawk. Marie was trying to hold her husband down as he thrashed wildly.

"He's having some kind of seizure," Marie cried out.

Martin crouched down beside his brother, holding both his shoulders. The muscles on Tom's face were pulled unnaturally tight, his eyes rolled back into his head and his mouth frothed. Numerous large, red welts covered him from the multiple stings he had suffered. They numbered far in excess of those on Teddy's hand.

"Tom, Tom, can you hear me?" Martin asked, trying to stop his brother from hurting himself with his jagged movements.

Pink spittle began oozing from the corners of his mouth as every muscle in his body tensed. A deep, guttural moan emanated from deep within Tom's chest, his back arched, his body shivered from head to toe and then he relaxed. Tom had stopped breathing.

"Tom," cried Marie. "Tom, no."

Martin pushed her aside, preparing to commence CPR. He ripped open Tom's shirt buttons and then quickly withdrew his hands as several stinging ants scurried in aimless patterns over Tom's bare chest at the realisation they'd been discovered.

Tom covered his hand in the material of his sleeve and crushed the murderous insects. Through the material he could feel how hard their bodies were and how violently they struggled to escape as he crushed them. He didn't put any thought into whether they could sting through his clothes. His single-minded focus was to kill each and every last one of the hateful things.

With the last visible ant dead, Martin sat back and cried a long, sorrowful cry. Tom was dead and Martin feared that soon, the rest of them would follow him.

CHAPTER 15

Simon kept his head down as he rode his scrambler along the meandering road up to the main house of Yellow Hills Ranch. The heat of the day was intense now and he kept his visor down to avoid the bright glare of the sun from blinding him. The visor tinted the colours of the landscape from a yellow/orange to a deep dark blue.

Simon cursed his luck and questioned the absurdity of what he had seen. Had those ants really killed Franklin? Or had his death been the result of something else and the insects had merely been picking his bones clean? When he's been there, he felt for sure that the insects were deliberately chasing him. Now that he had made some distance between him and them, he wondered if perhaps his mind had been playing tricks on him.

Fuck, he didn't need this shit in his life. He should be on his way to Marlene's, to enjoy Thanksgiving dinner with all the trimmings. Not running from brain eating ants that had crawled from the eye sockets of a man he considered a friend.

Regardless, he was in it now, up to his neck. He couldn't just leave or else the law would likely try and finger him for it somehow. He decided he would mention finding Franklin's body but leave out the part about the ants. If the police decided to give him a drug test, he didn't want to think what its results would show.

Rounding a corner, the main house came into view. Simon pulled to a stop and kicked out the bikes support bar. He pulled off his helmet, not believing what it was he was seeing. The house and the grounds around it were absolutely covered in tens of millions of the large fire ants.

He guessed maybe his mind hadn't been playing tricks on him after all.

The ants were running over the ground, crawling up and around the two SUV'S parked outside the front of the house, as well as a quad bike. Simon recognised one of the vehicles as belonging the boss' wife. The other was new. It had to belong to the boss' brother.

Simon spat to the ground in exasperation. He wished he'd never agreed to meet Franklin for a couple of drinks. No amount of free beer was worth this shit.

* * *

Nobody said anything as Martin gently draped a sheet over Tom, giving his brother what dignity he could. Martin had dragged Tom back into the living room and lay him in one of the corners so that people wouldn't need to step over him. His eyes stung with tears and he had a lump in his throat.

He crouched beside his brother's still form and hung his head in mourning. Louise stood beside him, resting a hand on his shoulder. Marie sat at the table in the kitchen, watching the procession with dead eyes. She looked emotionally and physically gutted, her eyes dull and cold. She had poured herself a new glass of wine. It didn't seem smart to Martin for her to inebriate her senses, though he understood why she wanted to. Dean remained in the corner, quietly weeping to himself.

"Martin," Louise whispered. She hated to disturb his grief, but their situation hadn't changed. If anything, it had become more dangerous. It was almost a certainty that at least a handful of the ants had escaped into the living room. Everyone had their eyes constantly darting over the floor, searching for any movement that would betray the insects.

The fireplace was completely filled with the struggling ants, desperate to get out and only a single pane of glass kept them contained. It looked disturbingly fragile and could break at any moment. When it finally broke it would all be over.

"Martin," she whispered again. "We have to do something. We have to get Teddy to the hospital."

With supreme effort Martin stood up, trying to overcome the hole in his heart he felt. "I'm sorry, brother," he whispered. He then walked, zombie like, into the kitchen. Marie glowered at him. He wanted to say so many things to her. All he could manage was a weak "I'm sorry."

"Sorry isn't going to change anything," Marie sneered. "He's dead. Your brother is dead, and nothing will change that."

"He died being brave," Martin acknowledged. "He saw those things coming down the chimney. If he hadn't have acted, we'd all be dead now. He saved us."

"He saved your family," Marie spat with venom. "You still have your family. I have nothing left."

Martin and Louise exchanged worried glances. Louise calmly walked over to the kitchen table and began stroking Teddy's hair tenderly. "I think his fever has broken," she said, eager to change the direction of the conversation.

Martin gave one final look at his brother before joining her. He checked on Dean, who was now sitting on the counter, watching what was going on. It seemed he'd ran out of tears to cry. That was good, Martin had been concerned Dean wouldn't be able to act if the time came. His alertness was a marked improvement. He needed the capable Dean who had acted and saved his brother. Inevitably such actions would be needed again.

"That's good," Martin said to his wife.

"He still needs the hospital, though."

"I know."

"What are we going to do?"

"Yes, fearless leader, what are we going to do?" snapped Marie, gulping more wine.

"I'm trying to think," he shot back.

"Better hurry. Those things will be in here before too long."

"I know."

"Better come up with a good plan, otherwise we'll be wading out of here, waist deep in the fucking things."

Martin snapped. "Marie, will you shut the hell up for one minute." She glared at him.

"Maybe she's right," Dean said from across the room.

"What do you mean?" Martin asked.

"Maybe we could wade out."

"Come again?" said Marie, irritably.

"This is no time for jokes," Louise warned her son.

"No, no I think I follow him," Martin said.

Louise looked exasperated. "Please explain what you two are going on about?"

"My fishing gear. I've got several sets of waders and wellies."

"You think we can just walk out there in your fishing gear?" Marie scoffed. "You've seen how many things there are out there. How quick they move. The waders might buy us time, but that's all. We'll just end up dying slower."

Louise looked from Marie to Martin. "What do you think? Is she right?"

Martin wanted to be optimistic. At the same time, he couldn't bring himself to lie. Not when their lives were on the line. "Marie's probably right. The waders would buy us time, but with how many of them there are out there at the moment, we still wouldn't last long."

"Maybe we could thin their numbers?" Dean asked.

Martin nodded. "If that were possible then yeah, it could work. I can't for the life of me think how, though."

The four of them jumped as a loud crackling sound filled the room. They turned suddenly, expecting some kind of threat from the ants. Instead, they looked over to the counter, where the walkie talkie left by Franklin the night before crackled to life.

"Boss? Boss, can you hear me?"

"Who the hell is that?" asked Marie, not believing her ears.

Martin jumped across the room and picked up the walkie

talkie. He felt as if his prayers had been answered. "Simon? Simon, do you read me? Over." He had to keep himself from talking too fast, his excitement overtaking his faculties.

"I read you, Boss. What the fuck is going on with the ants? Over."

"I don't know, but they're highly aggressive." He paused. "They've killed my brother. And my niece."

"They got Franklin too, over."

Martin hadn't expected that. "Where are you? Over."

"By the barn, looking at the ants. There's got to be millions of the things on your house."

Martin walked through to the living room and looked out the large bay window. Between the multiple six-legged bodies of the ants searching for a way in, he could see the barn just past the drive. Simon was standing there, beside his scrambler, watching the ants in a manner too passive for Martin to bare. For whatever reason the ants hadn't noticed him, despite him being just a few hundred feet from where they were concentrated.

"Jesus, be careful, Simon. These things are dangerous. Don't let any sneak up on you."

"It'll take more than a bunch of bugs to get the better of me," he laughed. Martin found Simon's jovial attitude offensive, considering the tragedies they had been dealt. He'd have been more pissed if he wasn't so ecstatic to see his labourer. "What do you want me to do?"

Martin thought for a second. "Can you call for help?"

He watched as Simon pulled his phone from his pocket and checked it. "No bars. Want me to go get some help?"

Martin turned, looked at Tom's body, hidden under the shroud they had given him.

"No. We'll be dead by the time you get back."

"There's pesticide in the barn. Shall I spray them? Over."

Martin imagined how the scenario would play out. He couldn't shake the feeling that if Simon tried to douse the ants there would simply be too many of them. He had no doubt that as soon as Simon started spraying, he would be attacked. That said, the insects could turn their attention to the labourer at any moment. If that happened, Simon would have no choice but to leave and get help. It would take at least an hour before he returned. And that's if he managed to convince someone of what was happening. He was aware the police weren't exactly fans of Simon and his delinquent past.

"Negative. There's too many."

Simon tutted. "We should'a thrown more gas on these sons of bitches when they were in the nest."

"What did you say?"

Simon hesitated, as if worried he'd said something wrong. "Just that I wish we'd thrown more fuel on them when we had the chance, is all."

Martin punched the air as an idea formed in his mind. "Simon, you're a genius."

CHAPTER 16

"You're sure this is going to work?" asked Louise, the incredulity in her voice impossible to hide.

"Look, there's no guarantees about any of this, but I think it's our best shot. I really do." Martin looked at the face of each person in turn. "If we stay here much longer, the ants will get us. That's a fact. At least his plan gives us a chance."

Louise chewed her bottom lip, unconvinced.

"Sounds like suicide," Marie slurred, taking another gulp of wine.

The enthusiasm for his plan wasn't as high as Martin had hoped. "Come on, guys. It's all I've got. As far as I can reckon, it's the best chance we have."

Dean stood up from the counter he'd been sitting on. "I think it could work, Dad."

Martin smiled, relieved he had someone on his side. "That's great. That's great. Louise?"

She hesitated, looking down at Teddy. "You're sure we'll be able to take Teddy with us?"

"I'd sooner die than let those things get at Teddy again," Martin said, and he meant it. "I wouldn't be suggesting this unless I thought it was the best possible chance for him. For all of us."

Louise looked deep into Martin's eyes, searching for his confidence and honesty, desperate to believe the plan had even the remotest chance of working. She looked back down at Teddy, running her hand through his hair. She took a deep breath. "Okay. I trust you."

"Thank you," Martin responded. "I promise I'll do

everything in my power to get us all through this." He turned to his sister-in-law. "Marie?"

She investigated the half empty glass cradled in her hands, as if the answers she searched for were at the bottom of the glass. After much internal deliberation she looked Martin in the eye. "I think it could work."

"Excellent." Martin was relieved everybody was on board. If Marie hadn't wanted to go along with the plan, he would have been willing to leave her behind for the sake of his family. He was grateful it hadn't come to that. He owed it to Tom to get Marie out. It was the least he could do.

Martin ran down the plan again so that everyone fully understood what was going to happen. In the barn he had over a dozen large drums of gas. What Simon had said about not having used enough fuel to burn the bastards the first time had sparked the idea that the gas could be used to finish the job Franklin had started.

The barn was uphill slightly from the house, so the first part of the plan was simple. Simon would roll out the barrels and open them up and tip them over so the gas would run down the hill and over the ants. Due to the front of the house being raised two stone steps off the ground the fuel would pool against this structural barrier, rather than dousing the timbers of the house. As soon as the fuel hit the ants it was likely they would react, and so before the insects could scatter or attack, Simon would light them up like so much charcoal. The only gamble was if the steps between the drive and the house would keep the house from catching alight also. The distance between drive and house was about four feet so he felt it should be safe. With a little luck the smoke from their burning comrades would cause confusion and scatter the insects crawling over the house itself. He'd heard smoke could be used to help control the bees in their hives, and ants were sort of like bees, so he hoped the smoke would have a similar effect.

There was no way all the ants would be killed by the fire. They were crawling all over the house, as well as all around the back perimeter. Their numbers were simply too large to be killed that way. A least not without the house burning down, along with them inside it.

Hence part two of the plan; one of them would have to get to one of the cars parked out front. Fortunately, the cars were parked against the house a little way from the front door. The nearest of the two cars was the rental SUV Tom's family had hired. It was impossible to reach at the moment, for no matter how close it was, the vicious insects were too aggressive and would soon cover anyone making the attempt. Even wearing the fishing waders, as Dean had suggested, wouldn't buy them enough time. He hoped that once the fire had burnt out the ants' numbers would disperse enough for the car to be reachable. The issue was that Teddy, in his unconscious state, would need to be carried. There was a high risk that whoever carried him would be moving slower and may potentially drop him in all the chaos, and thus someone would have to wait behind with him until the car could be spun around to the door.

The ants were all over the cars at present, so ants would need to be burnt off as quickly as possible. To achieve this, a makeshift flamethrower would need to be utilised. Checking under the kitchen sink, Martin had found various aerosols that could do the job. All it took was a lighter held up the nozzle and a thick jet of fire was produced. It was scary to him how easy it was to create such a devastating weapon. This flamethrower would also be used to burn the insects from the front door upon their return, giving whoever stayed inside the house enough time to jump into the car with Teddy.

It was unlikely that zero ants would get into the car so they would have to try their best to keep their numbers to a minimum and hope that if they did receive stings the doctors would be able to treat them.

There were enough waders and thick clothing for everyone, so it was hoped the ants could be kept at bay long enough for them to make their getaway.

They went through the plan a couple of times, psyching

themselves up for the trial ahead. Louise insisted she be the one to remain with Teddy, something Martin wasn't the least bit surprised about. A mother's love trumped all, so he didn't even attempt to argue.

Upon further discussion, the potential for ants getting in through the front door once it was opened was raised. Martin had imagined they would be able to run out and shut the door before any ants managed to cross the threshold, until Marie reminded him of just how fast the insects had darted through the guest bedroom door the second it was open a sliver. After further deliberation, they decided Dean would remain behind with his mother.

They managed to find two lighters in the kitchen, which equalled two flame throwers. Martin would wield one and make a break for the car with Marie, who would have the keys at the ready. Dean would wield the other and close the door behind his father. He would then burn any of the ants that managed to get inside.

Finally, they went through the plan in detail with Simon. He would release the fuel and set it alight. The gas would burn fast and hot against the house. Due to the intensity of the flames, Martin and Marie would have to wait until they died down enough for them to leave without being burnt. This part of the plan is where the timing had to be the most exact. If they opened the door too early, their path would be blocked by choking smoke and flames, or worse, a backdraft would suck the flames inwards. If they waited too long, the flames and smoke would die down enough for the ants to regain their foothold and their escape window would be lost.

Martin and Marie would run to the car, Marie with the keys whilst Martin watched her back and burnt any insects that threatened them. Meanwhile Dean would burn any insects that managed to get into the house and wait until the car was pulled in front of the door. Marie would honk the horn and Martin would open the rear car door as soon as he saw the house front door open. Dean and Louise would jump in carrying Teddy and they would drive, leaving the swarming ants in the rear-view mirror. As soon as he could see them making their escape, Simon would jump on his dirt bike and follow.

The idea of leaving Tom to the ants didn't sit well with Martin and he would insist the authorities return as soon as possible. He may even return with them. He'd enjoy watching the bugs get destroyed. Regardless, that was something that could be decided later, and realistically he knew that as soon as he was away from the hellish scene he wouldn't want to return. And even if he did, Louise wouldn't let him.

CHAPTER 17

Martin checked himself over in the mirror of his bedroom, trying to ignore the constant skittering of ants as the scuttled over the window plane, their numbers robbing the room of most the natural sunlight and forcing him to switch the lights on. By some miracle they still had electricity, but for how long?

He was fairly certain the ants were now in the walls. A number of times he could hear a noise, like rice crispies, emanated from within them. No doubt it was their insect foes, scurrying, chewing, and probing for a way to get inside. Martin was now more thankful than ever that he had modernised the building shortly after purchasing it. It meant the number of tiny holes caused by wood rot, pests and general movement of the timbers wasn't really an issue and this had saved their lives, he was certain. Beforehand the ants would have found a million ways in. As it was, they hadn't managed to breach the building further. Yet

Give them time, they'll get inside soon enough, he grimly thought to himself. He knew the roof would be an easy way inside, so he had forbidden anyone from entering the attic. It was likely infested with the hateful insects and was providing them access to the spaces between walls. They really didn't have a lot of time. The problem with the attic being infested was compounded when Martin and Louise realised that was where the waders had been stored. Now the waders were beyond retrieving so it had been agreed that thick clothing would be best alternative option.

"How do I look?" he asked, turning to Louise.

She looked him up and down, appraising his effort to protect himself as best he could. He was wearing a thick sweater and jacket alongside his thickest jeans and boots. He also wore gloves, though he felt the ants would be able to sting through them. He wished he'd taken up a sport like skiing so that he had a reason to have balaclavas in the house.

She scanned him, checking for any obvious vulnerable areas that could be fixed. "Looks good," she said. Her voice was strained and her eyes looked to have developed the hundred-yard stare that shell-shocked soldiers developed. It was the look of someone who had been through too much, as if something had detached in her brain. He prayed he would be able to help her reattach it when all this was over.

Upon seeing her lip begin to tremble he held her close. She was wearing a similar getup to him and the heat of the day was making the heavy padding unbearably hot, though it was a small price to pay to avoid the heat of the ants' stings.

"It's going to be okay. We're going to get through this," he said, trying to convince himself as much as his wife.

"All of us?"

"All of us."

"Promise?" She looked up into his eyes, searching, pleading for him to say the right words to ease her fear.

"I promise," he said and kissed her, praying he would be able to fulfil the commitment he had just made. Despite the uncomfortable, sticky sweat running down his back Martin savoured the embrace, not wanting it to end. It was Louise who eventually pulled away. Her eyes once again met his, although the look on her face had changed. Gone was the near-broken woman who had been seeking comfort. She'd been replaced by a woman with cold, detached determination.

"If the worse comes to the worse. If the plan fails, if you and Marie die or can't get back to the house, I want some control over what happens to us."

Martin felt a lump in his throat. "What do you mean?"

"I saw the pain Tom was in before he died. I can only imagine what Cassie felt. I know a normal fire ant sting feels like a bee sting, and I know those things out there," she glanced to the shapes moving over the window, "are anything but normal."

Martin nodded numbly. In the deepest most unspeakable recesses of his mind, he feared where his wife was going with this. Even so, when she spoke his legs turned to jelly.

"I want a gun."

"You won't be able to keep those things at bay with bullets," Martin stuttered, hoping that had been her intent.

"Not for them. For us. Me, Dean and Teddy."

Martin had to sit down on his bed, taking deep breaths.

"I don't intend to use it, unless there is no option," Louise soothed, a hand on Martin's shoulder.

"I don't... I don't think I can allow that."

"It's not a decision you'll be making." Louise spoke softly and sternly.

Martin's vision blurred and he rubbed at his eyes, which were suddenly stinging. "I don't want you to die." His voice almost failed him, coming out as a whisper.

"Then don't let us. Make your plan work."

Martin nodded his understanding. "It'll work. It'll work."

"But if it doesn't, I don't want Teddy, Dean and I to be massacred by those monsters, screaming and burning. I want to spare them from that. Let me have that power. Don't leave us out of options. Don't let them win."

Martin nodded again and stood up. He made his way to the side draw, where the keys to his gun cabinet were kept. He pulled it open and shuffled through the small tin box in the bottom draw, alarm dawning on him.

"They're gone."

"Martin?"

"The keys. They're gone."

Louise gave a look of pity and sadness. "Martin, please."

"I'm serious," Martin protested. "The keys, they should be here. But they aren't. They're gone."

Louise's doubt in her husband's words faded. "Where could they have gone?"

"I don't know. They were right here, besides the keys for the quad bike. Do you think Dean could have taken them when he took the quad keys?"

"Impossible," Louise replied. "I checked that they were there earlier."

"You checked?"

"Yes, with Marie. She was worried the kids had taken a gun when I told her the gun keys were kept with the quad keys."

"And you put them back? You're sure?"

"I could have sworn I put them back," Louise shrugged. "At least, I'm ninety-nine percent sure I did."

Martin began scouring the floor, looking for the missing articles. "Perhaps you dropped them?"

"Maybe," Louise replied. She wasn't convinced.

"I can't see them anywhere. I'm sure I put them back," Louise swore.

Martin gave up searching. "Well, they aren't here now. Fuck."

"Could someone have taken them?" Louise went to double check the draw while Martin strode across the room to the cabinet, set in the wall. He tried to yank it open, but it was still locked. This gave him no relief, as there was no way to tell if it had been opened and then relocked, or if anything had been taken from it.

"When Marie and I were up here checking the bedrooms, she ran to block the plugs in the ensuite. She was in here a while."

"You think Marie could have taken the keys? Why would she have done that?"

"I didn't say that," Martin quickly said. "I'm just saying, she knew where the keys were and was in here alone."

"That fucking bitch," Louise uttered.

"We can't be sure," Martin warned. "Let's leave it for now."

"Leave it? Are you crazy?"

"No I'm not. I also know what Marie's state of mind is right now. Throwing accusations at her might end badly, whether she has the gun or not."

Louise couldn't believe what she was hearing. "So we just

pretend we haven't noticed the missing key?"

"That's right," Martin said firmly. "We don't mention it. What else can we do?"

* * *

In the kitchen Marie sipped some wine, letting the liquid sit on her tongue, hitting all her tastebuds before swallowing it, her eyes scrutinising Dean as the teenage boy sat melancholy on a chair beside the table. His hand rested gently on his younger brother's, who still lay prone on the table. His eyes were downcast, looking at the floor.

She thought of Cassie, of the horror she must have experienced in the end as the ants overwhelmed her. The thought burnt through Marie's heart like a cigarette being stubbed through a photograph. Marie loathed that she hadn't been there and she also loathed that she had no real idea what fate had befallen her daughter. Had the ants come suddenly? Had they overwhelmed her in seconds? Or had the attack been more prolonged, with Cassie's agony and fear stretched out for an unbearable length of time? Had she called for her mother in the end? She deserved to know, goddamn it.

Dean appeared to be doing everything in his power not to look at her. Was it guilt? It sure looked like it. Good, Marie thought. He should feel guilty. He'd taken her baby for a joy ride and gotten her killed. He'd taken something from her she could never get back, all with the stupid flippancy of youth. And now she wasn't allowed to talk with him about it, wasn't allowed to call him out because it might hurt his feelings? Fuck that. He was hiding something. She was certain of it. She had a right to know what.

"How's Teddy doing, Dean?"

Dean's body stiffened; he didn't look up. "Okay," he mumbled.

Marie sipped another mouthful, contemplating her words. "And how about you? How are you doing?"

"I'm okay." His voice trembled.

"Just 'okay?'"

"Scared," he stated, finally looking up at her. He was wearing his thickest clothes, like Marie, like the rest of them. They just had to wait for Louise and Martin to finish getting ready and the plan would be enacted. The thick clothing made him look more like a boy than he had done since she'd arrived yesterday.

Marie stood and walked over to him, sitting down on the chair next to his. Dean flinched as she sat. "I'm scared too. This is a pretty messed up situation, isn't it?"

"It is."

"I can imagine how scared your mother must be. For you and for Teddy. Losing a loved one is scarier than dying yourself, sometimes. Isn't it?" Her words were soft yet calculated.

Dean nodded, tears began welling in his eyes once more as he set his sights on Teddy.

"This one time, Tom and I, we took Cassie to the boardwalks in New Jersey. Just for a little weekend break. Nothing fancy. We had a lovely morning. Cassie was only about eight or so. The perfect age for all those rides and things. She went crazy for cotton candy. Does Teddy like cotton candy?"

Dean nodded.

"I guess all kids do. Anyway, what I was getting at is that after lunch she ran off ahead of us to play on this one arcade machine, through the crowds. We lost sight of her. It could only have been for about ten seconds before we got through the crowd. And she was gone. She wasn't on the machine she'd been heading to. It was like she'd just evaporated.

"I remember being so, so scared. More than I'd ever known I could be." She gave a laugh. "I mean, I'm a New Yorker, you know? I wasn't scared of anything. But I was scared that day. I was terrified for my daughter. For my little girl, not knowing what had happened to her."

"What had happened to her?" Dean asked.

Marie rested her hand gently on Dean's and smiled, cherishing the memory of her Cassie. "She'd spotted a young boy she'd been playing games with earlier on in the day and the two of them had jumped into this two-player cabinet, shooting zombies and such. She didn't know what all the fuss was about. She was just hanging out, doing what kids do. Having fun. She wasn't scared at all, but I was terrified."

Dean shifted his attention to Teddy. "It is scary. I'm scared for my brother."

"I'll bet. But do you know what the scariest thing of all that day was?"

"You said. Losing her, right?"

"Close. It was not knowing what had happened."

Dean looked confused. "Isn't that the same thing?"

"Not quite. It was the not knowing. It was so horrible, thinking I might never know what had happened to her. It was such a relief when I found out she was safe and sound." She paused. "Dean, I know my daughter is dead. I know the ants got her. It hurts. It hurts more than I can bare. And to lose Tom so soon after. I've lost everything today, Dean. Everything. At least... at least with Tom I know what happened. I was there. I saw. As horrible as that information is, it's infinitely better than not knowing. Do you know what I am saying?"

Dean looked back at Teddy. "I think so."

He remained silent so Marie decided to push a little further. "I wasn't there, Dean. When Cassie passed. And it's killing me. You were there. You know what happened. Tell me, please."

Dean bit his lip, looking like a rabbit caught in headlights. Marie squeezed his hand and pleaded again and this time he relented. Remembering the incident that had taken place made him feel like he was reliving it and his whole body began to tremble.

"The ants got her, Aunt Marie. They covered her."

"How did they surround you so quickly? You were on those bikes, weren't you? Surly you could have gotten away?"

"We weren't on the bikes when they came."

"Weren't they near?"

"I'd left mine a ways away. I'd ran to help Cassie."

"Help with the ants, you mean?"

Dean's trembling grew stronger and stronger as he began to sob again. He shook his head.

"Not the ants? Then what?"

"She fell."

"She fell?"

"From her bike."

"She fell from her bike?"

Dean looked to the floor again, the shame and grief overwhelming him. "We were doing stunts. On the bikes. She fell…"

Marie pulled away her hand, her body stiffening as she blinked multiply times, trying to process this new information. "Because of the ants?"

Dean managed an uncommitted shrug.

"Dean, this is important. Did she fall because of the ants or did she fall before the ants came?"

Dean opened his mouth to speak but was cut off by his parents entering the room.

Martin glanced between Marie and his son. "What are you doing, Marie?" you said accusingly. Louise hurried past the woman and hugged Dean, stroking his face and soothing him as he wept into her bosom.

Marie stood up, defiantly. "I'm trying to find out what happened to my daughter," her voice raised in fury.

"You know what happened," Martin yelled back, trying to project authority. "The ants got her."

"So says you. Dean said she fell."

Martin hesitated. "Fell?"

Sensing she had the upper hand, Marie continued. "He said it himself. Before the ants showed up, they were fucking about on your quad bikes. The bikes your son effectively stole from you. She fell. She probably got hurt, bad. That's why she couldn't get away from the ants." She stared hatefully back at Dean. "Your boy practically murdered my daughter with his thoughtless behaviour."

Despite the shock of learning what Dean had stated had occurred, Martin hid his hesitancy. The missing gun cabinet keys were at the forefront of his mind. "Marie, if you don't stop pointing fingers and looking for blame, none of us are going to get out of here alive."

"Out of here alive? That's a laugh. I've already lost my family."

"Don't forget Tom was my brother. Cassie was my niece. I've lost them too. We're all hurting."

"Well you should be," Marie spat. "Their blood is on your hands too. If you had done a better job keeping the key hidden then they'd both be alive now."

Martin didn't know what to say, dumbfounded by the accusation. The logical part of his brain told him she was wrong. That it wasn't fair to backstep on events, searching for blame in an unforeseen event. The emotional part screamed much louder, however.

"You're right," Martin said weakly. Walking to the table, he pulled out a chair and sat down, head in his hands.

Marie was clearly caught off guard by Martin's admission of guilt. "What?"

"You're right," he said again. "If I'd been more discreet about where I kept the keys, Dean wouldn't have been able to get them. When me and Tom discovered the ants in the shed, we could have all simply got in a car, there and then and left. It's all my fault. All of this."

Louise stood by her husband. "Martin, you can't think like that."

"It's true." He looked up at Marie, who still looked utterly puzzled on how to react. "Marie, this is all my fault and I'm sorry. Please, blame me, not the boys. I know I do. I'll never forgive myself for what's happened here today. For what we... all of us have lost. It's my fault and I'll have to live with that for the rest of my life."

Marie took her seat once more, the fight leaving her. "Let's just get out of here," she uttered. She didn't feel like drinking any more wine.

"We will, I promise you that," Martin said. "We haven't always seen eye to eye, Marie, but we are family. Nothing changes that.

Marie said nothing, stood and left the room. She looked profoundly defeated. Martin turned his attention back to his son. "You holding up there, Dean?"

Dean pulled away from his mother's protective embrace and wiped at his eyes. "I'm sorry dad, for not telling you everything straight away. I was scared. I still am."

Martin showed his understanding. "I know." The radio crackled, making Martin jump. He picked up the walkie-talkie. "Simon, you there?" Silence. "Simon, are you there?

"You're meant to say 'over', over," Simon said over the crackling radio.

"I really don't give a fuck about radio etiquette right now," Martin snapped. "What's the situation?"

"I have four barrels of gas stationed and ready to go."

Martin looked pensively at his family. "Okay, give me five minutes then open them up."

"Will do," Simon responded.

Martin stood and held his elder son and wife close, whilst looking down at Teddy, still sleeping soundly. "Everyone, remember the plan. In twenty minutes we'll be far from here."

CHAPTER 18

Simon grunted as he forced the crowbar into the lid of the barrel and prised it open. The aroma of fuel filled his nostrils as the liquid poured out across the dry ground and flowed downhill, towards the amassed ants. Wiping his brow, he observed his handiwork before walking to the next barrel and with another grunt prised its lid free.

He had rolled out eight barrels of fuel to use, no mean feat in the blistering midday sun. Once out he began setting them at strategic locations so the fuel would run down to the house. He ensured the gas had a fairly wide berth from the parked cars. If the flames engulfed the cars the plan would become an abject failure.

After leaning four of the barrels on their sides at the desired locations he realised that perhaps eight was overkill so left the remaining four standing.

After the fourth barrel had been opened and its contents flowed into the swarm of angry insects, he pulled the walkie-talkie from his waistband. "Boss, you receiving? Over."

His employers voice crackled through the airwaves. "Here, Simon. How's it going? Over."

"The fourth drum is open and the gas is leaking out over those God-forsaken bugs."

"Good stuff. How are they reacting to it?"

Simon squinted against the sun, watching as the hordes of ants attempted to scatter as the liquid ran over them. Many of them appeared to curl up and die from mere exposure to the fuel, while others made deliberate attempts to escape it, pausing to desperately clean the toxic fluid from their antennae and legs.

"They sure don't like it," Simon chuckled.

"They'll like it even less when it's all lit up like the fires of hell."

Simon laughed at that. "Of that I have no doubt."

"Okay, keep an eye on things and inform me when you are about to light up. If the fuel is spread pretty thinly across the ground it should only burn for one to two minutes tops, so make sure we are ready before burning those fuckers."

"Received," Simon sighed as he jogged back to the central location of the barrels, watching the gas drench a large area of the drive and drowning some of the smaller ants. "I hope I'm getting overtime for this," he grumbled to himself.

*   *   *

Inside the house, everyone prepared themselves for what was about to occur. Louise waited in the kitchen, beside Teddy who was wrapped in bathroom towels to protect him as much as possible.

Martin stood nearest to the front door, aerosol can and lighter at the ready. Marie stood close behind him, car keys in her hand.

In the living room, Dean waited by the bay windows, ready to call out when the fire had burnt away enough for his father and aunt to make a run for it. Although they had Simon acting as their eyes outside, Martin had been concerned that his distance would mean his perspective on the flames could be flawed. When Simon gave the go ahead, Dean would confirm before running to the hallway to close the door behind them and killing any ants that managed to get inside. He shared the room with Tom, who's body had been covered over with a sheet to keep his dignity. A crucifix rested on top as a mark of respect. It went a little way towards soothing Martin's guilt for his brother's fate.

Although he was supposed to keep his attention focused on the windows, trying to peer through the writhing red mass of insects, his eyes kept darting to the corners of the room. He was all too aware that a handful of the ants that had managed to escape from the fireplace may still be in there with him, hiding and waiting for their time to strike. When not searching out tiny attackers, his eyes flitted towards his uncles' still shape under the sheets. The body freaked Dean out and made him feel sick. Worst still, admitting to these feelings made him feel an overwhelming amount of shame. His uncle had died saving them all surely he shouldn't be feeling grossed out by him.

"You ready?" Martin asked Marie. She nodded silently, body poised, even though they still had a few minutes of waiting before the mad dash which would either save them or doom them. He turned back to Louise, visible beside Teddy in the kitchen. "You ready, Lou?"

"As I'll ever be," she stated.

"Dean?"

Dean thought that for a split second he saw movement under Tom's sheet, as if he was moving his face, ever so slightly. He blinked away the phantasm and when he refocused his attention, the movement had ceased.

"Dean, are you ready?" Martin called again.

Dean returned to observing the area outside, beneath the blanket of malicious stinging insects. "Ready," he called. He rested his hand on the windowsill for a split second before remembering the potential threat and pulling his hand away.

"Now or never, I guess," Martin said. He waited a couple of seconds in case someone had a sudden reservation. Nobody did. He raised the walkie-talkie to his lips. "Ok Simon, light them up."

* * *

"Consider it done," Simon said. He held a clump of dried straw in one hand and lit it using his lighter. Cautiously approaching the spilt gasoline, he threw the lit torch. The instant it hit the ground a bright red flame spread out, heading towards the house as well as towards the nearly empty barrels. Expecting this, he darted into the doorway of the barn to give him shelter and peeked from inside, watching as the flame reached the barrels and they exploded with gusto one by one. Simon held his hand over his ears to protect them from the explosions.

The flame proper continued to lick over the ground towards the house, engulfing tens of thousands of the insects. The ants barely had time to struggle as they were instantly incinerated. The flame reached about two feet in height and acted as a cleansing fire, burning away the thousands of hellish ants that couldn't escape it. Thick black smoke rose from the burning ground and Simon couldn't help but feel he was witnessing Hell on Earth.

The ants that weren't immediately in the path of the fire scurried away as fast as they could, desperate to get away from the heat. This included those that were on the front of the house above the flames.

Simon was pleased to see that even a large number of the ants that weren't set alight were curling up and dying, the heat cooking them inside their skins. Masses of them dropped from the front of the house, dead before they hit the fires and were burnt to ash.

"How's it working?" came Martin's garbled voice over the radio.

"It's working well. Stinks like hell, though. I reckon you'll be able to make it to the car once the flames die down."

"Understood. We're waiting on you to give the go ahead."

"No problem, Boss. No problem at all."

*   *   *

"The door's hot," Marie stated, gingerly putting her hand against it. The door's frosted glass gave some indication of fire and smoke though not much else.

"We're about to get a lot hotter," Martin said, adopting the same stance as his sister-in-law, prepared for action. "Remember, when he says the flames are low enough, we run."

"Out of the frying pan…" Marie muttered.

Martin called out to Dean. "How's it looking out there?"

"Flames are still pretty high," Dean reported back. "Although the smoke's making it hard to see. There are definitely less ants than before."

"That's good," Martin called in response. "Just keep us updated, son."

Dean kept his eyes on the horror for as long as he could before feeling the need to look away, his mind threatening to revolt against him. He felt itchy and sticky under his thick clothes and kept telling himself the sweat was caused by heat and not his own cowardice.

His eyes darted to a corner of the room where he could have sworn he saw movement, though there was nothing there now. Trying to reconcentrate, the unnerving thought of what would happen if ants got in under his thick clothes made him feel even itchier and he knew he was on the verge of freaking out.

Looking away from the window, he drew deep breaths, trying to keep his panic contained. His family were counting on him, he couldn't let them down.

Like how you let Cassie down, you mean? Asked a vile voice inside his head. Dean groaned slightly, searching for anything to break this spiralling train of thought.

His eyes focused once more on his uncle. Brave Uncle Tom, who'd saved them all and died a painful death because of it. Dean's guilt felt unbearable as he recalled Marie's words in the kitchen. If only he hadn't taken those keys, none of this would be happening now. They could have easily left before things got so bad. Now they were all going to die, like poor Uncle Tom. Like Cassie. And it was all his fault.

Dean was almost staring into space when movement caused his eyes to snap back onto Tom's shape and the movement coming from his face, beneath the sheet. Dean felt for sure that he had to be imagining it, had to be going crazy when he saw the movement again. It was slight, so slight he almost missed it, but now he was searching for it, the movement was a definite fact.

It almost looked as if Uncle Tom was opening and closing his eyes, or raising and lowering his eyebrows. Some sort of discreet facial movement.

Dean's mind reeled with the potential ramifications. Could it be his uncle wasn't dead? Had the ant stings merely stunned him, knocked him unconscious and now he was waking up? It seemed almost ridiculous, but who knew what the hell was going on with these ants?

He thought to call out to his father in the hallway and almost did, until he began to wonder how it would go down if he was wrong. His dad would think him crazy. Aunt Marie would hate him even more. It would be all types of bad. On the other hand, he wanted his suspicions to be true with every fibre of his being. If Uncle Tom were still alive, it was one less weight on his crushed conscience.

Glancing out the window, Dean confirmed to himself that the coast was clear before approaching his uncle's covered form. Nervously he checked the doorway to see if his father or anyone else could see him. There was nobody. His dad and Aunt Marie were fully focused on the orange flicker of flames through the front doors' frosted glass. Mom was in the kitchen, guarding Teddy. Dean felt another pang of guilt. Poor, defenceless Teddy. He'd only ever wanted to hang out with his older brother, yet that had been too much to ask. Dean had been cold towards him, and now Teddy was hurt. He might not even wake up.

Shaking away the invading thoughts, Dean slowly crouched beside his uncle. The tiniest of movements played out beneath the sheet over his uncle's face.

"Uncle Tom?" he whispered, so quiet as to be barely audible. He gently cleared his throat as his shaking hand reached for the sheet. "Uncle Tom, can you hear me?"
He pulled off the sheet and tried to scream, though it died in his throat. Dean froze in horror at what he beheld.

Upon his dead uncle's red, swollen and misshapen face fifteen to twenty ants crawled. Some ran in erratic circles; aware they had been exposed and searching for their attacker.

Others continued with their gruesome business. Several of the ants gripped at Tom's bloated face with their mandibles and drove their stingers deep into his flesh. Others ran in and out of his nose and slack mouth, some of them carrying grisly red packages, as if they were trophies.

Whether they knew he was dead or if they were still attacking what they perceived as a foe, Dean could not even formulate. Even worse, a number of the hellish insects were concentrating on his eyes. They'd either opened or mutilated Tom's eyelids and now were either piercing the whites of his eyes with their stingers or using their biting mouths to cut unto them, pulling small chunks away.

Dread and disgust overwhelmed Dean as he surveyed the ants at work, only to be broken out of his malaise when he realised several of the ants were crawling over the white sheet he had lifted, heading straight for his vulnerable hand.

"Ants!" he screamed at the top of his lungs before reflexively bringing his lighter and aerosol to bear, aiming at the demonic insects. Without thinking, he lit the lighter and pressed down on spray, engulfing the ants and his dead uncles' face with a jet of fire. He continued spraying Tom's face with the flame, even as the skin peeled and cracked under the intense heat. In that moment nothing else existed for Dean expect the ants and his desperate need to destroy them.

"Dean, stop," yelled Martin as he came charging into the room. He quickly took in the grisly spectacle of his son blow-torching his dead brothers face, filling the room with the stench of burnt hair and flesh. He was upon his son in two strides and grabbed at his hand, pulling them away and breaking off the jet of flame.

"Oh my god!" screamed Marie, who was two steps behind Martin.

"There were ants!" Dean yelled insistently. "There were ants!"

Martin had to restrain his hysterical son who was even now struggling to raise his hands and continue his assault on Tom's corpse. He looked over at his brother's body, at his face, now black and charred, the skin cracking and peeling like a jacket potato that had been left too long in the oven. He couldn't see any ants.

"I believe you, I believe you," Martin affirmed, holding Dean tight. "Now calm down. Calm down."

Dean looked at his dad, suddenly realising what he had done. His eyes widened in shock. "There were ants," he repeated numbly, no longer shouting.

"You fucking monster," Marie screamed, as if Dean's hysteria had been passed to her. "What have you done? What have you done?" She launched herself at Dean in murderous rage, her hands turned to claws, eager to get at him. Martin quickly jumped up and caught her, keeping her away from his boy.

"He said there were ants, Marie. Ants."

Louise came running in, her protective instincts in overdrive as she immediately helped pull Marie back from Martin.

Marie pushed away from Martin and Louise but glared with hatred. "Where? Where are the fucking ants?" She looked again at Tom, his burnt visage breaking her heart and tearing her soul.

Louise wasn't fully aware of what was happening so looked to her husband for guidance. Martin forced himself to look down at Tom, but try as he might he couldn't discern any of the insects in the charred mess, nor on the sheets. It was likely any ants that had been present were incinerated by the flame or had fled from the heat.

"Where are they?" Marie demanded, pacing back and forwards.

"They must have burnt up," Martin tried to explain.

"Burnt up?" she sounded incredulous. She then spat at Dean. "You're a monster, first you get my Cassie killed, then you burn my husband's face off? I won't forget this." She stormed out of the room and Martin watched as she went. As soon as she was out of sight he turned back to Dean. He looked pale as a ghost, the experience shaking him to his core.

"Dean?" There was no response. "Dean?" Martin said sharply, shaking him. Louise stepped in, holding him.

"There were ants, dad. I swear."

Louise looked to Martin and he nodded. "I believe you son, we both do."

Louise was justifiably afraid the experiences Dean had suffered were causing massive psychological damage. There was no way he would ever be the same after this. Hell, there was no way any of them would be the same. "We do believe you baby, we do. Try to keep it together, this is almost over. Be strong. Be strong."

As Louise stroked his hair, Dean looked back at Tom's burnt and disfigured face and was hit by a wave of nausea that was compounded by the stench of burnt hair and flesh. "I'm going to be sick," he groaned as he could feel the vomit begin to rise in his oesophagus. He repeated himself as he pulled away from his parents and ran into the downstairs bathroom. He slammed the door and the sounds of him vomiting into the toilet could be heard above the whirring of the extractor fan which had come on as the light had been flicked.

"We need to get out of here. Now," Louise stated.

Martin agreed as he covered Tom back over with the sheet. Holding his breath, he cautiously checked for ants as he handled the covering. "Get back to Teddy, those flames outside can't be burning for much longer."

Without acknowledging she strode from the room, avoiding looking down at Tom any further and headed back to the kitchen. Martin followed her out and waited in the hallway outside the bathroom door. Marie stood silent by the front door, contempt still burning brightly in her eyes.

Martin held her stare silently as Dean could be heard, still throwing up behind the bathroom door. "Dean, you okay in there?"

Dean could be heard spitting. "I'm okay, dad. I'll be out in a minute."

"We don't have a minute," Marie said coldly. "The fire will

burn out any second. He needs to be ready." Although there was spite in her voice, Martin had to concede she was correct.

"He just needs a second," Martin replied. "Dean, I know it's hard, but you need to be as quick as you can. We've only got one shot at this."

*   *   *

"I said I'll be out in a minute," Dean protested, spitting the remnants of his stomach into the toilet water. The acidic vomit burnt his throat and nose and made his eyes water. Flushing the toilet he reached across, teared a strip of toilet tissue and wiped the sick from around his mouth as his tongue run over his teeth, dislodging half-digested lumps of his breakfast croissant.

He spat again before turning to the wash basin and cupping some of the water in his hands and bringing it to his lips. Swirling the water around in his mouth, hoping to purge the final remnants of the sickly taste before he spat into the toilet once more. Flushing the toilet, he stood up straight, willing himself to get it together and studying himself in the mirror.

His face was pale and sweaty and he felt shudders despite being in thick clothing. It took everything he had to try to keep his body tremors to a minimum. He felt as if he'd had enough and that he just wanted to curl up and hide. To deny the terrible events that had occurred. Then he thought of Teddy. How there was still hope for him, but that he himself had to play his part to give his brother the best shot at getting the help he needed.

"Be strong," he whispered to himself. "Be strong."

The extraction fan above him began making strange noises, as if the electric motor was suddenly struggling and Dean's attention was instantly diverted. "What the hell?" he whispered to himself in bewilderment.

That was when the fan cover gave way under the weight of millions of ants and Dean screamed in abject horror as he was showered in the tiny, vicious creatures. Instantly his world turned to that of pain as an inconceivable number of stings pierced his body all over, the ants finding every possible entrance beneath the thick clothes, sensing the warmth of his body.

Dean's flesh felt as if it were burning from the excruciating pain and he tried to pull the door open, his panic exceeding its limits when the door wouldn't budge, it had stuck again and he realised he was trapped, with a seemingly endless supply of killer ants still pouring in on top of him.

Dean screamed for his parents in desperation as he fell to the floor in the foetal position, as if it could offer any protection against the murderous army of insects. Before his brain snapped and he was lost in a world of pain and nothing else, Dean could hear his dad calling to him and hammering on the door. Dean knew his dad was too late as he could feel himself falling down into the very pits of hell. The burning sensation felt as if it were turning his flesh to ash, destroying his nerve endings.

The unmitigated pain of a million burning stings and merciless bites were all he knew in the end.

CHAPTER 19

From beyond the door, Dean screamed.

"Dean!" Martin screamed as he hammered and raged against the bathroom door with all his might, desperate to gain access and help his son. His lighter and aerosol had been dropped, his all-consuming thought was to save his elder son.

"What's happening?" cried Louise in distress and confusion as she ran to join him.

From beyond the door, Dean's screams continued.

"Ants must have got into the bathroom somehow," Martin wailed, himself now on the verge of losing it. He rammed his shoulder against the door. Marie watched anxiously from by the front door, unsure what to do.

"Can't you get in?" Louise cried out, helping him in his efforts.

"It's stuck again," he yelled, again throwing his wait against the seemingly immovable door. "It's fucking stuck. I can't get in!"

From beyond the door, Dean's screams died. Only the sounds of a million biting insects crawling over one another emanated from the bathroom.

Louise wailed, pulling at her hair. "Can't you do something? We have to get to him."

"I'm trying," insisted Martin as he rammed the door again. It budged slightly, allowing the slightest gap at the bottom edge for a split second. In that miniscule amount of time, twenty or so ants scurried into the hallway. Louise jumped back, her screams growing louder still. Martin cursed, stamping on the insects, reducing them to stains before mindlessly preparing to force the door again.

"Don't open that door," demanded Marie.

Martin and Louise looked at her in outrage. Martin hit the door again.

"He's dead. If you open that, we'll all die," Marie called again, keeping her distance from the hysterical couple.

Martin blinked, as the rational side of his brain tried to comprehend what she was saying, knowing it to be true.

"Fuck you!" Louise screamed like a madwoman; her brain very much dominated by sheer emotion. "You hate Dean! You want him to die! Fuck you!"

Martin prepared to charge the door again, the paternal side of his mind winning out.

"If you charge that door again, I'll shoot," Marie yelled, clear and concise.

Somehow, through the haze of panic, fear and rage, Marie's words reached Martin and he stopped, twisting his head to look at her again. He stopped cold, as did Louise. By the front door, Marie stood poised, Martin's Glock handgun in her hands. It was trained on them both. Martin was instantly sobered. Despite everything, he could tell the safety had been released. He held up a defensive hand in front of him, the other warning Louise to step back. Reluctantly she did, although it took every ounce of her self-control to do so. She wept, pleading for Marie to let them save their son.

Martin's mind was racing at the sudden, new scenario he found himself in. His son was dead, he knew that and sorrow ripped him in half. Even so, he knew now wasn't the time to become lost in grief.

"That's my gun," he stated. He was out of breath from the exertion from trying to knock down the bathroom door.

Marie said nothing, her eyes were glazed over, her hands trembled.

"Marie, why are you pointing the gun at us?" Martin asked. He tried to stay calm.

"I don't want to die," she uttered. The gun remained

pointing at them, wavering slightly. It was more unnerving than a million ants.

"I don't want to die either," he said. He looked to Louise for help but she had slid down against the wall, sobbing into her hands, grieving the loss of her son. He looked back at Marie. "How did you get the gun?" he asked, tentatively, already knowing the answer.

"When I was filling your ensuite basin with water. I remembered you saying the keys were in the drawer. I took them, opened the case. Took the Glock. Locked it." Her voice quivered as she spoke and she appeared shocked by her own words, as if she were describing the actions of a stranger.

Martin took a step towards her, keeping low, hand still held out to show he meant no harm. "Okay." He paused. "Why did you take it?"

Marie let out a gasp, a stuttered sob. She said nothing.

"Dean," Louise hissed, accusatory in tone.

Marie blinked, as if unsure of her own thoughts or what her next move should be. "I, I don't know."

Louise remained seated, although the look on her face was so full of malice it made Marie baulk and take a step back. The gun went from Martin to Louise, to Martin again.

"Marie?" Martin asked.

"No, it's not true," Marie gasped, although it was clear her own motivations for taking the firearm were beyond even her own reasoning. "I was, I was angry. And afraid."

Louise pressed her point. "You blamed Dean for Cassie. You hated him."

"I, I, I don't know. I did hate him. I didn't want to hurt him."

"My son is dead now. You stopped us from saving him. Does that make you happy? Does that make us even?" Martin was afraid of the coldness in Louise's voice and was desperate to lower tensions before Marie did something terrible.

"Marie, it's okay. Give me the gun." He took another step.

Marie trained the gun on Martin. She looked like a trapped

animal, desperate for a way out. Behind her the fire still burnt behind the frosted glass, though not as intense as before.

"You've always hated me," she whimpered. "Always. Even before Tom tried to screw you over."

"Marie, I just want us to get out of here. We can discuss this later, when we've all gotten out to somewhere safe." He took another step. Martin was so close to her now.

"We won't all get out of here, though. Not now. You'll leave me. You'll leave me and I'll die."

"Nobody's leaving anybody behind. Isn't that right, Lou?"

Louise took a deep breath, stilling her anger, thinking of Teddy. He was still alive. He was her paramount concern right now, even if it meant relying on a woman she had always disliked and now hated. She would have made a deal with the devil if it meant getting Teddy to safety, although making a deal with the bitch who had a gun trained on her and her husband felt supremely worse. Regardless, she nodded slowly. Her words were steady and measured. "Martin's right. We need to work together. We can't lose anybody else."

Snot and tears ran down Marie's face as she contemplated Louise's words. She so wanted to believe Louise's words, yet a part of her brain, the part that always felt it was her against the world, didn't let her. "You're lying," she cried, pointing the gun at Louise. "You hate me. I can see. You're going to leave me."

Seeing his moment, Martin jumped for the gun. He miscalculated. Either he was further than he thought, or Marie was more deft at using a firearm than he had realised. She swung back around to him and pulled the trigger.

The gunshot rang out, filling the hallway with noise and gun residue as the bullet shot from the barrel of the Glock and hit Martin in the gut. His attempt to disarm her had failed and he crumpled pitifully to the floor, awash with pain. Louise screamed in utter despair and rapidly moved across the floor until she was holding him. Martin squeezed at her forearm, grunting in pain as his other hand held the bleeding wound in his belly.

"You bitch!" she cried out. "You've shot him! You've shot Martin!"

Marie remained motionless, disbelieving her own actions and unable to account for her own motivations.

The walkie-talkie crackled on Martin's waistband. "Boss, the fire's dying down. Now's your chance," said Simon.

"Fuck this," cried Marie, regaining the movement of her limbs. Twisting around she pulled open the front door. As she did so, several ants fell from above the door onto her arm that held the Glock. One fell immediately onto her hand and, sensing it had landed on vulnerably flesh, it sank its stinger in, injecting its poison.

Marie screamed in agony at the hot pain, as if someone had stabbed her with a heated needle and she dropped the Glock to the floor. Frantically she swatted at the insects climbing her arm and before disappearing out the door.

Louise watched her go, relieved to no longer have a gun pointed at her and cradled Martin's head. After a few moments they could here Marie's car start up and drive away at speed.

"The door," he struggled. "Close the door."

Marie looked up in horror as she saw ants begin crawling in though the open door. Thankfully the heat from the fire had killed many and had forced many more at bay, otherwise she'd have been overrun by now. Hastily she jumped to her feet and ran to the door. Being as careful as possible she avoided the insects before kicking the gun back inside the hallway in case it was needed later. As she reached for the handle an ant fell onto her hand, as one had done to Marie. She succeeded in shaking it off before it had purchase enough to sting.

Louise reached for the handle again and this time succeeded in slamming the door shut, barring any further access to the marauding ants.

"Lou, help," Martin managed as he tried to push himself down the hallway and away from an advancing column of ants. He left a smear of blood on the wooden floor as he pushed himself along.

Louise let out a squeal at the sight of several ants climbing her boots and shook them off the best she could before formulating a plan. Running back past her wounded husband, she picked up his discarded aerosol and lighter and turned her attention to the numerous insects. Try as he might, Martin's progress was too slow to outrun the killer bugs and they were gaining fast. Stepping over him, Louise levelled the aerosol at the malicious creatures and felt a sense of victory as she sprayed the entire column of ants with a jet of fire and watched them burn.

When the ants on the floor were little more than ash and scorch marks, Louise turned her attention to the insects crawling over the walls. As tenacious as they were, they too were easily incinerated.

With the immediate threat of the ants over, she dropped the can and lighter and crouched beside Martin. He had managed to pull himself into a seating position against the wall, face contorted in pain as a bloodied hand held the bleeding bullet wound in his abdomen.

"How is it?" she asked, removing his hand to try and examine the wound. All she could see were blood-soaked clothes.

"It… doesn't feel good," Martin managed through gritted teeth.

"Marie's gone with the car keys." The hopelessness in her voice was inescapable.

"We can try for our car. Simon has enough fuel, we can try again. We can still make the plan work."

Martin's attempt at optimism was admirable, however Louise was unable to see the plan working. "How can it work? There's just the two of us now. Teddy is still asleep. Dean is… Dean is gone. You can hardly move. And our car is parked further away than Marie's was. We're going to die." She cast her vision upon the Glock, laying on the floor. "We can still go on our own terms…"

"No," coughed Martin. "There must be a way. There must. Marie might come back, or…"

"She's not coming back, Martin. She shot you."

Martin was silent for a moment, reliving the recent events, how everything went to hell. He reached for the walkie-talkie and held down the button. "Simon, do you read me?" he said. After waiting several seconds he tried again. "Simon, do you read me? Over."

The radio remained silent.

CHAPTER 20

Simon had been forced to back away from the huge swarm of insects and the incalculable number of individuals therein. It was clear that they realised they were under attack from some such hostile force, although they still hadn't managed to sense him. He wondered how good the vision of the ants was.

Immediately after the barrels had exploded he had emerged from the barn and re-approached the swarm, not daring to get any nearer than the initial line the row of barrels had occupied.

Since the fuel had been begun burning the ants had widened the area they covered, meaning he's had to again retreat, although not all the way back to the barn. He leant back on one of the four remaining barrels he had rolled out and watched the fire do its work, shielding his eyes from the sun with his hand.

Now the ants were less densely concentrated than before, though they still teemed over the ground in vast numbers and would easily be able to overcome him if he wasn't careful. Although the bulk of them was still concentrated on the house, the swarm had spread uphill towards him, likely tracking the gas to its route, albeit at a safe distance so as to avoid the flames. They now encompassed the areas where the barrels had been tipped, cutting off any possible escape route on foot that may have been laid down by the scorched earth.

The flames were dying down now and Simon prayed to God that the Boss's plan worked. Simon's pondering as to whether the family would be able to simply run for it along the ground where the flames currently burnt were now dismissed.

There would be no Plan B.

Trying to ignore the stench the burning fuel gave off, he watched as the flames began to die down until they were practically non-existent. Amongst the crackling of the fires he heard a gunshot emanate from the house and had to guess the ants had broached the family's defences.

He waited a few more moments before speaking into the walkie-talkie. "Boss, the fire's dying down. Now's your chance." He then watched tensely, fearing it wouldn't take long before the ants begun to reclaim the burnt ground they had been forced to flee from.

Watching intensely, he saw the front door open. This is it, he thought. A woman emerged in thick clothes, no doubt to offer protection from the biting insects. She paused, flailed her arm, dropping something and then used her other arm to rub the first one down. It was clear she was trying to brush off attacking ants, and then she ran for the car.

"What the hell?" Simon voiced his confusion. Why wasn't anybody following her?

*   *   *

Marie ran over the charred ashen ground, avoiding the numerous patches that were still burning as she made for the car. She felt as if she were running through Hell itself, the landscape becoming an infernal backdrop to her struggles.

Hundreds of ants had dropped from the side of the house, clearly with the intent of landing on her. They had missed and now eagerly scampered after their prey. The swarm as a whole reacted to her presence, infuriated by the hot earth that seemed to frustrate their efforts to reach her. Some of the main swarm started making its way across the charred ground, though the progress was stunted and slow. Many of the attacking ants curled up in writhing defiance, roasting on the burning ground. Others continued their advance.

Marie could comprehend their struggle, even though she

was running at full speed. Many of the ants died. Many more were continuing their advance. She was nearly at the car and she realised that as long as she didn't slow, she'd easily make it. Reaching into her pocket she pulled out the car keys and pressed the 'UNLOCK' button.

The car's lights flashed once, indicated the doors had unlocked. She bemoaned the sight of the car, still covered in thousands of ants. She had no time to hesitate, however. For to hesitate would give the rest of the vicious insects time to reach her. She'd have to incur some stings and hope to reach medical aid in time.

Reaching the car, she pulled at the handle, ignoring the ants crawling all over it. Immediately they were on her appendage, stinging and biting. She gave a scream as the searing hot pain of her existing sting was extrapolated tenfold.

Carelessly she flung the car door open. Ants on the car roof spilled over the edge, many landing upon her as she leapt in and with a burst of adrenaline she reached out and pulled the door closed.

Now in the driver's seat she put her foot on the brake and turned on the ignition, ignoring the attacking ants as the engine came to life. Two or three ants stung the side of her neck and she gasped as everything went red and her head felt as if it would burst. She quickly reached up and swiped at the insects, crushing them against her skin. The dead ants remained hanging, their stings still firmly imbedded in Marie's flesh.

Marie reversed at full speed, backing away from the house and spinning the wheel to line up with the road that led away from this living nightmare.

She hit accelerator again, screaming and crying in pain, fury and fear as ants managed to crawl under her clothing, their stings on her legs, stomach and back causing her to lose the finer aspects of her motor functions.

Fuck it, she thought, *I just needed to accelerate and steer, get away from this place. I can worry about the stings later.* Marie's vision began warping and going red and she wondered if it was because of the intense pain she was in or a side effect of the ants' venom. She'd been stung far more than she'd contemplated and functioning was becoming difficult in the face of the sheer pain that was overriding her senses.

The loss of control was similar to being drunk, although the haze was anything but pleasant. The car swerved violently from left to right as she made her escape, crushing countless tiny bodies beneath the car wheels as she kept her foot down until finally she had escaped the swarm.

She cried out again as an ant stung her above her right cheek and she swatted at it, splatting the offending creature against her face. Already the damage was done, a new injection of white-hot pain causing her face to swell and her eye to water.

The act of swatting the ant had caused her to swerve severely to the right and she gave a surprised scream as she saw the body of a man bounce over the top of the bonnet, followed by impacts as her car ploughed into the four gas barrels that had been pulled outside.

The barrels bounced down the hill and into the swarm of furious ants who ignored them, single minded in their attempts to reach their fleeing prey.

Marie glanced into the rear-view mirror as she sped away down the dirt track and away from the house. She only took her eyes off the road for a second, she was sure. When she tried to refocus on the road, she hit the brakes and spun the steering wheel hard to avoid the large longhorn cow that had trotted absent-mindedly into her path.

The car left the dirt road and spun into the rough desert terrain at a dangerously high speed. A large boulder caught on the front axle and gave a sickening metallic crunch which reverberated through the car's chassis. The axle had instantly snapped.

Carried by its momentum, the car went into a half spin before the right-hand wheels left the ground and the car flipped. Marie was tossed about inside the vehicle as it landed on its roof with a bang and continued sliding for several more feet before finally coming to a rest. The longhorn gave an irritated moo in displeasure at the incident before galloping away indignantly.

Steam raised from the wrecked car. Marie lay crumpled upon the car's inner roof. She was battered and bruised, covered in her own blood and broken. Unbeknownst to her a lung pierced by one of her ribs and was in the process of filling with her own blood. Her breathing was raspy and wet. She was covered in the remnants of the shattered safety glass windows, and the glass made a crunching sound as she struggled to move.

She knew it was hopeless. Her body was as beyond repair as the car, one of her legs had bent the wrong way, she couldn't twist her neck without shooting pains going down her back and one of her arms was shattered in numerous places. The hand was mangled and ruined, barely recognisable for what it was. And that wasn't even considering the numerous lacerations, some shallow, some very deep, that covered her. The stings she had received still burned ferociously, the searing pain they caused had only increased and the swellings added to her misery.

Marie was dying and she knew it. Her injuries were grave enough to end her, she realised that as fact. Despite this, it was the ants that would spell her doom. Even now hundreds of the insects scurried over her, stinging and biting, causing her to go into shock. Her whole body felt as if she were burning alive, although the burning was beginning to be replaced by numbness. She wanted to welcome the cold numbing feeling, wanted to be beyond pain. The sweet release evaded her.

As she lay there, broken and bleeding, gasping for breath and drowning in her own blood, a mangled heap, covered in the pitiless insects that stung and bit and violated her wounds, she wondered one thing over and over; *'Is this how Cassie felt?'*

CHAPTER 21

Jesus Christ, that bitch is going to hit me!

That was the thought going through Simon's head the instant before Marie's weaving car ploughed into him. He cursed in pain as he bounced and rolled off the side of the bonnet, landing in a heap on the hard ground, flat on his face, busting his nose and splitting his lip. The large barrels of fuel also took the brunt of the car and toppled and rolled like pins in a bowling alley.

Struggling to stand, he gave a groan before forcing out a snort to clear his potentially broken and bloodied nose of sand and dirt.

The first thing he noticed, beside the fact his face felt as if he had just ran into a brick wall, was that his right wrist was broken. He yelled out in pain as he tried to push himself into a sitting position.

His right knee also hurt. He didn't know if it was broken, but it sure as hell felt like it was. He groaned, rolling his head to loosen his sore neck. "Fucking bitch," he shouted at the receding car. It was a futile gesture and within seconds the zig-zagging car had disappeared down the dirt track.

His mind was fuzzy as he tried to make sense of what had just happened. The last he had heard the Boss-Man and his wife and kids were still alive, as was the Boss's sister-in-law. The Boss and his sister-in-law were supposed to make the run to the car, then swing around for the rest of them. So, what the fuck had happened? Why had the escaping woman fled on her own? Why hadn't she swung back around to pick up the others? Was everyone else already dead? If so, a heads up would have been nice. And why the hell had she appeared to deliberately veer the car into him when he was the one putting his ass on the line to save her?

His mind was racing with questions and possibilities. Eyeing the house, he could see that the front door had been closed. That meant the others were still alive, or at least, one of them was. Eyeing the house, looking for any other evidence people were still inside, he reached down for the walkie-talkie. He drew it up and started speaking into it before noticing the light that denoted it was working wasn't lit. Swearing, he fiddled with the dial before admitting defeat. The impact had damaged the radio in some way. It was fucked.

Casting the device aside, he then reached for his phone to check for signal. He hadn't expected there to be any reception and wasn't disappointed. He'd have to return to the barn and pick up another walkie to see if he could get hold of anybody.

Trying to stand, he yelped in pain and fell back to the ground, realising just how damaged his leg truly was. The barn was only a hundred of so feet behind him. It would feel like a mile.

Looking back toward the house, the fuzziness in his head abated a little more and he focused on the raging ants. His frustration at the situation suddenly turned to terror as he realised the ants were now crawling eagerly towards him.

"Holy shit," he exclaimed as he forced himself to stand despite his protesting body. He could barely put any weight on his right leg and he held his broken wrist close to his body. Whether it was the erratic driving of the escaping woman or they could smell his blood, but either way the ants were now advancing on his location and in about thirty seconds they would be on him.

All thoughts turned to escape as the icy fingers of fear gripped his heart. Throughout this experience, despite what he had witnessed, he'd almost felt like a spectator or someone outside of the whole scenario. He'd witnessed the aftermath of Franklin's encounter. He'd become embroiled in the Bevaux's own siege. Respectively, he'd been able to easily escape or gone unnoticed by the ants at large. That status quo had now changed, and he didn't like his new situation one bit. The ants were coming for him and there was a serious chance they would overwhelm him.

No way I'm going out to a bunch of bugs, he thought as he twisted and began hobbling towards his bike. He cursed as he realised the ants had performed some kind of pincer movement and millions of their tiny bodies now stood between him and salvation.

The gulf of insects was insurmountable. If he tried to run across them in his crippled state they would absolutely bring him down. His only hope was the barn and he limped towards it, grunting and cursing his fate as he moved as quick as possible. He put some distance between himself and the ants, though they were surrounding him to the left and right. Both sides were closing in fast.

With no other option he stumbled into the barn. He limped towards the walkie-talkie charging cradle and pulled one out. Quickly tuning it to the correct frequency, he brought it to his lips.

"Boss? Boss? Do you read me, over?" There was nothing except static. "Boss, anyone, do you read me? Over?" Again, just static responded to his desperate calls. "Jesus Aitch Christ, is anybody alive?" When once more there was no human voice replying he gave up, cursed the heavens and pocketed the radio, just in case someone decided to start speaking through it in the indeterminable future.

Through the open barn doors he could see the ants begin crawling over the threshold. Even more crawled in over the walls, eager to get to him.

Simon turned to limp away, even though he knew there was nowhere left to go. The barn lacked any kind of back exit, the ant infested main doors the only way to escape.

Past the remaining fuel barrels, at the back of the barn the haystacks, stored for feeding the cattle, were stacked high and

Simon decided the only thing left to do was to climb. Perhaps it would only buy him time, but time was the only thing he had left right now. For an instant he neglected to avoid placing weight on his leg and cried out in pain from his damaged knee. If he hadn't been injured, he could have easily climbed to the top of the stacks. As it was, his progress was pitifully slow and agony inducing.

Through sheer determination he managed to get two thirds of the way up the stacks before the bulk of the ant swarm had begun blanketing the far side of the barn floor and walls. He looked back at them and spat in disdain.

"You bastards ain't getting me," he yelled before beginning to climb ever higher. As he grasped at the hay bales, he yelped in surprise as he suddenly became aware of the fact the hay was crawling with the goddamned bugs.

He automatically pushed backwards to avoid being stung by the thousands of insects that darted for his hands and he tumbled down the stacks before landing hard on the ground.

The violent jolts amplified the pain inside him and brought tears to his eyes. "Oh Jesus, oh Jesus," he moaned in distress as he struggled to his feet once more. Evidently the ants had completely surrounded the barn and now a number of them were working their way in through the back wall. He was well and truly fucked and he knew it.

With all options of flight exhausted, Simon's mind switched to fight mode. No way was he going down without a fight. The main body of ants pouring in through the entrance hadn't yet reached the storage area for the gas, and that was when Simon had an idea.

He admonished himself for being so stupid. The fires outside had worked well in keeping the fuckers at bay and burning many of them to a crisp. He'd simply use the same method here and hey presto, barbequed bugs.

He didn't have long before the insects surpassed the barrels of fuel and so he hurriedly stumbled towards them. "Fucking Franklin and his beers. Should'a kept on riding all the way to Marlene's," he uttered as he managed to reach the barrels. Using a nearby crowbar he wrenched the lid off the first barrel he got to and tipped it over, sending fuel flowing across the ground and over the ants. The insects didn't seem to like it one bit and did their best to avoid the flammable liquid.

"I could'a been enjoying Thanksgiving dinner. Turkey with all the trimmings," he continued as he popped the lid from a second barrel and send the liquid spewing. He then moved onto a third. He popped it, this time he tipped it over in the opposite direction to the previous barrels so the liquid splashed over the ground and ran towards the piles of hay. It puddled at the foot of the stacks. There was still five more barrels. He wished he had the time to pop them all, but the ants were still advancing from all angles and were nearly upon him. Looking up he could see the roof of the barn absolutely coated in them, as were the walls. There were less on the ground, due in large part to the spilt fuel, although still too many for him to run through.

"And after tucking into my turkey dinner, I could have been tucking into Marlene." Grimly he pulled his lighter from his pocket. The petrol fumes filled the air, making Simon feel lightheaded. He coughed, the fumes clogging his lungs. "Instead, I'm stuck here, fucking around with a bunch of ants with rabies, or something." He raised the lighter, regarding it grimly. The ants were seconds from crawling up his boots. "Oh well, bug barbeque it is, I guess. See you fucks in hell." His thumb applied pressure to the lighter and a spark ignited.

CHAPTER 22

Martin and Louise threw themselves to the floor and covered their heads in defence as the barn exploded with the force of a half-ton bomb. The entire building's structure was shattered into pieces as the flames rose forty feet into the air and sent debris flying in all directions.

Upon Martin's suggestion, Louise had aided him into the living room when it was discovered Simon was no longer responding on the radio. Each step was painful and Martin struggled to keep going into shock from the gunshot wound. They had approached the large bay windows hoping to see why Simon had ceased transmitting and what Marie's fate had been.

By the time they got there Marie's car was gone and Simon was nowhere to be seen. It seemed Marie had gotten away. Neither of them acknowledged the fact, wanting to focus more on the person who could potentially save them rather than the person who had abandoned them to die.

Their hopes diminished further when Simon was nowhere to be seen.

"Do you think he left when Marie left?" Louise asked.

Martin didn't think so. He shook his head.

"But who knows what that crazy bitch could have said to him? She could have told him we were all dead, so you couldn't report her for shooting you."

Martin dismissed the idea. "The state she was in, she wouldn't have stopped for Simon. Even if she had, Simon hasn't left."

"How do you know?"

"His bike is still there." He pointed to the scrambler, still standing further up the large driveway.

"He could have jumped in the car with Marie."

"Doubtful. He loves that bike. And do you really think Marie, of all people, would have let him into her car?"

Louise had to admit the Martin had a point. Marie was so up herself it was hard to imagine her sticking her neck out for anyone she believed to be beneath her class, even in a life and death situation such as this. "So where is he then?"

"He has to be in the barn. Maybe his walkie-talkie has ran out of juice and he needs another. Maybe he has another idea."

"You really think so?"

"I don't know. But look, the ants. They're swarming over the barn now."

"They've seen him?"

"It looks like it. This just doesn't make sense."

"What do you mean? Clearly Marie's getaway alerted them to where Simon was."

"Probably, but even so. If the ants turned on Simon, he should have had plenty of time to hop on his bike and get away. So why didn't he? Why instead would he have ran into the barn? He'd be trapped like a rat in there."

"You think he went in to change radios and doesn't know they've followed him."

Martin turned the idea over in his head. "Maybe. But look at the fuel barrels. Simon had them all standing together before. Now they're scattered."

Louise could see that he was correct. The barrels had indeed been knocked over. One of them was on its side where it had stood, another had begun rolling down the drive towards the house before stopping a third of the way. Another and rolled a third further before coming to a rest and the final one had rolled all the way to the house and now rested against the stone steps leading up to the front door. A dent could be seen in the closest barrel.

"Jesus, what did we miss?"

"I don't know, but right now, we've got to hope Simon

makes it out of that barn."

At that moment the barn had exploded, causing the couple to drop to the floor. The windows rattled from the sheer force and Martin feared they would shatter. Thankfully they didn't.

When the reverberations of the explosion finally ceased, and the noise of flaming debris hitting the house had stopped, Martin and Louise climbed back up and surveyed the damage. The barn was gone, nothing of the structure remained except a burning heap of timber and rubble, thick black smoke choking the air around it. Debris from the explosion had flung out all over the drive and still burnt where it had fallen.

The ants were in disarray, clearly unsure how to react to the massive blast. Their numbers seemed less than they had previously been. The ground was no longer as blanketed as it was previously and the bay window was certainly clearer to see through. It was still too dangerous to chance running, although clearly the ants' number had been depleted. It seemed a large number of them had pursued Simon into the barn before he had blown it up, himself included. The concussive force from the explosion had simply blown thousands of the ants away. Bourne to the wind, Martin felt it was likely the blast wave would have killed many of them.

"Oh my God," said Louise in awe of what she had witnessed. "Martin, do you think Simon made it out? Before it blew up, I mean."

Martin shook his head. "I don't think so. There was nowhere in there he could go. Unless he lured them in somehow while he remained in hiding somewhere else."

Louise grasped at the slither of hope. "You think he could have?"

Martin's look quashed that line of thinking. "I think Simon took a shit-ton of those bastards with him."

"Enough to allow us to escape?"

"I don't think so."

Louise gave out an exasperated huff. "Then what does it

matter? We're still trapped. Nothing has changed. No, scrap that, things are worse. Simon's gone and you've been shot."

"Perhaps help will come when Marie reaches civilisation."

Louise scoffed at the thought. "You think we can hold on until then?"

"I don't know," Martin groaned, sitting down on the armchair as the bullet wound gave a jolt of pain that knocked him from his feet.

Louise's face softened as she saw her husband in pain. She eyed the blood trail he had left, stumbling from the hallway to the window. "You've lost a lot of blood."

"I'll live," he said, instantly regretting the choice of words.

She spotted the medical kit Tom had been using to patch his wounds earlier. She held her breath as she stepped around Tom's body to retrieve it, eyeing the ants in the fireplace warily. Even they seemed less in number. She guessed some of them had crawled back out, searching for another way inside. She returned to Martin. "I'll patch you up as best I can."

Martin wanted to protest. He nodded instead and breathed deeply with exertion as he removed the heavy jumper and lifter up his shirt to allow Louise to tend his wound. Although now more vulnerable to ant attack, he had to admit he was relieved to remove the stifling clothing.

Louise worked in silence and Martin watched her, falling more in love with her than he had ever had before. She was truly an amazing woman. "I don't know what I did to deserve you," he smiled.

Louise gave a weak laugh. "Me neither." Once she was finished Martin pulled his shirt back down over his bandaged middle. "How does that feel?"

Martin downed some pain killers he had found in the medical kit. He slowly stood. "Better," he gasped through the waves of pain.

"For all the good it'll do. You need the hospital."

"I know," he grunted as he started walking around the room, adjusting to the pain.

Louise watched him and felt her sorrow build up inside her. It broke her heart watching her husband barely able to walk. With that sorrow came the heart break of reminding herself of Dean's fate only ten minutes before. And before that, Teddy's condition. How had her world fallen apart so fast? Hopelessness once again set in. "Oh Martin, what is the point? What are we going to do?"

"I'm thinking." He wanted to be calm. To be strong. But what options were left open to them? Louise watched him, her hopes sinking by the moment and Martin was about to say something, anything, to try and raise her spirits when a scared voice called out from the kitchen.

"Mom? Dad? Dean? Where are you?"

Martin and Louise looked at each other in disbelief before immediately heading out through the hallway. Despite Martin already standing and being nearer to the door, his injury slowed him and Louise rushed passed him. She tried not to look at the bathroom door as she jogged, feeling sorrow and guild pervade her at the thought the small downstairs bathroom was now her eldest son's tomb.

Running into the kitchen she nearly broke down at the sight of Teddy sitting upright upon the table. He looked dazed and confused and his skin was pale and wet with perspiration, but his fever seemed to have broken. "Mom?" he said, again with confusion and unable to understand what was going on.

"Oh, my baby," Louise cried as she embraced her son. Martin entered the room a moment later and joined in the hug.

The tender family moment lasted for the briefest of times before Teddy pulled away, destroying the blissful diversion his parents were holding onto. "What happened?" He sounded scared as he surveyed his surroundings. "Are you hurt, Dad?"

"It's nothing," Martin lied.

"Why is everything such a mess?" he looked at the various items that had been knocked to the floor around the kitchen and the various burn marks and signs of the conflict with the ants in the hallway. Both Martin and Louise exchanged glances, neither one of them able to explain the madness they had endured. "Where's Dean and Cassie? Are they in trouble?"

Louise fielded that question. "Nobody's in trouble, baby. Well, not in that way."

Martin had sat, the pain in his belly flaring up. "Do you remember what happened, son?"

Teddy stared blankly ahead as he struggled to recall the morning's events. "I was stung. By ants." His expression turned from confusion to horror as he recalled being stung and what had happened afterwards. "They got Cassie. The ants did. They nearly got me and Dean. Dad, you saved us. And then…"

"I did save you," Martin explained gently. "But those ants, Ted, they followed us back here. They attacked the house."

"The house?"

"They still are."

"They're trying to sting us?"

Martin thought back tears. "Dean and your uncle, Tom. They got stung. They got hurt, real bad."

Even at his young age Teddy could read what it was his father was struggling to tell him. "They're dead," he said flatly. His face brimmed with sadness.

"They are. Your aunt, Marie, she managed to get away, but we're, well, we're trapped."

"Trapped?"

Louise quietly cried as Martin explained things as delicately as he could. "The ants are all over the house. We can't get any help."

"Aunt Marie will get help?"

Martin wet his lips. "Maybe. But we can't wait that long. It's best if we leave too, as soon as we can."

Teddy looked blank as he absorbed the information. "I'm thirsty."

Louise hugged and kissed him before walking to the counter, the spoiling Thanksgiving food now looked unappetising and excessive. She filled a glass of water and tried her hardest not to focus on the insects crawling over the outside of the windows.

"Are those the ants?" Teddy whined as he spotted them, his breathing increasing as his father's story suddenly became a lot more real. He instinctively reached down, holding his wounded hand.

"Don't worry, they can't get in," Martin said.

"Really mom? They can't get in?"

"Not at the moment, baby." Louise's lip trembled as she returned to the table and handed Teddy the water to drink.

"So, what should we do?" she said, eyeing Martin.

Martin watched as Teddy drank, determination welling up inside him to the strongest it had been since Dean had passed away. "I'll think of something." He believed those words now. He would think of something because he had to. There was no other choice.

"Please do, because I'm all out of ideas and we are not letting those things win."

CHAPTER 23

Trying to ignore the pain, Martin stood from the table and wondered back through the hallway. Like Louise, he couldn't bring himself to look at the closed bathroom door. He knew that if he ever witnessed with his eyes the grisly, soul-destroying truth he knew was hidden behind it he would be truly crushed and unable to function. No doubt more grief would come, but not until he and his family were safe and far away from this cursed land.

As he limped towards the living room, he noticed the Glock, the very gun Marie had shot him with, laying by the scorched front door. He approached it and picked it up before grimly placing it in his waistband. He didn't want Louise to know he had picked it up. He was afraid what she would do with it.

He then walked back into the living room, looked sadly at his brother's still body and sat down on his armchair. He groaned in pain as he did so, though it was good to be off his feet. Regarding Tom's form beneath the sheet and the sickly smell of the burnt hair that prevailed in the air, he really hoped he could avoid bringing Teddy into the room.

He then glanced over at the fireplace, at the thousands of creatures that crawled over each other, still united in their single focus to get into the house proper and murder him and his family. How he hated them, more than he'd ever known he could hate anything. He felt an almost uncontrollable urge to put his foot through the glass in some futile gesture of defiance. The idea was discounted. It was unlikely such an act would kill even a handful of ants, and then they would be upon him. And after they were through with him, they would search out Louise and Teddy. It was a thought too horrific to even contemplate. The Glock felt heavy in his waistband. With all its compact power, it was a hopeless weapon against the hoards of tiny insects. Treading on the damned things would be more effective than shooting into them.

He stared again at the crawling ants in the fireplace, focussing on his disdain for them. "How do I do it? How do I kill you?" he sneered at the insects. The ants, of course, said nothing. "Damn you all." He stood up and made his way to the window, looked out at the swarming drive, at the remaining four barrels, rolled to random locations across its span, at the burning ruins of the barn and finally he looked at Simon's bike, still standing, undamaged by the explosion and unmolested by the insects. It was only a few hundred feet away yet the expanse of marauding ants between the bike and the house meant it may as well be on the moon. "There has to be a way."

He was taken over by a coughing fit, each convulsion sending fresh agony shooting up from his gunshot wound, throughout his body. When the coughing had ended he realised he had coughed up blood, numerous specs of it sprayed across the window glass. He tried to wipe them away and succeeded only in smearing the glass further.

He was dying. He realised that. He thought the prospect of dying would have scared him more than he felt. Now it seemed like little more than an afterthought. For any man, the prospect of his own demise meant little when weighed against the lives of his family.

"There has to be a way."

*   *   *

Louise leant back in the chair, watching her beautiful, perfect young boy as he drank more water. He'd been thirstier than she'd thought and requested a second glass, which she's instantly jumped up to get for him. From the living room she could hear Martin yelling to the ants and at himself, followed by his coughing. He was hurt worse than either of them cared to admit, though the risk of him bleeding out seemed somewhat muted at the present. She was only thankful he hadn't gone into shock and could still function, even at the limited functionality he was operating at.

Before Teddy had awoken she would have ran to Martin's side upon hearing his coughing, forced him to rest and remain comfortable the best she could. As it was, she didn't dare leave her beautiful Teddy's side, and she really prayed he wouldn't have to see Tom's body lying on the living room floor. Even under a sheet she didn't know how Teddy would react. It was one thing for him to understand Tom was dead. It was another for him to see the body. And she dare not mention Dean's location, so close to where they were. He was scarred enough as it was.

Louise watched her son slowly sip his second glass of water for ten whole minutes and in that time she realised just how tired she was. She'd been running on adrenaline since the ants had turned up and everything had been happening so fast. Now, with some time for introspection, she realised she was close to dropping. Teddy let out a gasp after gulping down the last of his water. He looked at the empty beaker in his hand for a while before putting it down. "Mommy, I don't feel well."

She placed her hand on his. "I know, baby. As soon as we've got away from here we're taking you straight to the hospital."

He pulled away, scratched at the swelling on his hand. "I hope it's soon."

"Me too. We're working on it."

"I miss Dean."

Louise felt as if she were a mirror that had been shattered into a million pieces. "Oh baby, I miss him too," she sobbed and embraced Teddy's tiny, slight frame once more. She squeezed him tight and never wanted to let go.

Eventually, she released him after kissing his head. "We must be strong now. For Dean. For ourselves. You understand?"

Teddy's body went rigid. "Mom," he whispered, barely moving.

Louise was instantly alerted by Teddy's sudden change in posture. He'd switched from tired and uncertain to being frozen in fear. "What's wrong, baby?"

He struggled to talk, he was so scared. "Mom, there are ants."

She glanced at the glass window by the door, feeling revulsion for the insects as the crawled over the glass, blocking much of the view with their numbers. "I know, I know," she soothed.

"Not out there," Teddy whispered. "In here, with us."

Louise felt a prickling at the back of her neck, the same feeling one would get if they were being watched. With dread she slowly turned around to see the kitchen counter behind her. She didn't risk a scream at what she saw. The ants were indeed in the house. There had to be thousands of them, scurrying over all the food she had been preparing with such care earlier on in the day, before abandoning it.

Her eyes followed the wide column of ants to their origin, as they went up the tiled wall and into the oven's extractor fan. So that was how they had got in.

Looking back to the counters, she could see the ants were working on the food, using their tiny cruel jaws to cut chunks from everything edible and carrying it away with them, back into the extractor fan. Even more ants were running in, making a beeline for the food.

A second column was running down the front of the cabinets, away from the food and onto the tiled floor, where it broke up into thousands of insects seemingly searching at random for either more food, or perhaps for her and Teddy.

She cursed herself for not noticing the ants until it was too late and now, as she observed, the kitchen floor between her and the hallway was covered in the things. She gave a shriek as she realised some of the ants were inches from crawling up her boot and she quickly lifted her feet from the floor to elude them.

Grabbing hold of Teddy she then stepped onto the table, taking him with her. At the moment the ants still hadn't seemed to have noticed her and appeared to be searching, almost at random. Not at all like the direct attacks they had been committing to before.

Teddy began emitting a high-pitched moan. "Mommy, they're going to get us. I don't want to be stung again. It hurt so bad."

She held him close. "I'm not going to let them," she promised. "Martin," she called out, "the ants are here, help." As she heard him groan in pain as he began hurrying to help them, she calculated the distance between the table and the hallway and judged it too far to jump without landing amongst the bugs.

"I'm coming," Martin called as he appeared. "Jesus Chris," he yelled as he immediately spotted the ants, scurrying all over the tiled kitchen floor.

"Martin, help us," Louise pleaded in desperation. Teddy had started crying.

Martin tried to get a handle of the situation, trying to come up with the fastest solution possible. Even now the ants were climbing the table legs. By some miracle they still seemed oblivious to the people so close to their swarm. None had yet ventured into the hallway, where they'd be able to make easy prey of Martin. Louise wondered if all the food stuff had made them somewhat docile or was overwhelming their senses somehow.

"Can you burn a path?" Louise suggested tensely.

Martin tossed the idea over in his head before dismissing it. "If I tried that they'd overwhelm me. The only reason that has worked before is because we've been able to close doors between us and the swarm. That isn't an option here."

"Then what?" she squeezed Teddy so tight she worried about breaking him. He didn't complain, returning the embrace, seeking the safety of his mother.

"Hold on a second." Martin limped away down the hallway and shortly after returned with the small red rug from the living room, rolled up beneath his arm. He moved as quick as he could, even though every step was torture.

"The rug?"

Martin nodded. "I'm going to throw it down and roll it out to you as quick as I can. It won't bridge the gap entirely, but it'll make it most the way. As soon as I do that, you need to jump down onto it. The biggest jump you can, and then run for me. Understand? Run straight past me, don't stop. As soon as you are through the door I'll slam it shut. You need to run upstairs and grab some towels from the bathroom so we can stop them following you under the door. Have you got that?"

Louise nodded, imagining the scenario in her head.

"You won't have a lot of time, once I roll this out," Martin warned. "You've seen for yourself how fast these things can be when they've got your scent. As soon as the rug goes down, they'll be on it. There isn't enough time for Teddy to jump first, you both have to jump together. Do you understand that, Teddy?"

Still in his mother's arms, Teddy gave affirmation.

"I don't know if I can do this," cried Louise, knowing that if she failed, Teddy would be the one paying the price.

"You're the only one that can," Martin said. "If I was in your situation, with this wound, I'd be a goner. But you can do this. I know it. You'll keep Teddy safe."

Martin's words gave Louise the courage she needed. She looked behind her to see that the ants had begun crawling up over the tabletop. "Are you ready?" she asked Teddy. He nodded. "As soon as we hit the floor, you just run, okay? Just run."

"Are you ready?" Martin asked them both, preparing to toss down the rug. They both said they were and Martin unfurled the rug. It rolled out, over the kitchen flooring, crushing and pinning down the multitude of ants which had been scurrying in its path. As soon as it was down ants began invading it from either side. "Now, jump," Martin cried.

Louise eyed the jump, lamenting that the rug hadn't covered quite as much ground as she had hoped, necessitating a larger jump than she's realised. Regardless, she yelled "now!" and leapt alongside Teddy, keeping his hand gripped tightly in her own.

They both hit the rug and went to run, the rug slipping from the force of their landing and nearly sending Louise to the floor. Even while stumbling and nearly tipping over, Louise used all her strength to heave Teddy off his feet with her momentum, carrying him forward so he didn't fall. Teddy took another stride and he sailed passed Martin into the relative safety of the hallway, with Louise right behind him.

Martin immediately slammed the kitchen door as the behaviour of the ants changed, their almost aimless wanderings replaced by a singular purpose as the scampered after the fleeing family. No sooner had the door slammed shut did the tiny creatures begin squeezing under the door. "Louise, towel, quickly," he demanded and his wife shot up the stairs two at a time, quickly descending with a couple of towels. She threw them to the floor and pushed them against the bottom of the door with her feet. The few ants which had managed to crawl through were swiftly crushed under her heel.

Relieved that the current crisis had been dealt with, Martin succumbed to the gunshot pain and slid to the ground.

"Thank God we made it," Louise exclaimed. "Teddy, are you alright? Were you stung anymore?" When Teddy said that he wasn't she then turned to Martin, realising just how bad a shape he was in. "Oh Martin, you saved us. How are you feeling?"

Martin forced a smile. He was elated he had managed to save them, but the pain of breathing was becoming nearly impossible to bare. He gave a thumbs up before being racked with coughs. Louise watched on in silence until the coughing stopped. "Not too bad," he lied. He didn't realise blood was showing at he corners of his mouth. "You okay, champ?"

Teddy was busy looking at the carnage the siege had had on the hallway, the burnt flooring, the blood. He nodded numbly. He went to walk into the living room and Louise stopped him.

"We need to get out of here fast," she sighed, holding onto her son. We're running out of rooms."

Martin knew she was right. "Let me sit again," he gasped through pain, his pretence of being able to cope with the pain and blood loss began to slip.

Louise chewed her lip, uncertain. "But with Tom in there…"

"I know." He understood her concerns, bringing Teddy into the living room, though it seemed unavoidable now they had lost the kitchen. "Like you said, though. Not many rooms left."

CHAPTER 24

"Mommy, the ants are scaring me," whimpered Teddy, sat on the sofa, his eyes fixed on the ants inside the fireplace.

"I know, just try to ignore them," Louise replied, thinking how ludicrous her suggestion was. In a weird way she was thankful that Teddy was more fixated on the insects. The more of his attention that was on focused on them, then the less it was on the body of his uncle.

She then turned back to Martin. He was becoming weaker by the minute, one bloodied hand permanently clamped over his blood drenched belly. The bandage she had applied had bled through and Martin refused to let her look at it. As he had stated earlier, bleeding out now seemed like a luxury he wouldn't have time to be afforded.

Outside the ants were working on the building, tunnelling in through the timbers and brickwork. It really wouldn't be long before the house was completely infested. The ants' activities within the walls could be heard whenever the trio fell silent and so silence was now something that the family were trying to avoid.

Martin kept his eyes focused on the window and the ants outside, desperately trying to come up with an escape plan as he breathed laboriously.

Louise joined him, scrutinising the insects scattered over the drive. The barn was still burning, clogging the air with thick, choking black smoke. The smoke seemed to have dulled their senses somewhat, although she was under no illusion that they would be able to simply make a run for it.

"Our car is pretty close, maybe I can reach that?" she asked.

"I mean, I know the quad bike is covered in them, but the interior of the car might still be okay. Marie seemed to get away okay."

Martin shook his head. "There's no way you'd make it. It's too far and we haven't got the cover of fire to keep them at bay anymore."

She looked at the fallen four fuel barrels, scattered across the drive. "What about them? Can you shoot at them?"

"Look at the blast marks of the original four barrels that went up when Simon set the gas alight." She looked. "They're about ten feet across, but that won't get you close enough to then reach the car."

"What if I carried a rug? I could roll it out, if you exploded the one nearest the door?"

"Potentially. But I don't like it."

"Those things can barely walk over the scorched areas from the initial fire. I'd have enough time."

"Maybe." He glanced again at the ant covered car. He dismissed the idea. "No, it's too much of a distance. You couldn't carry anything that heavy alone and I'm in too bad a shape to help you."

"Then what? Wait here and die?" Louise shouted. Teddy looked up with alarm and she lowered her voice. "Like I said before, I'm not letting them get to us. I'm not going to let what happened to Dean happen to Teddy." She paused. "Where's the gun, Martin?"

"The gun?"

"Don't play stupid, you think I wouldn't notice you had picked it up?"

Martin thought about protesting before relenting. "I have it in my waistband. What do you plan on doing with it?"

"I don't know. Maybe it'll come in handy against those things somehow."

"Maybe." He wasn't hopeful.

"If those bastards come for us, I might just shoot that nearest barrel anyway. I want to take as many of those things out as I can."

Martin agreed with the sentiment. "Let's hope it doesn't come to that." He gave her a slight smile. "Besides, you've never shot a gun before, you'd be a terrible shot. Best leave the shooting to me."

Louise scoffed, appreciating the gallows humour. "Well, you wouldn't be much better. She eyed the furthest barrel. "Reckon you could hit that one, at the back?"

"With the Glock, not a chance."

"Ha, well we can see, if we run out of options. See if you can shoot them all. Get a little target practice in. You get extra points if you manage to hit the last one before the flames of the first one die down."

Martin chuckled and that. It hurt, but it was worth it. He held his wife's hand. "I love you, you know that?"

"Of course I do. I love you too." They kissed gently and both relished the meaningfulness and affection of the interaction.

"Gross," groaned Teddy, giving them both a disgusted look.

Martin managed another chuckle at that. He thought about the human spirit, how, despite all they had been through, Teddy was still the boy he had always been, even with the terrible losses they had endured he hoped they could one day rebuild and live as a family once more.

He looked again at the closest barrel and decided to keep up the light dialogue, not wanting to let the grimness of their situation infect their minds. "Well, I'd have about ten minutes to hit each barrel. I'd take that bet."

Louise rolled her eyes. "Now all you need is an unlimited amount of bullets to try."

It was then that an idea clicked. "I've got it," he exclaimed suddenly. He stood bolt upright before crying out in pain and sitting back down.

Louise's concerned face returned. "Jesus, Martin, calm down. You want to bleed out any quicker?"

"I've got it," Martin said in excitement. "I know how to get through the ants."

Louise looked at him in disbelief, as if she had come to accept there was no way of escaping their fate. She glanced over at Teddy quickly before returning her gaze to her husband. "You do?"

"I do. It's like you said before, the barrels that exploded before, they took about ten minutes to burn out, after covering an area roughly ten feet across, right?"

"Right," said Louise, unsure where he was going with this.

"And look at the ants. Even now there aren't many of them on the burnt areas of ground."

"They don't like the ash, I guess."

"I think it's more than that. I think the ground is still too hot. I don't think they can walk over the scorched areas. The heat could kill them."

"If that's correct, we should have just burnt a path earlier, we might have been able to make it."

"Maybe," Martin conceded. "Although as soon as the fuel was leaked, the ants appeared to follow the trail. They would likely have cut off the escape route before we reached the end of it."

Louise had to agree he was probably right. "So where are you going with this?"

"Look at how the barrels have fallen. One by the house, one a third up the drive, another a further third, roughly."

"And the final one at the drives end," Louise finished. "How does that help us get to the car?"

"Not the car, Simon's bike."

Louise gasped as she realised what Martin was talking about. Simon's dirt bike was still outside the radius of the mass of angry ants. And even from the distance they could see the keys hanging from the ignition.

"We can use the barrels to create steppingstones, so to speak. I'll explode the first barrel, then the next, then the next. Once the first one stops burning, we run on. Hopefully we can time it so that by the time the second one dies down the ground underfoot is still too hot for the ants to attack us. I'll give them a minute between taking them out. Hopefully that'll mean the ground is too hot for them to walk on, but okay for you in thick boots. We repeat until we're through them."

Louise chewed her lip. "That might work, but look at the angles, you'd be shooting through smoke to hit those barrels further away. They line up *too* perfectly. Plus, are you sure you'd have enough shots to pull it off? If it went wrong, could we retreat back to the house? The timings would need to be pretty close. Remember, the ants aren't walking on the scorched areas because they have no need. If we are standing on them, they'd be more motivated to try."

"They would, but I still think it would work," asserted Martin. "The issue is, the first one if too close to the front door. If I explode it, it'll likely rip the front door off its hinges. The blast would probably shatter the window in here as well."

Louise didn't like the sound of that. "Then they would have won. We'd be stuck hiding in a bedroom with nothing to do but wait for them to get us."

Martin furrowed his brow, trying to see how his plan would play out. "Not necessarily. We could close the living room door so they couldn't get into the hallway."

"What good would that do if the front door has been blown off its hinges?"

"Remember the front door is within the radius of the barrels' blast. It would be on fire. That would probably stop them from coming in, at least in high numbers."

Louise relented the point. "Maybe, but even so, you'd still have to shoot through smoke. Is it realistic to think you'd be able to shoot blind?"

Martin's face darkened. "If I was standing with you guys, I'd be shooting blind. Not if I was shooting from elsewhere."

Louise became panicked at what her husband was going to suggest. "Where would you be shooting from?"

"Our bedroom. From the window I'd have a clear vantage point of all four barrels."

"Then how would you escape?"

Martin lowered his voice further, noticing Teddy was listening to their hushed voices, even though he was acting as if he wasn't. "Let's be honest. I can barely walk anymore. I'd just be a liability out there. We'd still need to make short sprints between the scored areas. There's no way I could manage that in my shape." Louise looked as if she was about to contest his point. He didn't let her. "And remember the mode of transport is Simon's scrambler. It doesn't seat three people. Hell, it doesn't even seat two. You'd only be able to get away with it because Teddy's small enough to sit in front of you. And the way that thing bounces, I wouldn't be able to take it. I'm in excruciating pain just sitting here. I wouldn't be able to take bouncing over the desert."

Louise looked defeated. "I don't want to leave you."

"I'll shut myself away somewhere, safe and sound as soon as the shooting is done. Just try and return with help as quick as you can. The most important thing is that you get Teddy out of here, right?"

Louise nodded, her maternal instincts once more taking over. "It's dangerous, but I think it could work. Do you think you could hit the barrels okay from the bedroom with the Glock?"

"Not with the Glock. But with the rifle there would be no problem."

"But the gun cabinet is locked. We don't know what Marie did with the key."

Martin smiled grimly and pulled the Glock from his belt. "That's not a problem, I've got a new key right here."

CHAPTER 25

The couple went over the plan in more detail a further two times to ensure that they weren't grasping at straws and believed it could work. After they had convinced themselves, they explained it to Teddy, who already had a pretty good idea of what the plan entailed from listening to his parents discuss it. He didn't take any convincing at all. He was eager to escape and was willing to believe anything his parents told him. If they said it would work, that was all he needed to hear.

Once they were committed to the plan in earnest, they went about making it happen. The trio made their way up the stairs. Martin's condition was deteriorating to the point he had to lean onto his wife as he ascended. As they did so, Martin was more certain that he was right to remain behind. There wasn't a chance in hell that he'd make it past the blood-thirsty insects. If he could save his family, that was good enough for him.

Louise kept making mention of sending help to recover him as soon as possible. Martin went along with her belief that people would return in time to save him, even though he knew there was little chance of anyone returning before the ants could breach what was left of the house. He felt she knew that too, though she didn't want to admit it to herself and that was just fine with Martin if it meant his wife and son had a shot at surviving. Martin feared that if Louise admitted the truth to herself, that she was likely leaving her husband to die, then she might not be able to go through with it, even for Teddy's sake.

Once upstairs, Louise supported Martin as they made their way to the master bedroom and he was left resting on the bed. She then went with Teddy to his bedroom, where she picked the thickest clothes he had for him to wear.

Sitting on the bed Martin could hear his son complain about the clothes being hot and stuffy and Louise snapping at him. The sound of them bickering made him smile and almost added a degree of normality to the world. Drawing the Glock, he eased himself off the bed and took a few shaky steps until he was at the gun cabinet. Aiming at the lock, the barrel of the gun mere inches from its target, he pulled the trigger.

The loud gunshot rang out and the lock was shattered. Dropping the handgun to the floor, he reached down and easily pulled the cabinet doors apart, revealing the AR-15 rifle. Admiring its sleek design, Martin picked it up, as well as a box of bullets and sat back down on the bed. He slowly loaded it, wishing he had spent longer becoming accustomed to the mechanism. The blood covering his hands from his gunshot wound made his fingers slippery and compounded the difficulty of the task at hand.

Once the rifle was loaded he shouldered it, looking through the sight. His hands trembled a little, though he felt confident he'd be able to hit his targets when the time came.

Louise and Teddy came back into the room. Teddy was dressed in thick clothing and looked even more miserable because of it.

"How are you going to shoot out without those things getting in?" she asked.

"I'm going to have to shoot through the glass, there's no way around it." Louise didn't like the sound of that, so Martin continued. "Look at the nearest barrel," he said. "It's right below this window. I've got to hope on the blast, heat and flames pushing those bastards away or killing them before they get in here. Same as the front door."

"'Hope,'" Louise looked uneasy. "What if that doesn't happen?"

"If it doesn't happen, then I'll be a goner."

"I don't like it."

"Me neither. Either way, even if I think of an ingenious way of shooting out without making myself vulnerable, the force of the bang from that first barrel will likely shatter this window. There really isn't a choice."

Louise nodded, looking no more convinced by the way Martin was selling the scenario to her.

Martin painfully made his way to the window. A multitude of ants still scurried over it. "As soon as the shooting starts, you guys need to be prepared to run, okay? We don't know for sure how long these fires will last."

Louise nodded. "So, this is it then." Abject sadness was written over her face.

"Until you send help," Marin tried to smile. It only faltered a little.

Louise embraced her husband, kissed him and buried her face in his chest. "I love you so much. Don't you ever forget that," she said, close to tears.

"I've never doubted it," he replied, fighting to stop his own voice from devolving into sobs. He noticed Teddy watching them and he opened an arm, gesturing for his son to come. Teddy rushed across the room and into his parents' arms. His arms squeezed Martin's middle, causing the pain there to grow worse. Martin didn't let Teddy know about the discomfort he was causing. He just held his son.

"You be brave, son," he said. "I love you. You do me proud, you hear?"

Teddy sobbed. "I will, dad. I'll get help. I promise."

Martin smiled with sadness. "I know you will. Just focus on getting you mom to safety first, okay? You're the man of the family now."

"Just until we get help, you mean."

A lone tear ran down Martin's face. "Of course, Ted. Of course that's what I mean." After a few moments the hug broke apart and Martin cleared his throat. "Now, you guys get going downstairs. Don't stand too close to the front door though, when I blast that barrel it's going to cause a big bang."

Louise nodded and went to leave the room. Before she

exited, Louise turned around to look at her husband one last time. "You take care of yourself, Martin."

"I always do," he smiled back. With that she left, closing the door behind her.

*   *   *

Once downstairs in the hallway, Louise ensured the living room door was shut so that if the bay window shattered they would still have a door between them and the ants. She then armed herself with the aerosol can and lighter, prepared for any ants foolish enough to try and attack them.

"Are you sure this is going to work, mom?"

"It'll work," Louise said with an absolute certainty she wished she felt. "If your father says it'll work, it'll work."

At that moment, in the upstairs bedroom, Martin angled the rifle down and pulled the trigger. The barrel closest to the house exploded into a ball of fire, the force of it killing all ants in its immediate vicinity as well as forcing those further away back with the blistering heat.

Louise screamed in shock and shielded her eyes as the barrel exploded with far more force than she'd expected. The front door was blown completely off its frame and hurled against the stairs, smashing into multiple fragments as it did so. The hallway was bathed in an orange glow as the flames burnt wildly just outside the front doors' threshold.

Louise stood with her body between the door and Teddy, the heat almost blistered her as she protected him from the wave of hot air. Teddy cried, holding onto Louise's leg. She wanted to hold him desperately, but the aerosol and lighter in her hand had to take precedent. As soon as her eyes adjusted, she prepared herself for the potential onslaught of six-legged death.

The onslaught never came. The entire area which had once been the entrance to her beloved house was now an inferno, flames from the burning fuel catching on the doorframe, rising high, licking the ceiling greedily

My god, she thought. *The fire is going to burn down the entire house. We're trapped. Doomed to either choke to death on black smoke or burnt alive in red-hot flames!*

She started coughing as thick black smoke began building up, filling the hallway from the heights of the ceiling and beginning to work its way down. Pocketing the aerosol and lighter she covered her mouth and crouched, helping Teddy to cover his own mouth and nose.

Another explosion ran out, this one further away. Louise realised Martin had just shot the second barrel. The force of the second explosion fanned the flames of the first barrels' remnants, pushing them further into the hallway at a more rapid rate.

Louise's mind raced as Teddy began coughing hard into her hand, unsure what to do. The fire had already reached the stairs so retreating to the second floor was now impossible. The flames were also blocking the entrance to the games room, to the point the exit appeared to have partially collapsed. The door to the living room was beside her and she wondered if it could provide refuge. Her wondering was answered when through the glass panel she noticed the shaking from the explosion had shattered not only the main window, but also the thin glass of the fireplace. Ants swarmed everywhere, although somehow, they seemed to be acting differently than before. Clearly the violent explosions and the heat of the flames had them alarmed, the tiny creatures no longer moving in the singular fashion they had previously displayed. Now their movements were panicked and confused. Regardless, she had little doubt they would set upon her if she opened the door.

That left the downstairs bathroom door and the kitchen door. Both led to certain death, as well as other unspeakable horrors she dare not think about at that moment.

"Martin, we're trapped," she called up, hoping to be heard over the roaring fire. There was no reply.

* * *

In the bedroom, Martin held his breath and pulled the trigger. The rifle shot off, the noise causing the painful ringing in his ears to become all the louder as the bullet found its mark and the third gas barrel exploded in a fountain of red-hot flames.

As he had predicted, the glass on the window had completely shattered from the first explosion. He hadn't realised quite how much force would be behind those glass shards as they flew towards him and had tried to move out of their way. He'd only been marginally successful. Multiple lacerations now covered his upper body, though he ignored the pain. It wasn't as if pain was anything new by this point. The real agony was still burning in his belly that continued as his lifeblood slowly seeped out. He had succeeded in protecting his eyes so he could hit his mark. That was all that mattered.

The floor of the room was now covered in broken glass and Martin had to wonder what had become of the ants that had been on the window. It was likely they were hurled into the room along with the glass from the first explosion, though he hadn't managed to spot any of them crawling around. He hoped they had all died from the blast force. No other ants swarmed into the window, the heat from the raging fire below had stopped them, as he had hoped.

Martin realised the house itself was on fire and wasn't likely to stop, and he had heard Louise calling up, saying that she was trapped. This only strengthened his resolve. There was nothing he could do for his family now, except keep taking his shots. He had to pray the fire would ease enough for his wife to take his son and escape the burning building.

Thick smoke billowed up, choking him, each cough wracking his body with fresh hell. Covering his mouth, he counted to thirty before taking aim, the wind at the height of the second floor dissipated the blinding curtain of smoke just enough to provide narrow openings.

He gave a grimace as fresh pain made itself known in his leg. At first he thought it was glass, or that he was on fire;

the wound felt as if his leg were burning. Looking at his thigh, he spotted the culprit, a lone inch long fire ant, its stinger embedded in his leg, penetrating his thick jeans. Swearing he crushed the insect under his palm before taking aim once more and pulling the trigger.

The fourth shot ran out and the final barrel exploded, taking with it another few tens of thousands of the ants as an area roughly ten feet across erupted into flames. The final fire breeched the outer perimeter of the massive ant swarm. He prayed the ants wouldn't move to cover the getaway that it may provide.

His main task complete, Martin lowered the rifle and shuffled back over to the bed, broken glass crunching underfoot. The heat from the nearest barrel was intense and seemed to becoming not just from the open window, but from beneath the floor. Either way, he knew it wouldn't be long now. He was so tired, the fight all but gone from him. The heat becoming more and more intolerable by the second.

He scanned the room, searching for anymore ants. He spotted a handful, moving between the glass shards, though he didn't pay them much mind. Their numbers were too small for them to overwhelm him and besides, they didn't seem to be particularly aware of him. He guessed they had more pressing priorities right now, namely not being burnt to a crisp. He wondered how many of the fucks he had managed to burn that day. Not enough, he decided. It could never be enough after what they had taken from him.

Thoughts of the ants receded into his mind as the smoke threatened to take his consciousness from him. Martin closed his eyes, everything becoming blurry.

He just needed to sleep. Just for a moment.

Everything began fading to black.

* * *

"Martin, can you hear me?" screeched Louise from downstairs.

Martin opened his eyes suddenly, his duty and desire to save his family forcing him to put death on hold for a little longer. He realised the room was growing hotter still. "Yes, I can hear you," he yelled from the bottom of his smoke charred lungs.

"We're trapped," his wife called back up in sheer desperation. "The house is burning."

Now that he was concentrating on what Louise was saying, the ringing in his ears diminished and he could hear Teddy coughing on the fumes of their burning home. Could this really be how it ended? Burnt to death, after all their struggles?

Fuck that, he thought as he stood up. "Can you still get to the front door?"

"It's on fire. We're trapped in the hallway."

"You're going to have to run through it. There's no other option." He approached the window and looked down through the blinding smoke. It was so hard for him to discern what was going on.

"We'd be running to our deaths. The fire is outside too."

"Listen for my voice, I'll shout as soon as the barrel fire dies. When I do, you need to run though the flames and get outside as quick as you possibly can."

*   *   *

Upon hearing Martin's suggestion, Louise felt more afraid than she had done that entire day. Half the hallway was burning, the flames angry and red, and Martin wanted her to run through it?

"I can't. I'll be burnt."

"You have got to," Martin's voice shouted down from upstairs. "It's the only option."

"Martin, I'm so scared," she wailed, feeling as if she were being asked to do the impossible.

"I know, but I know you can do this. Pick up Teddy and wait for my signal. As soon as it's possible for you to run outside, I'll tell you."

"Okay," Louise called back before crouching back down

and hugging Teddy.

"Mummy, it's so hot. I don't want to burn," he wept.

"I know, baby. We'll be in the flames only for a moment. Then we'll be outside. You just have to hold onto me as tight as possible and keep your head down. Can you do that?"

Teddy stifled a cough and nodded. "I can." He wrapped his arms around his mother's neck and his legs around her waist, holding his face against her chest.

Louise struggled to stand, her head becoming dizzy, her vision distorted. She held Teddy tight. She prayed, something she hadn't done in a long time. She'd always been a believer, although she hadn't truly thought about it for a while. Whether or not God heard her prayers, she knew that right then, in that moment they were giving her the strength and clarity to stay strong for her son.

"Now, now, now!" Martin shouted from upstairs.

With her husband's voice echoing in her ears, Louise fought against her natural instincts and ran, full speed into the hungry flames ahead.

CHAPTER 26

Louise scrunched up her face as much as she could and kept her head down against the top of Teddy's head. Teddy, so small a frail, holding on to her for dear life, his head buried in her chest as the flames licked around him.

Teddy screamed as the heat blistered and burnt him. He struggled to wriggle free from Louise's grip, his primal survival instinct kicking in as he reacting to the searing, oven level temperatures he was being subjected too. Louise kept her eyes shut and her head down. As her son attempted to wriggle from her grasp, she held onto him all the tighter, desperately aware that if he were to escape her grip, he would surely die in the flames.

Each footstep felt like agony as her legs blistered and popped, the material of her thick jeans catching alight. If she had been alone in the hallway, she knew she would never have had what it took to run through the flames. She would have waited in the hallway, trapped and lamenting her fate until the flames spread and consumed her. It was only because of Teddy that she had managed to summon the strength of will to endure the trial.

As she was running blind Louise could only pray the fire hadn't caused the flooring to collapse and cause her to trip. To fall now would lead to a miserable death. She held her breath and kept one hand clamped over Teddy's mouth, fearing that every inhalation he made was scarring his lungs via a combination of heat and smoke.

The ordeal couldn't have taken longer than a few seconds, but for Louise it felt like hours until finally she was through the fire and out of the house. The heat and smoke receded, though were far from gone. Thick smoke still rising from the scorched earth still choked her, but was far less thick and invasive, the open space helping disperse it into the air.

Teddy coughed viciously, struggling for breath and she moved as far away from the smoke as possible before unclamping his mouth. She put him down and ordered him not to move as she quickly whipped off her heavy jumper, the back of which was still smouldering hot against her skin. Her jeans were scorched black and had melted onto her skin, though she disregarded the thought of taking them off and exposing her legs.

"Are you okay?" she urgently asked Teddy. The boy kept coughing. She squatted beside him the instant she had thrown off the burning jumper. She coughed herself as she attempted to draw fresh air into her lungs. "Look at me, Teddy. Are you alright?"

Teddy stopped coughing and gave her a weary look before giving a thumbs up. Louise smiled and hugged him, thanking God they had both survived. Despite being covered head to toe in blackened ash, Teddy appeared to have made it through relatively unscathed. He was far less burnt than Louise, that was for sure. Her head, legs, back and arms all felt as if they were burnt bad, although she decided it wasn't worth worrying about until they got through the mess they were in.

"Your hair," Teddy coughed.

Louise felt her hair, realised it was a singed mess. It was likely most of it would need cutting off, yet in that moment she couldn't have cared less. "Don't worry about that," she smiled, kissing him on the cheek.

A gust of wind rolled on, clearing much of the blinding smoke and revealing the situation the two survivors now found themselves in. The ants were everywhere, all encompassing and angry by the affront that had been given to them. Despite the fire and smoke, they reacted with determination and surged towards the scorched haven the two survivors were standing on, though the heat still emanating from the ground kept them at bay. Thousands of them tried running straight to their intended prey before curling up and cooking amongst the ashes, their tiny bodies popping and sizzling.

Beyond the relatively small number of ants that cooked, the majority of the swarm stayed back from the heated earth yet were closing in from all angles. The density of the ants increased to the point that it wouldn't be long before the ground beneath them was no longer visible. Their malign presence threatening to engulf everything.

"Stay close to me," Louise warned Teddy, guiding him nearer the centre of their haven. The ground was hotter and Teddy began complaining the heat was too much. Louise agreed with him, the soles on both their boots beginning to melt. Still, burnt feet beat being eaten by killer ants. "I know, baby," she said. "Try moving from one foot to another, don't let your feet get too hot."

"Are they going to get us?"

Louise glanced at their intended path, still burning bright ten feet from them. She needed it to start dying down soon, only too aware that as soon as the ants could safely approach the cooling earth, they would attack. She glanced back at the burning house, itself the same distance in the opposing direction. The flames had really taken hold and she had no doubt it would soon be reduced to ashes. The bodies of Dean and Tom would never be recovered. She looked up at the window, trying to spot Martin. Black smoke blocked any hope of seeing if her were still alive or in his vantage point.

From the outside she could see that many of the insects that had been crawling over the house were now gone, either they had burnt up or they had fled to the ground. Hopping from one foot to another and encouraging Teddy to do the same, she was now out of options, except to trust in her husband's plan.

"The fire's going down," Teddy exclaimed and Louise saw that he was right. The flames were indeed faltering, and faster than she had imagined they would.

"Okay, as soon as the flames are gone, we need move onto

that second spot."

Teddy nodded. Louise was acutely aware that slowly the ants were advancing, which meant the outside of the circle of burnt earth was cooling. It would still take them time to reach the centre, although they could begin running between the first and second haven, which was less than ideal.

The flames began dying further. "Now?" Teddy asked between coughs.

"Not yet," Louise replied, wiping thick sweat from her forehead. The flames died down to smouldering ash and just as a thin column of ants had tried to cut the survivors off from the second burn site. "Okay, now," Louise shouted.

The two ran, easily striding over the thin column of ants. They then stopped as close to the centre of the second blast-site as possible, the heat rising from it more acute than the first. Still, the plan was working. It was actually working. Louise was almost incredulous at the thought, as if the plan was enacted out of desperation and she hadn't really thought it would succeed. Now they were half-way to freedom and she allowed herself to truly hope they could make it.

"Keep hopping, Teddy," she urged her son, holding onto him upon noticing he was slowly started to veer from the centre to the cooler rim of the second barrels blast-site. She turned back to the house again, hoping to spot Martin at the window. Again, she was disappointed. The entire bottom floor of the building was now burning. It wouldn't be long before the entire structure collapsed. When it did, it would spell Martin's demise, if he wasn't dead already. She hoped as many ants as possible were burning in the flames.

She surveyed the merciless insects again, only partially obscured by the thick smoke. Their eagerness seemed to be increasing, ever more of them were attempting to scurry over the hot sand and stones. So far none of those ants that attempted to reach them had avoided boiling their insides.

"It's taking too long," Teddy whined.

"Be patient," Louise said before a coughing fit overtook

her. She feared they would both be suffering breathing difficulties for the rest of their lives if they survived this ordeal. She spied Martin's quad bike, just outside the barrel's blast radius. It was close to the still burning third barrel also, almost touching the flames. It appeared the ants that had been crawling over it had been blasted off by the two close proximity explosions, although a few had since reclaimed it. She toyed with the idea of taking it if the third fire didn't burn down in time.

"It's beginning to burn out," Teddy exclaimed excitedly.

"That's good, that's good," Louise said, eyeing the insects beginning to close in. They all died in the attempt, though some seemed more able to survive the heat for longer and managed to get closer than Louise would have liked before curling up in death, their insides boiling. Regardless, the third barrel's fuel finally burnt out and Louise and Teddy quickly ran onto the blast-site that had been a raging inferno mere moments ago.

"One more, one more," Teddy chimed, his hope growing with his mother's.

"In the centre. Keep hoping," Louise instructed. As she spoke she breathed in sharply as a patch of her left boot's sole failed and the searing heat of the ground caused her foot to blister. It hurt so bad it brought tears to her eyes. She cried out in shock as her flesh blistered.

"Mom, are you okay?" Teddy asked, picking up on his mother's sudden change in mobility as she struggled to keep the burnt foot from the ground as much as possible.

"I'm okay, baby," she lied, not wanting to add to her son's fear. They were so close, only one fire now blocking their escape. It was burning fiercely, even more than the others.

"Is it going to burn out in time?" Teddy asked, his hope replaced with fear once again.

"It will. It has to," Louise said. The very idea that they could make it so far only to fail was almost inconceivable. It would be unimaginably cruel. The ants slowly began to close in on the rim behind them, the fire in front stopped them from

DAY OF THE ANTS

creating a column to cut off Louise's escape.

"They're getting closer," Teddy shuddered, his hopping increasing in speed as he became more and more stressed out by the situation.

"It's okay, we're going to make it," Louise assured her. She looked back, saw the ants were surging forwards from behind. The route back to the previous burn sites now being reclaimed, the ants appeared to have realised that the scorched path might provide refuge to their human enemies. She turned back to the fourth fire, the last one to still be burning and her heart sank. It was still burning fierce. There was no way it would die down before the ants reached them. After all she had endured, she was going to die. Her and Teddy both.

She glanced over at the quad bike. It was tantalisingly close. Out of options, Louise came to the conclusion that she would have to take a step through the ants and leap onto the quad and try to escape on it. She felt she'd be able to withstand running over the swarming insects, although as the bike was no longer close to the flames, the number of ants on it had increased dramatically. It seemed unlikely she would be able to ride it away with Teddy on her lap without the ants painfully stinging them into agonising submission. Louise cried out, utterly grief struck as she realised she had missed her chance to try and escape on the quad. Martin's plan had failed. She had failed Teddy. It was all over.

*   *   *

Martin held the rag over his face to try and buy himself some time as the thick black smoke filled his lungs and burnt his skin. The fire beneath his bedroom was burning so intensely it was now coming through the floor. He realised there was no hope for escape. Even if he hadn't been shot, there was just no way. The fire had now made its way up the stairs to the landing. He was fucked.

Still he held on, each cough causing him more unbearable

pain. His head spun and his eyes were scratchy from how dry they were. He could see no ants remaining in the room. He doubted any of them that had been present were still alive.

With his last remaining strength he pulled himself to the window, hoping for some air that wasn't poison in inhale. More than that, he was hoping for a final glimpse of his wife and son before they managed to escape from this hell. What he saw instead horrified him.

Louise and Teddy were still on the third barrels blast radius, hopping from one foot to the other, obviously trying to stop the heat from attacking their feet. At the moment they were safe where they were standing, yet not for long. The new burn trail they had created was now in the process of being reclaimed be ants, the ground cooling enough for the evil creatures to march over. They were already beginning to encroach on the third burn zone, yet the fourth barrel's fuel still hadn't burnt out, leaving Louise and Teddy trapped. They were sandwiched between ants and an inferno, completely out of options.

The quad bike was nearby, though the ants had reclaimed it, making its suitability as an escape vehicle null.

"Come on, come on," he said under his breath, willing the fourth fire to burn out, although it was clear the ants would reach what remained of his family before it did.

This is truly hell, he thought. To witness Louise and Teddy's plight and be powerless to save them was intolerable. He thought of Dean's fate, how he had been unable to save him from the terrible ants. The feelings of helplessness made him feel as if he were being smothered.

The fourth barrel's fuel still burnt brightly and the ants continued their advance. What was left of Martin's family was about to be swarmed by the stinging insects.

He almost tore himself away from the scene, unable to bear witness. The fact he didn't is what allowed him to concoct his last desperate effort to save his loved ones. He aimed the rifle, its barrel swaying as the smoke affected his vision. He blinked numerous times, forcing his eyes to moisten to improve his vision.

*   *   *

"What are we going to do," cried Teddy, all too aware of the advancing ants. The ground beneath their feet had cooled enough that hopping was no longer necessary. That was a very bad sign, as it meant it wouldn't be long before it was cool enough for the ants to march upon.

"Hold on to me, baby," Louise said, wrapping her arms protectively around her son. She toyed with the idea of leaping into the fire, wondering which death would be the least painful. She wished she'd insisted on Martin giving her the Glock, at least then she'd have another option to end it all. She still couldn't believe this was how it was going to end, after all she had suffered through and endured.

A gunshot rang out from the house, causing them both to squat low. "Jesus Christ," Louise swore. Then hope began to build in her. "It's your father, he's alive."

Teddy held his mom tight as another shot rang out, making them squat lower still. "What's he shooting at?"

Louise felt a cold dread as she admitted; "I don't know." Could he be aiming at them? As a sort of mercy act?

Another shot rang out and the ants advanced closer still.

*   *   *

Martin cursed his aim, although he wasn't surprised by his sloppy marksmanship. He was a rookie marksman at best, and that was when he hadn't been shot in the stomach and left trapped in a burning building.

His head pounded and he coughed again, the fumes and his wounds threatening to overcome him. He fought to stay conscious, denying himself the sweet oblivion his protesting body longed for. *Just for a little longer*, he told himself. *Just for this one, final act.*

He held his breath, aimed and pulled the trigger.

The bullet found its mark.

*   *   *

Louise and Teddy flew to the floor from the force of the quad bike exploding into a ball of flame. Martin's final shot had pierced its fuel tank, causing the explosion and instantly vaporising the closest of the advancing ants and creating a wall of fire that protected Lousie and Teddy from the encroaching horde.

"He did it," shouted Teddy gleefully. "He stopped them from getting to us."

Louise ignored the further burns and scratches she had just received from falling to the ground and got to her feet. She smiled, eyes fixed on the bedroom window. "He sure did."

*   *   *

Martin didn't know if Louise could see him smiling, but he smiled all the same as he watched his loved ones pick themselves up off the floor and realised Martin had managed to buy them more time.

The floor was becoming too unstable now, the heat from it unbearable, the smoke too thick. The sound of joists failing beneath him were undeniable. He was surprised to realise that he wasn't afraid of dying. Not anymore. As his last act he had bought his wife and their son the time they needed to escape the nightmare that they had found themselves in. It was a good death.

That thought stayed in his head as the floor beneath him collapsed and he plunged into the fire below.

*   *   *

Louise held back the tears as she saw the front section of the house collapse, undoubtably spelling the demise of her beloved husband.

"Dad," Teddy cried, and made as if he was about to run across the ants to save his father. Louise held him firm. "Dad, he's in trouble. We have to save him," Teddy implored his mother.

Louise simply looked at him with sorrow, tears running down her cheeks. She'd promised herself she would save them for later. She doubted she'd even had any tears left to shed. Yet now she was unable to hold them back. She shook her head and kept her lips pursed.

Teddy wailed. "He's dead, isn't he? He's dead and we couldn't save him."

"He saved us," Louise said through stifled sobs.

"What do we do now?" the boy cried, seeking his mother's comfort.

Louise watched the fire consume more of the house, the heat of the fire before her blasting heat over her body. Normally it would have been too hot for her to bare. Now it was a symbol of the protection Martin had afforded them with his dying breath.

The fire behind them began to die out, whilst the quad bike still burned brightly, the ants frustrated by so much heat. They encroached as close to Louise as they could before their insides boiled.

"Be ready," Louise squeezed Teddy's hand. "Once that fire dies, we run." She knew that if the ants decided, they could block their final escape run. As it was, the ants' high density around their escaping prey had meant the swarm covered less of an area than it had done earlier in the day.

The fire burnt down, turning to smoking ash. "Now," Louise shouted and they both ran, holding hands. Ants indeed covered the sandy ground beyond the final flame, though their numbers and density were far less than the swarm's main bulk. The tiny creatures weren't much of a threat without their massive numbers and they couldn't react fast enough to find purchase on the boots of the fleeing humans.

Louise didn't try to avoid the insects, crushing them as she ran, speed the only priority now. If the swarm managed to chase them down, it would be over. Soon the ants became less and less and within half a minute Louise had run past the burnt down barn and reached the dirt-bike, still propped up.

Louise jumped on, reached over and helped Teddy hop onto the seat behind her. "Hold on tight," she ordered and felt his arms squeeze her middle. Reaching down she turned the key and the engine spluttered to life. She revved the bike a number of times, making sure it was working okay.

The ants advanced, but their movements were now so much more erratic than the concentrated efforts they had displayed earlier, the heat and smoke taking their toll. Still, the ants advanced in vain. Giving one last look at the burning house, Louise felt hollow inside. The house had meant to be a new start for her and her family. A place where their boys could grow, and her and Martin could grow old together. A place to escape the hostile trappings of the city and live a simpler yet more fulfilling life. She supposed it had been an illusion, though it had been nice while it lasted. Now it was nothing more than a grim reminder of the nonsensical death and tragedy that had befallen them all and she was glad to know it would burn.

The ants still advanced and so Louise focused on the dirt road and pulled down on the throttle. The bike rolled out down the trail, away from the ranch. She rode slowly, ensuring Teddy would be safe and wouldn't fall. It meant more time before they reached help, but then, the urgently had seemed to have fallen away. There was no one left to come back to, and she knew she would never return.

"Mommy, look," Teddy said over the revs. Louise had already seen what he had spotted; Marie's hire car, off the side of the road and flipped on its roof. She didn't care to see what was left of her sister-in-law after the ants had gotten her. She felt neither anger nor sadness at Marie's passing. It had become just another part of the amalgamations of horrific events that had occurred that day and was now behind her, a sense of calm and detachment now settled over Louise's mind. Louise knew she'd try her best to forget much of what had happened that day, and she knew she'd never succeed.

Riding on, the sun to their backs, the mother and son rode

off over the horizon.

Printed in Great Britain
by Amazon